PUBLISHER'S NOTE

Blue Moon Books is proud to present this collection from the best-selling Ironwood saga (*Ironwood, Ironwood Revisited, Images of Ironwood, Ironwood IV: The Taking of Jane, The Many Pleasures of Ironwood,* and *The Master of Ironwood*) Each passage has been personally selected by the author from the original volumes, some have been rewritten, and all have been edited exclusively for this deluxe Blue Moon edition. We would like to thank Pink Flamingo Publications (http://www.pinkflamingo.com) for permission to include excerpts from *The Many Pleasures of Ironwood* in this collection.

THE BEST OF
IRONWOOD

The Best of Ironwood
© 2002 by Blue Moon Books, Inc.

Published by
Blue Moon Books
An Imprint of Avalon Publishing Group Incorporated
161 William St., 16th Floor
New York, NY 10038

All rights reserved. No part of this book may be reproduced or transmitted in any form without written permission from the publisher, except by reviewers who may quote brief excerpts in connection with a review.

ISBN 1-56201-311-4

9 8 7 6 5 4 3 2 1

Printed in the United States of America
Distributed by Publishers Group West

THE BEST OF IRONWOOD

DON WINSLOW

BLUE MOON BOOKS
NEW YORK

CONTENTS

ix   Foreword by Richard Manton

xv   Preface by Don Winslow

xvii   Introduction

1   Lush Preludes

51   Unique Arrangements

73   Classical Pieces

85   Measure for Measure

119   Dominant Chords

147   Curious Counterpoints

185   Elegant Concertos

AROUND THE WORLD WITH DON WINSLOW

Somewhere in the sunny Roman empire, they're having a day at the races. Female entrants in the filly class could not be called overdressed, only harness straps at neck, wrists and ankles, unless we include an individually-coloured pony-tail which dances saucily from its anchorage somewhere between each girl's rear cheeks. The first event has young ladies racing, reined tight and upright, pretty feet pounding, knees rising high, heads held aloft by high leather collars. Next come team events with four or six girls, harnessed between the shafts of each lightweight chariot, driven by a younger girl with riding-switch in hand and a meaning look in her eye for the six dancing bottoms in front of her.

Before you can think of the Latin for "Horsey, horsey don't you stop," bets are placed by the excited audience and the competitors are off at a cracking pace. Riding switches flash wickedly because each slim young mistress knows she, like the ponies of her team, will be bending before a chastiser unless they win the race. That way, the folks who lose their money get a little consolation.

These sports of *Slave Girls of Ancient Rome* are one of the many worlds of Don Winslow. The scampering fillies of Bernesium might envy the "torture" of the Lady Alea in the Two Lands of Rahn the Warrior King, in *The Fall of the Ice Queen*. Lady Alea, tied naked to a pillar, endures an exquisite and intimate tickling of her nooks and crannies with cunningly teasing feathers. The bucking of hips and rattling of chains during prolonged and repeated orgasm ends in the silence of beauty hanging exhausted and swooning in her bonds.

Dotted round the globe there seems always some corner of a foreign field that is for ever Winslow. Yet one name rings more sombrely than the rest. Ironwood. The very sound suggests glowering landscapes and old-style reformatories. In truth, the settings are a celebration of the English manor house. A short tour through Virginia or South Carolina would suggest that the English don't exactly have a monopoly of these. So good times may be just around the corner. Ironwood, Rosedale, Cheatem Manor are monuments to Don Winslow's narratives. They are real and credible places, protected from the curiosity of the world by long carriage drives, woodland and rolling turf. The shrillest scream of outrage falls silent long before it reaches the boundary wall. The estates are not just instant countryside but have an impressive past. Cheatem, for example, belonged once to the medieval Lord Cheatem. His lordship scored high in civil warfare, sometimes fighting for the king and sometimes against him, but with a flawless sense of timing always emerging on the winning side. And if all the female captives ravished by his lordship were laid end to end, one wouldn't be at all surprised. In more civilised times, Castle Cheatem becomes a manor house with fine gardens, sumptuous drawing-rooms, and girls.

How did the girls get there? In this day and age, if you want to live in such luxury you have to make money from it. Letting tourists in would end the privacy. How about education? If it works for Broad Green or Cyres schools, why not here? Young ladies whose formal education is over and whose families can lay their hands on a small fortune are sent to be "finished" or "polished." Of course, the teaching may not be quite what it seems in the brochure. Riding lessons are suggestive of stables, harness, and whips, but don't you get real horses too?

The young ladies of Ironwood get a fine rocking-horse, with a neat phallus rising from the saddle, on which the stripped pupil lowers herself, lying forward along the steed's neck. As the wooden rockers plunge to and fro, pleasure and correction mingle wildly.

At Ironwood, Don Winslow skillfully weaves his story in and out of historical reality. The erotic antics of teachers and the taught are very close to history. James Miles, the real-life Dickensian reformatory master, was never more content than when his girls were lying astride an ironing-board with their bottoms bare as he tested a new "rod" of birch twigs. Others boasted the mastery of a disobedient girl by "a strong narrow table, straps, cushions and a good strong pliable birch-rod, telling her to prepare by removing her dress, knickers, etc. I fasten the knees together, the wrists the same, unless I anticipate a struggle, then I use anklets and wristlets. Taking the birch I measure my distance. For screams increased strokes must be given." No, this is not an extract from someone's spanking novel but the 1889 prospectus of Mrs. Walter Smith's chastising service, patronised by those with a troublesome girl in need of discipline. Mrs. Smith did, however, misprint "knickers" as "kinkers." Her service occupied a house in a select road near Hyde Park and another in a leafy suburb. She showed the press her premises, pointing out the apparatus over which girls were fastened, the ritual of undressing, and how the strokes of the whip were given. Anyone who thinks Ironwood couldn't happen should ponder Mrs. Smith in her special chastising uniform and think again.

One of the subtle skills of Don Winslow's plotting is that we never have to wonder why the girls are in such establishments. It seems their natural habitat. No one locks them in or ties them up, except during necessary instruction. Once again, reality echoes. Krafft-Ebing recounts a young woman who had spent her childhood unaccountably excited by words like "cane" or "whipping." When she read of an institution whose director would throw back a woman's bedclothes and ply the lash, she was eager to be sent there. Cheatem and Ironwood may be less earnest in their pleasures but the credibility of the situation is unfailing.

Don Winslow's novels also succeed in a most difficult trick of erotic fiction, the transformation of unwilling masochism into versatile sadism. This is splendidly done in *The Secrets of Cheatem Manor* whose hero begins as the victim of its female inhabitants, notably Lady Amanda. Even as a boy, they enjoy using superior numbers to pin him down, remove his pants and play "hospitals" with his naughty bits. In young manhood, with wrists strapped behind his back, he is used naked in sex education lessons by Amanda to demonstrate the nature and functions of male sexual anatomy to the girls in her class.

The "sex education" lesson is a powerful ingredient with its repeated promise of punishment if the victim fails to perform or control himself exactly as commanded before the rows of girl. The punishment is always implemented before the class is dismissed. The boy's revenge on the giggling class of girls is as natural as the whip of the hangman's boy across the pretty bottoms of such malicious youngsters as Vicky Sylvester or Caroline Auderssen, for whose sexual education he was also used as a live model.

The dramatic tension at Cheatem is skillfully raised as rescue arrives for the much-masturbated hero. His second cousin, a military man, storms the house and imposes a "new order." Amanda and her girls will obey—or else. The proud taunting Amanda lies, "upended over my lap like an errant schoolgirl," black silk panties dangling round her thighs. Remembering Amanda's sexual vindictiveness towards the hero, the readers are cheering over the narrator's shoulder as the first spanking and the muffled shrieks begin. Amanda is then forced to thrash her own girls, plugged in every socket, and paddle-thrashed to break her bottom's resistance to the narrator's impaling, bringing the drama to a thunderous conclusion.

This is powerful writing. It draws a useful distinction between Amanda and a character like the career-girl vixen Cat Clarke in *Captive V.* Cat Clarke with her auburn tresses and resentful man-hating is whipped to submission for the sort of young woman that she is, Amanda for what she does. The enforced reversal of roles in Amanda's case gives an explosive impulse to the novel at mid-point.

The world of Don Winslow's creation is richly varied and compellingly readable. In a genre where characters are too often cartoon automatons, Ironwood is populated by those that may be as rare as James Miles or Mrs. Smith, but seem no less real.

Richard Manton

PREFACE

To some people sex is sex,
To Lisa, sex is theater,
To me sex is opera,
But then, I'm another story
   —Tiffany Clark as Renee in *Hot Dreams*

And to some, sex is a symphony, the seductive music of the eternal dance. We find ourselves fascinated by the many variations on the theme, returning again and again to those especially favored parts, the delicious passages that excite and gratify, and move us most profoundly.

Try this experiment for yourself. Go to your public library. Take from the shelf one of those books that are meant to titillate, some call them "soft porn," the sort of thing written by Judith Krantz, Jackie Collins, or Danielle Steel. Hold the book by the spine and let the pages fall open. Before your eyes will appear a steamy sex scene, well-thumbed pages visited by legions of readers looking for a bit of pleasure; the juicy parts inserted, the author might tell us, to advance the cause of realism, but which, incidentally, manage to do a pretty good job inciting the passions.

Unlike such mainstream fiction, literate pornography holds no pretensions as to its purpose. It is a genre of fiction designed with one aim in mind—to excite, to induce in the reader the delights of sexual arousal. If the work does so, it is a success. Offered here are some choice passages from erotic stories designed solely for one purpose—to give pleasure.

           Enjoy!
           Don Winslow

INTRODUCTION

The story goes that Ironwood began life as a rather mediocre finishing school for middle-class girls, one that, for several years, barely managed to survive as a going concern. After a chain of financial setbacks, it was only saved from bankruptcy by a clever Headmistress and her ingenious agent, who managed to transform the place into the premier training school for the world's elite ladies of pleasure. In many ways the Ironwood Estate continued to resemble that strict girls' school of its origin, a place where young women were expected to acquire grace and charm, deportment and polite manners, all instilled by a healthy dose of proper discipline. But Ironwood differed from its sister institutions in one important way—at Ironwood the students were also thoroughly and vigorously trained in the many ways of Eros. The students of Ironwood were willing slaves to long hours of dedicated practice, and they grew under this iron discipline to acquire a level of expertise in pleasure-giving unrivaled by the most exquisite of the legendary geishas.

Upon graduation, an Ironwood girl could command any price; her pedigree would open any door. She might be enticed to accept an offer to serve as mistress to a rich and powerful man, as a trophy wife, or as a prized filly in the stable of one of the civilized world's more discriminating Houses of Pleasure. Ironwood graduates were much sought after, and the enterprise made a healthy profit providing a service for which a clientele of wealthy connoisseurs were more than willing to pay.

LUSH PRELUDES

MY HOSTESS MOTIONED me to chair behind a massive reading table that dominated the room, and I took a seat and settled back, crossing my legs, taking out a cigarette, and generally trying, without too much success I'm afraid, to appear relaxed and nonchalant . . . a jaded man of the world. It took only a few minutes for a bevy of lovely young women to appear in the doorway, hushing their girlish giggles, as they edged into the room. The whispered chatter died down as one by one they spotted me sitting there. Discreet, sidelong glances of definite interest came my way from under coyly lowered lashes. Fresh-faced and eager with an appealing innocence that was not quite innocent, the gaggle fell silent as they lined up, respectfully taking their places before their Headmistress and her mysterious male guest who, word had it, had arrived that very morning.

They seemed to know the drill. Without a word, the troop lined up across the table from where we sat, arranging themselves before us as though in presentation: a row that ran from the youngest on the left end to the oldest at the far right. I counted eight girls standing shoulder to shoulder, at loose attention, eyes front, assembled as though awaiting inspection.

The girls were identically clad in traditional schoolgirls' uniforms. My eyes passed down the row of healthy young women, well-groomed, with freshly-scrubbed faces and neatly trim hair, all fetchingly clad in tailored blazers of deep navy blue worn and loose pleated wool skirts. Beneath the jacket each girl wore a crisp white blouse, and a vaguely regimental tie. Knee-length white stockings of ribbed cotton, and black patent leather sandals completed the regulation uniform. They might have passed as pupils at any of the more respectable finishing schools that dotted the English countryside . . . except for one rather obvious detail.

For even the most casual observer would have certainly noticed that the length of the uniform skirts the girls wore would have drawn a severe frown from the Headmistress of any reputable girls' school. The skirts had been cut short so that they covered no more than the top third of nubile young thighs. I delighted in the pleasing sight afforded by those shockingly shortened skirts: a row of bare girlish thighs, dawn together and lined up side by side so that the inevitable comparisons might easily be made. The girls now waited in respectful silence, standing erect, shoulders thrown back, heads held high, eyes front, as though on parade.

Mrs. Blasingdale could not help but notice my obvious interest, and she allowed a cunning smile to curl the very edges of her lips. "I see that you are a man who appreciates feminine beauty, Mr. James," she remarked in a casual manner.

The "Mr. James" seemed a bit affected to me at the time, but I soon found out that such was the traditional manner of address used at Ironwood—a place where male guests were referred to only by their first names. I believed I flushed at being caught, suddenly feeling guilty for staring at that irresistible sight; the best I could do was to return her smile with a polite nod.

"They *are* pretty aren't they?" she mused thoughtfully. "Such pretty things." Her admiring sigh might have been meant for me, although otherwise I merited not the slightest attention, as her eyes ran down the trim form of a small-breasted blonde who stood at loose attention before her. The slight girl stiffened under her Mistress' attention, straightening up and drawing back her shoulders. Big blue eyes remained expressionless; an unseeing gaze locked on some distant horizon.

"And of course young girls who damn well know they are pretty, are not above a bit of display, especially when in the presence of a handsome young man. In fact, we positively encourage our young ladies to take pride in their good looks, and we quite insist that they rid themselves of foolish notions of false modesty. At Ironwood, our young ladies must learn that it is proper, even desirable to permit a bit of display from time to time. Here, I'll show you."

"Ladies, be so kind as to lift your skirts, please?"

This most irregular request was given in the calm, matter-of-fact manner of one who fully expects instant obedience. I couldn't believe what I was hearing!

I was further astonished to see eight pairs of hands instantly move to obey. Slim fingers clutched the sides of skirts, gathering up fistfuls of fabric and raising hems to reveal coltish young legs, smooth bare thighs, and white cotton underpants. As they lifted their skirts, I was struck by the girls' astonishing composure. With the casual indifference of high fashion models, they would blithely expose themselves to the curious gaze of a male visitor, with a total lack of concern. As they stood there, skirts hoisted up, showing me their panties, that equanimity never faltered. Their pretty faces remained devoid of all expression, eyes kept locked straight ahead, simply showing themselves—as they had been taught to do.

Needless to say, I was thrilled by this most delightful display.

My eyes bounced joyfully down the line, stopping briefly to admire each unique set of inviting thighs in turn. There were limbs that were graceful and fawn-like; others more narrow, straight and supple; some legs were smoothly tapered, while others showed the subtle but richer promise of more mature womanly contours.

For several minutes the girls of Ironwood obediently held the pose, allowing me to drink my intoxicating fill of all that was offered to me. I could feel Cora's eyes on me, watching as though she were gauging my reactions. And I turned to her, grinning foolishly I suppose, not at all sure what was being expected of me. I could do no more than grin, for I found that I was speechless!

"Enough," the primly correct Headmistress ordered in a clipped voice, and I was left with a twinge of regret as the curtains came down on that most agreeable show. But my disappointment was short-lived, for the lascivious Mistress of Ironwood, having discerned the extent of my interest, was eager to get on with her little game, the purpose of which I could not fathom.

"As you can see Mister James, our well-trained ladies have not the slightest compunction about showing off their feminine charms. In fact, you will find they are quite at ease in any circumstances when asked to exhibit themselves, and perfectly willing to present themselves *au naturel,* as it were. Allow me."

And with that, she turned to address the waiting lineup.

"Ladies, please remove your blouses."

Once again, there was not the slightest hesitation as the well-trained girls moved to comply, stripping with a nonchalance I found absolutely charming. The girls slipped out of their jackets, neatly folded them and laid them on the table. Then the blouses were unbuttoned, peeled off with similar indifference, and added to form a little pile of clothing before each girl. Now they stood before us, pleasingly nude from the hips up, clean line unbroken, save for the plain and serviceable brassieres that banded their lithe torsos.

"Very good," the Headmistress nodded her curt approval. "Now the brassieres, if you please."

I watched astonished, my amazement growing as brassieres were undone and casually sloughed off, freeing eight pairs of young breasts that jiggled before settling into place, and swayed softly as the girls bent over to add the feminine underwear to the growing pile of clothing.

As they straightened up and resumed their places in the row, they presented us with an enchanting picture indeed: Eight pretty maidens all in a row, proudly bare-breasted, standing shoulder to shoulder, with that marvelous, totally unaffected air. I was awestruck by these exquisite young women who could so casually undress with such a total indifference, who stood composed and calm, as though they were blithely unaware of the powerful erotic attraction they held for those around them.

I was later to realize that by carefully staging this show for me, Cora had purposely presented me an image of the Ironwood girl—that consummate blend of sexuality and innocence; a female creature with all the dawning sensuality and charming insouciance of a David Hamilton nude.

As the girls stood to attention, their youthful faces blank, hands loosely at their sides, my eyes took in the pleasing sight of those newly-freed young bosoms; breasts that ranged from slight rises budding with feminine promise, to gently sloping swells with firm undercurves. There were taut little crescents, small and neatly made with pointy nipples, and hard rounded mounds; saucy jutting titties and modest perky breasts, upturned and appealing, all bared for my edification and posed in open display. And then I was eyeing their nipples, pert, impudent nipples, brash nipples with wide aureole, nipples that already seemed to have stiffened by their exposure to the cool air. They were brownish and pink and dusky, some large, some small—all inviting the hand, all just begging to be sampled. I found that row of naked breasts to be endlessly and inexplicably novel; fascinating, delightful and most definitely arousing. I was suddenly aware that I had grown intolerably hard, and I turned slightly away, hoping that the tented front of my trousers was not too obvious to my hostess!

Cora smiled knowingly as she rose to her feet, and invited me to join her.

"Come, let me introduce you to our girls."

Then in a more formal voice. "Mister James, allow me to present: Jacqueline . . . Melanie . . . Danielle . . . Vanessa . . . Maggie . . . Sonya . . . Erika . . . and . . . Marianne."

We slowly trooped the line, stopping briefly to examine each girl as Cora spoke her name. They didn't move a muscle, except for a little nod of the head as they were introduced, but at that moment each would make eye contact with me, and their eyes seemed bright and exciting and full of promise.

I let my gaze linger lovingly over that choice assemblage, pausing to dwell on each unique example of the female nature. There were blondes and brunettes of every shade of hair. Some of the girls were taller with elegantly curved fuller figures, while others were shorter in stature, slim and slightly built with narrow shoulders. All stood nonchalantly barebreasted before me, as though it were the most natural thing in the world.

Cora, having completed the introductions, now turned about and returned to the center of the line. Standing at her side, I found myself face to face with little Danielle, a slightly-built young thing with a soft bell-shaped helmet of pale brown hair and silky bangs that fell in an even row above a pair of large dark eyes—eyes that sparkled with merriment. My gaze was drawn to the neat pair of small, crescent-shaped breasts that resided so close to me. Fascinated, I watched that nubile bosom rise and fall with the girl's even breathing, acutely aware of the tingling in my palms, the itch I felt as a renewed wave of lust surged up in me, feeding the aching desire I had to reach out and sample those tempting little treats.

Cora, watching me out of the corner of her eye, now leaned over, bringing her lips to my ear.

"Go on, you may touch her if you like," she murmured, in a voice so low and silky that it sent a shiver through me.

As though in a trance, I watched my own hand come up, as if disembodied, reaching out for the girl, straining fingertips eager to make the first contact with that conveniently-placed left breast. I touched that taut pendant, traced down the smooth slope and around the rounded curve marveling at the silken texture, the incredible softness of Danielle's pert little tit. The girl smiled up at me as I followed the seductive undercurve with my fingertips, hefting the delicate weight in my curved palm, bouncing it lightly, playfully, on the very edge of my curled fingers.

Tearing my eyes from Danielle's breast, I looked to the Mistress of Ironwood, to find her smiling her encouragement. Thus emboldened, I cradled that precious little tit, extending my thumb so that I might use the fleshy pad to brush across the rubbery nipple, rousing the tip, causing it to emerge from its dormant state tucked in the surrounding aureole of puckered flesh. I watched Danielle's face and saw her eyelashes flutter; her lips parted in a shivering gasp as that sensate nipple stiffened with excitement, the aureole expanding, darkening, the tip erecting under the constant stimulation.

Curious as to her reactions, I kept my eyes on the girl's elfin features, even as I closed my fingers on the captive breast, lightly squeezing, lavishly fondling, rotating the small mound of soft tittie flesh, feeling the nub of her hardening nipple stiffening, pressing against my palm with the hard urgency of growing arousal. The young woman arched her back and her eyes closed under the gentle pressure of my slow hand. I saw her tongue emerge to quickly pass over her mumbling lips. Then her lips tightened and curled, and two small white teeth indented the lower lip. I tightened my fingers. Danielle was watching me now, looking down at my rotating hand through half-lidded eyes, holding her breath, while I felt her up. Even though she did her best to retain her composure under the stern eye of her headmistress, the healthy, highly-responsive young woman was unable to keep still. She let her head fall back, swaying and twisting her shoulders, writhing under the rising tide of pleasure. A tiny moan escaped her tightly pressed lips.

I shot a glance to one side to see Cora watching me intently. As our eyes met, she flashed me a decidedly wicked smile. Something about the evil gleam in her eye, made me pause, wondering if I was going too far. Rather reluctantly, I brought back my hand, leaving Danielle to shudder and then to exhale a low shivering sigh of disappointment. I watched her swallow as she waited with eyes closed, slowly recovering her composure. In a few seconds, she squared her shoulders and opened her eyes, to stand before us with small breasts undulating, girlish nipples fully erect and proudly upstanding.

I idly wondered how much of this sort of thing a girl could take before she could no longer maintain her place in the parade line. I didn't know it then, but I was later to find that Cora had some definite ideas on the subject. It was, in fact, common practice to conduct just such trials to test the young ladies' self discipline. The girls of Ironwood, I learned, were expected to master their passions. They were to achieve a level of self-control that would have been the envy of the most dedicated Yogi.

Now like the impresario she undoubtedly was, Cora abruptly clapped her hands, twice, shattering my reverie, and ending that most singular interlude. Discarded clothing was quickly scooped up; those bare breasted naiads, dismissed with quiet authority. The room emptied magically; in no more than a fleeting moment, we were alone. It would not be the last time that I was left adrift in such circumstances, left with the curious feeling of having woken as if from a dream—no trace of which remained in the still and timeless library of this remote country estate. Ironwood does have that curious effect on one.

"Well Sir, I trust you found our little performance informative," Cora asked, arching a well-defined eyebrow.

I didn't know what she meant. Was she being cynical, toying with me, or was she being sincere? Cora was for me then, and would continue to be in a way, one of those "mysterious older women," one privy to secrets about which a callow young man can only guess. My feelings at the time were a jumble of confusion and, like little Danielle, I too needed time to recover from the exciting experience, especially since the painfully obvious bulge in the taut front of my trousers, would need some time to dissipate.

"Er . . . quite nice, really." I managed to get out, shifting uneasily. It wasn't much, but it was the best I could come up with at the time.

Cora gave me a reassuring smile, that was warm, almost maternal. I thought for a moment, the woman was about to pat me on the head and send me off to bed.

"Come. We have a lot to talk about," she said with new decisiveness. "Perhaps you'd care for a bit of lunch?"

* * *

Cora's voice rang out in its clear, imperious tone. The curt command summoned forth a striking apparition: a pretty, dark-haired lass of no more than twenty, clad in the seductive uniform of an Ironwood girl, appeared, as if by magic, in the doorway. I watched in silence as the willowy girl made her stately way toward us, self-composed, her demeanor that of a young acolyte in procession; gliding with head bowed, eyes downcast.

The slender girl came to within a few feet of us and stopped to stand before us, head tilted submissively forward, eyes riveted on the floor, hands held loosely at her sides. There was something fascinating about this young woman who could present herself to us with such detachment, with that almost Oriental serenity so characteristic of a well-trained Ironwood girl. And I knew, that like the obedient servant she was, she would stand there and wait, deferential, ready to be called upon to serve in any manner that might be desired.

The girl's shiny black hair, long and straight, had been pulled back and gathered up in a neat chignon. She wore the evening uniform of an Ironwood girl: a tunic jacket of pale burgundy that snugly tapered her lithe form, a matching pleated wool skirt, thigh-high stockings of a soft violet hue, and high-heeled, open-strapped sandals.

"Raise your head, Miss," Cora urged softly.

The eyes that met mine seemed large and dark, and unseeing. They gazed blankly from that placid countenance with its smooth brow and handsome features. Sensuously lined and shadowed, they were eyes that seemed to regard the world with a bored indifference from under those long silky lashes. They held a jaded quality that I found surprising in one so young.

As she stood before us, self-contained, placid, I let my eyes drink in the delightful picture she presented, visually caressing those thin shoulders; the reedy lithe body with its slender but well-shaped thighs, straight narrow hips; slim legs with a subtle taper, long smoothened contours encased in shimmering violet of her silky nylons.

"Vanessa, you remember Mr. James?" Cora began dryly.

"Yes, Mistress," her voice was low, respectful.

"He wishes to see a bit of display," the Mistress of Ironwood continued in her clipped, business-like manner. There was a pause. And then, in a low voice that was quietly understated, yet unmistakably meant to be obeyed: "Get undressed please."

I glanced up at the girl's face, curious to see her reaction.

But the expressionless lines of her set face never wavered; the dark eyes remained vacant and unseeing, fixed on some distant point. Like some lovely automaton she seemed to take a few seconds to take in the words, and then there was a slight nod. The girl moved slowly, as in a dream, taking the single step that would bring her to a place right in front of my chair, reaching up behind her head to remove a single clip from her hair. With a casual toss of her head, she flung free a brilliant mane of fine black hair sending it cascading down to halo her slim shoulders.

Immediately, a slim hand went to the O-ring set at the collar of the tunic; narrow fingers closed on the tab and rode the zipper slowly down the front of the jacket, opening the tunic in a steadily-widening vee which exposed first the girl's lovely neck and the high ridges of her collarbone, then the creamy smooth contours of her lithe chest and finally, as the jacket parted even further, a most appealing pair of firm young breasts: each slightly uptilted mound crowned with a fawn-colored nub embedded in a disk of crinkled flesh.

Even though her face betrayed no emotion, baring her maidenly breasts to our devouring eyes must have moved the girl because I was certain that the sensate tips had begun to stir immediately upon their exposure to the air. There was a subtle expansion, the brash nipples unfolding as the puckered aureoles grew into prominence before our very eyes. As she leaned over to peel back the jacket, her small pendants dangled appealingly under her bowed torso, elongating to the pointed nipples that swelled as they hung heavily. The hardening tips by now had darkened to a rich coffee hue, burnished with the first unmistakable blush of sexual arousal.

Twisting her shoulders free of the jacket, young Vanessa straightened, and let her arms fall down behind her so that the sagging jacket slid down her extended arms to crumple to the carpeted floor in a soft heap. With that characteristic indifference to exposing herself, Vanessa paused to stand before us, nude to the hips, yet quite unabashed. I admired the way she lifted her chin and squared her shoulders, hands loosely at her sides, prepared to let us fully appreciate those pert breasts—their hardened tips fully erected now, peeking out like tiny stems.

She held the pose for a long moment, waiting, and only after her Mistress' nod did she proceed, reaching around behind her to find the clasp of the brief skirt she wore. Leaning forward with a girlish wiggle she tugged at the sides of the sagging garment to assist its descent, till gravity took over and it too collapsed to ring her ankles in a crumpled heap. Vanessa pawed the carpet, lifting each foot in turn, stepping gracefully out of the puddle of soft wool, reaching down to free her heels of the fallen skirt, and nudging it toward the discarded jacket with a sandal's pointed toe.

When she straightened up this time, a twinge of electric excitement shot through me. A familiar stirring powered up from my loins. My palms were tingling, and there was a fiery ache of intense longing which grew in the pit of my stomach as I beheld that exciting sight of young Vanessa bare breasted, stripped down to a pair of low slung panties that banded her narrow hips. She still retained her high heels and tinted stockings—those long shimmering nylons with the embroidered topbands of wide elasticized lace which ended three quarters of the way up her choice young thighs leaving exposed those last few inches of succulent silken thighflesh.

My eyes traveled down her sleek clean lines of her nude torso, banded by those narrow briefs. The low-riding underpants were made of open mesh. There was a delicate webbing of organdy lace on either side of a wedge of thin satin which formed the crotch and which now molded the gentle mound of a modest pubis tucked between the girl's closely set legs. The dark shadow of sparse pubic hair was quite evident through the sheer, tightly-drawn crotch.

With the same graceful, trance-like movements, Vanessa held her upper body erect while she crooked one leg to bring a foot up in back. With her vacant eyes still fixed in front of her, she reached back to feel for the shoe and slip it off. I watched her remove the other shoe the same way, poised like a ballerina, delicately balanced on one stockinged foot.

Next, she moved closer to me and lifted her left foot to place her nyloned toes on the very edge of my chair. I watched her fingers pluck and twist the stocking's topband, forming a little roll of it and using flattened palms to rub the nylon down her leg. My eyes followed its clinging progress, entranced as she slowly bared those subtle feminine contours.

Her long black hair fell around her face which was just inches from mine as, bending low, she glanced sideways at me and, for the first time, allowed just a trace of a smile to crease her fine thin lips. Then, her eyes fixed on mine, she reached a hand out to steady herself on the arm of the chair while she pulled the clinging nylon off her toes. She repeated the process removing the right stocking, while my solidly erect prick pressed demandingly against my slacks, its tented outline only inches from her toes.

Straightening up, Vanessa brought her bare legs together in a straight line, slid her hands down her waist to her slight hips, there to dispatch the last item of lingerie, the hip-hugging panties. She hooked her thumbs in the delicate lace of the elastic waistband and, bending forward, ran the flimsy scrap down her thighs and straight down her legs, slipping off her underpants without ceremony. Straightening up once more, she presented us with an insloping, slightly curved vulva, bearded with a triangle of fine black pussyfur, which thickened into wispy tufts to all but obscure the neat tuck half-hidden between her bare legs.

Now, this naked ingénue stood at attention: motionless as a statue, her thin shoulders pulled back and framed with that cloud of long silken hair; her lithe body straight and erect; the pert little breasts simply begging to be caressed; her pretty pussy brazenly exposed between those lean young legs that were pressed tightly together. The fallen underpants still ringing her ankles lent a particularly wanton touch to the charming picture.

With delicate precision, she lifted each foot in turn, stepping free of the discarded undies, and then she struck a pose for us: widening her stance, giving a quick toss to her head and raising her arms to put her hands behind her head. The girl stood perfectly still, chin held high, proud and young and unabashedly nude. Her unseeing gaze was fixed on some point over our heads, distant, aloof, almost disdainful of the eager eyes that devoured her splendid naked beauty.

"Down, Vanessa." Cora's voice was lowered to almost a whisper, but a note of unmistakable urgency had crept in.

Those blankly staring eyes registered nothing, nor did the slightest trace of emotion flickered across that smooth brow, as the docile creature moved to obey. Holding her body perfectly erect, the young woman slowly lowered herself to her knees, to wait kneeling before me. Now she knelt in place, head tilted down, letting her silky hair fall forward to drape the sides of her face in a soft black cowl. Spreading her knees, she sat back on her heels, her hands at either side, open, palms up, as if in mute offering. This, I was to learn, was the ritual presentation at Ironwood, a pose automatically assumed whenever a student was introduced to a guest.

Mesmerized, I studied the pale beauty presented before me, my eyes caressing the top of the bowed head, the fragile shoulders and modest succulent breasts, the supple curves of her arms and lean torso, and my gaze traveled downward, inevitably drawn to the darker patch of wispy pubic hair just at the juncture of her gently sculpted thighs. Suddenly, I had the feeling I was being watched. I looked up, and was startled to find Cora staring at me. Her pale blue eyes had widened, and they held a oddly cold gleam of excitement. Over the head of the kneeling girl, her eyes found mine, and her thin lips curled in a slight twitch. On the mantlepiece, the clock ticked loudly, the only sound in the absolute stillness of that timeless room.

* * *

The "graduation" was the major event of the year at Ironwood. Actually, it more closely resembled an auction, an event in which clients could get to know the girls, and contracts were negotiated, contracts that might well make a girl wealthy beyond her wildest dreams, while substantially enriching our own coffers with the standard percentage.

The highly-prized and much sought after invitations had gone out some time ago to far flung addresses around the world. Guests had been arriving all day, and were now preparing for the magnificent dinner that kicked off the event. The dinner was the opportunity for our clients to get to know the young women who were being offered on a more personal basis. Later they would get to know them in even more intimate ways.

In order to provide the privacy for each couple, small tables were set in the dining room, each surrounded by folding screens composed of intricately carved frames that held embroidered panels arranged to form enclosing alcoves, like those found in some of the better restaurants.

Chic designer gowns were specially ordered from Paris for the young women who were meant to be showcased. These fashionable creations were then altered to meet the peculiar specifications of Ironwood, the bodice generously cut away so as to leave the wearer's bosom delightfully exposed.

In their elegant dresses, tastefully made up, their hair stylishly arranged, these prized beauties sat among us, excitingly bare-breasted, gracing our tables with their lovely presence on that memorable night.

At such events the younger girls were pressed into service. For the occasion, our serving girls were erotically clad in a pair of tights and high heels. They looked delicious: loins encased in a slick black nylon which smoothened hips and legs and was snugly fitted to the pert curves of those tight-cheeked young bottoms. On their stockinged feet were the open-strapped sandals, gleaming high heels which kept a girl high on her toes, elongating the tapering feminine contours of a lovely pair of legs.

The shiny tights and tall heels was all these serving girls wore. Supremely indifferent to a bit of nudity, these bare breasted waitresses went about their duties with a certain nonchalance, as though unconcerned as to the devastating effect they might be having on those around them. They were an inspiring addition with their trim hips encased in nylon, and their supple arms, nubile torsos and eager young breasts all left deliciously bare so as to be freely admired at the leisure of the assembled guests.

I watched with endless fascination as little titties shifted and swayed whenever our topless waitresses moved amongst us, reaching down to serve a plate, or bending over to fill an empty glass. And many an eager guest could hardly be faulted if he (or she) was unable to resist the tempting invitation to run a hand up the back of a slick nyloned leg, or to cop a quick feel of a nearby tit, reaching up to squeeze and fondle the smooth softness of a conveniently-placed dangling breast. Needless to say, our serving girls enjoyed a lot of attention that night.

* * *

This strange girl, who I hardly knew, glided into the room with that calm, detached air of a well-trained Ironwood girl. The fetching schoolgirl's uniform in which she was dressed gave young Justine's neat blond features a girlish innocence. I admired her trim figure and the straight folds of blond hair that hung down to kiss her collar. Dark gold with streaks of pale blond, her silken mane, neatly parted in the middle, was allowed to hang in two smooth even sheets, framing that fresh, youthful face.

She walked with head bent down, eyes downcast. Silently,

she came up to stand before me, presenting herself to me, waiting with head submissively bowed, her hair falling forward, partially draping her attractive features. She had come in answer to my summons; she would now await my commands.

"Look at me," I said quietly.

Slowly, the girl raised her head, and I found myself looking into blue eyes that were strangely soft. The gaze that met mine was compelling, yet curiously distant. I now examined her calm, set features.

Justine had the classical good looks of a high fashion model: high cheekbones, chiseled features, a straight narrow nose, and thin, precisely etched lips, parted just a little, as she gazed down at me. I let my eyes caress her lithe, small-breasted form: the sharply-tailored blue blazer with the embroidered crest over the breast pocket; the crisp white blouse; the regimental tie. The pleated wool skirt hung down loosely, barely covering her half of her young thighs and leaving exposed her almost the entire lengths of her smoothly tapering legs all the way down to the thin white cotton socks and patent leather loafers.

"Take your shoes off." I tried to keep the impatience from my voice, although my eagerness was palpable.

Without the slightest hesitation, Justine moved to obey. With the unaffected poise of a ballerina, the agile girl balanced on one foot, while reaching down and bringing the other foot up to slip off one shoe, then the other, all the while keeping her eyes on mine.

"Now I want you to undress, slowly. Begin with the jacket and skirt," I urged softly.

I watched her raise her narrow hands to the blazer's lapels, strip off the jacket peeling it back off her shoulders, extend her arms down behind her and let the jacket slip down to fall to the floor, all without the slightest change in her expressionless features. Then the hands were working open the tie, pulling it free, letting it flutter to the floor with the same indifference.

She never looked down to watch their progress, but kept her eyes on me, as her hands blindly sought the clasp at the aside of the skirt, opened it and lowered the little zipper. Bending forward, she worked the loosened garment down her hips, to let it drop onto the carpet there to form a soft heap around her ankles. With two delicate steps, she stepped free of the fallen skirt, and nudged it to one side with the pointed toe of her shoe.

Then she straightened and drew back her shoulders, as if coming to attention. Justine held her head high, her blue eyes staring unseeing into the distance, arms loosely held at her sides. A well-trained Ironwood girl, she would stand there, waiting for further instructions, presenting for my study, her slender, half-clad form. The snowy white blouse hung straight down from her narrow shoulders, covering most but not all of the thin white panties she wore, leaving exposed the delicious lengths of her coltish legs. Using a single finger I drew a circle in the air; Justine obediently turned in place, presenting me with a back view of her half-clad form. The hem of the hanging blouse rode just above the undercurves of the girl's pantied rearend. A surge of lust shot through me.

"Now take off your panties." My mouth was dry, and my words came out in a surprisingly husky voice.

Still standing with her back towards me, the obedient blonde reached up under the loose blouse and, bending over from the hips, quickly rode her underpants down to her knees. Straight- ening up, she crossed one leg slightly in front of the other in a girlish gesture, and with a final shove let gravity take over so that the displaced underwear dropped down her straight bare legs to collapse in a nylon heap about her slim ankles. She took two tiny steps backward, pawing the carpet with stockinged feet, stepping out of her puddled panties. Then she stood still, waiting.

"The blouse," I instructed. "No! Wait! Turn around first."

Slowly, as in a dream, the slender blonde turned to face me

once more. I watched as her hands went to open her cuffs, then she brought them up to the top of the blouse and they began to systematically undo the front buttons, one by one. Peeling the open blouse back, she twisted her shoulders out of it, and with a shrug, sloughed it off to pull it down her long supple arms.

My eyes caressed the pristine beauty of the blond girl's lithe, almost hipless, form; the sculpted neck and shoulders; the crisp ridges of her collarbones; the smooth even chest and taut flat belly, all delectably bare; clean lines broken only by the delicate, lace-edged brassiere that banded her slim reedy chest. My eyes were inevitably drawn to the pale, lightly furred vulva exposed so naturally, so freely, with all the casual indifference of a true Ironwood girl. My penis, which had been gradually stiffening, stirred expectantly, suffused with sudden power at the quietly erotic display.

"The brassiere," I nodded to the motionless girl, struggling to keep my voice even.

Without a flicker of emotion, Justine reached up behind to undo the clasp, and bending forward, swept the thin straps from her shoulders, shedding the tangle of straps and cups and letting the flimsy lingerie fall to add to the growing pile at her feet. This time when she straightened up it was to display to me an adorable pair of sexy breasts, small plump tits that sagged slightly, crowned with soft pink nipples, crinkled now in quiet repose. The sort of small delicate breasts that would make two neat handfuls. It was all I could do to restrain myself. But at Ironwood, creative restraint was paramount, and while I felt an overwhelming surge of desire for the girl who stood showing herself to me in nothing but a pair of socks, I resolved to wait. Taking a deep breath I continued.

"Now, go over to the bench, and take off the socks."

I watched the blond nude pad across the carpeted floor, holding herself erect like a well-composed model strolling the runway, moving with that remarkable *savoir-faire* that was so typical of a perfectly trained Ironwood girl. She placed her naked bottom on the cool leather bench and brought up each foot in turn, pulling off her socks, tossing them aside. And then, somewhat surprisingly, she took a step on her own.

With seeming languor, she slowly let herself ease back, draping her lissome form along the narrow bench and spreading her legs and bending her knees to straddle the bench with bare feet planted on either side. It was a brazen, sexy pose she struck for me, as though instinctively know what I would like.

She shifted a little, raising herself up on her elbows, and turning to look at me, and for the first time I saw a trace of expression cross her pretty blond face. It was a smile of mild curiosity; her lips parted as if to ask if the pose was okay. Did it meet with my approval? Did I like what I saw?

"Turn over," I nodded, smiling my honest and profound appreciation.

The naked girl pulled herself back a little further up the bench, dragging her legs up onto the leather padding before turning over to rest on her belly. Now she lay supine, her entire length extended along the padded leather. Her eyes were closed, blond head resting on her folded arms. Her features had relaxed in inner bliss, and her lips kept that Mona Lisa smile, as she rested in dreamy repose.

I feasted my hungry eyes on the sinuous lines of the taut young body laid out before me. The soft blond hair spilled over her slender neck flowing down onto the padded leather. Her folded arms were covered with the merest trace of golden down. The long slope of her naked back swept down in a shallow dip before rising in two neatly symmetrical domes. Starkly white, the firmly rounded contours were sharply bisected by a narrow slit that led the eye to the secret cove tucked up between her legs. In the shadows of that hidden place, I could make out a soft tuft of pale pussyhair, flaxen silk lightly dusting the partially hidden vulva.

My eager eyes traveled on, lovingly caressing the girl's sleek sides, on down the long streamlined haunches to the ridges of her compact hips, marked with a narrow strip of pale white skin, the ghost of a low-slung bikini. The stark band of white flesh, contrasting sharply with the lightly tanned legs and torso, made her bare white bottom seem shockingly prominent. I continued my visual journey, letting my eyes take in the silken flesh of her inner thighs, the long tapering contours of her shapely legs, sprawled loosely apart, the delicate ankles and finely-made feet.

As I contemplated that magnificent still life: the golden girl draped languidly over the bench, I felt a tingling in my palms, and a powerful upwelling of sexual desire. I sported a full-blown erection, yet I could not move. I was transfixed by that nude beauty laid out for me in that quiet, timeless room.

* * *

I stared down at the slightly disheveled girl who looked back up at me with a vague hope that overrode her fear that, for the moment at least, had replaced the anger suspended just below the surface. Her hands were still cuffed behind her, and the ballgag had been left in place. She sat on the bed, looking up at me, deep brown eyes peering over the tight leather strap that banded her gaping mouth.

I sat next to her, and looking directly into those wide fearful eyes, clamped a hand on her neck, running it down over her bare shoulder. She flinched at my touch and recoiled back. I smiled and brought up my other hand to grasp her firmly around the neck, while I began to caress her. Still holding her dark eyes with my steady gaze, I whispered to her in a hypnotic voice, calming, reassuring words, while all the while my fingertips were tracing a line from her delicate wrist up a slender arm over the rounded shoulder pausing toy with her thin shoulderstraps. I plucked at the narrow straps of dress and brassiere, lifting each in turn, and peeling them down over her rounded shoulder, getting a gurgling sound from behind the gag. Now I continued my journey, dipping into the shallow indentation behind the collarbone, along that delicate ridge to her sternum; down, just an inch or two, then back up to retrace my route to the side of her neck. Cupping my hand around her neck, I moved my fingertips up to sample the short silky hair at the nape. I rubbed her neck lovingly, caressed like a favored pet, all the while murmuring to her, patiently explaining her situation.

She was at a place called Ironwood, I told the girl, a sort of finishing school for young ladies. She had been brought here at Cora's suggestion and she would spend the next thirty days here. Those days could be easy for her, or they could be unpleasant, the choice was entirely hers. At the end of her thirty days, we would decide whether she would be invited to stay.

Now my hand was roaming once again, down her neck and shoulders and onto the smoothness of her upper chest, skating up over the ridge of her bodice and onto the thin cotton dress. Her eyes widened as I let it slip down the slope and along the undercurve of a cuddly little breast. I traced the outline of a silky brassiere cup through the dress, but I didn't linger there. My exploring hand continued down her body to trail across her belly and feel the ridge of a hip outlined through the thin fabric.

Should she choose to stay, and should we accept her, she would begin a regimen of study and strict training designed to introduce her to a world unknown to her, a world of total sexuality, I explained.

My hand glided on down to her nyloned leg to come to rest cupping her just above her knee. I let my hand rest there, spanning the silken-smooth thigh, squeezing it from time to time as I continued my monologue.

Graduates of our training program, I told her, went to some

of the finest houses of pleasure in the world, to a life of adventure, sensuality, excitement, and often the wealth that came with meeting the right people. If she chose *not* to stay, she would be given a mild drug designed to wipe out the last few weeks from her memory. She would then be given some money for her time, and released in London, none the worse for wear, except for being a little dazed and unable to remember the past month.

By now my hand was rubbing her thigh, sliding up under the loosely pleated dress, up along the column of slick smooth nylon, till my fingers felt the moist heat of her soft vagina through her thin panties as I probed high up under the folds of the soft billowy dress.

I slid my fingers under her crotch and used my thumb to rub the front of her panties. The girl let out a muffled bray of protest; her eyebrows shot up in sudden alarm, her wide eyes took on a desperate look over the top of the gag strap. Whether that reaction was because of the sudden intimate fondling of her cunt, or because the gravity of her position sank in, I couldn't tell. It didn't matter. I ignored her reaction, calmly explaining to her that we would begin her first lesson immediately. It was only necessary for her to follow my instructions, and there would be no unpleasantness.

* * *

As we strolled the gravel paths that meandered over the grounds, I explained how an Ironwood girl was taught to be of service, to give herself freely for one purpose, and one purpose only—the pleasuring of others. This would be accomplished when she came to realize that, when all was said and done, the essence of her femininity could only be defined by complementing masculinity.

Ever since Eve, it has been the female's lot to entice the male; the male's to take the female. In this principle's ultimate expression, the sexual act, the male triumphs by domination; the female, by submission. The secret to our success at Ironwood lay, as Cora Blasingdale, our Headmistress, liked to point out, in getting each Ironwood girl to re-discover this eternal truth for herself.

To accomplish this, we found it necessary to instill the proper attitude towards the girl's own sexuality. For we had found that many of the girls who came to Ironwood, even those who considered themselves quite "liberated" in their thinking, often harbored deep, brooding torments of guilt. We worked to systematically root out every shred of this destructive guilt by helping the girls develop a healthy pride in themselves, in their bodies, and in their femininity.

Thus, casual nudity was fostered; sexual experimentation, encouraged. An Ironwood girl would learn to revel unashamed, to delight in human sexuality in all its many manifestations. Inhibitions and false modesty were to be banished. The result was a frankness and openness at Ironwood that visitors found charming, if at first, a bit disconcerting.

As though to provide a case in point, we happened to round a bend in the path at that moment, and came upon one of the girls sunning herself just to the side of the path. She was sprawled loosely on a blanket, laid out on her belly, and wearing nothing but a pair of sunglasses. The girl was propped up on her elbows, and so engrossed in an open book between them, that she failed to hear our approach, as we came up on her behind. We stopped abruptly, regarding the perfectly still nude in silence.

For the longest time we simply stood there, mesmerized by the perfect study of the female form—the lightly-tanned flesh of her smoothly even back; the satiny inclined plane, broken only by the faint angular traces of her shoulderblades and the tiny ridges of her spine. I let my gaze trail lovingly down that sloping back through the gentle hollow to the definite upsweeping contours of her bottom, two neatly-rounded hillocks—high, perfectly symmetrical domes, separated by a tight crack. I savored the delicious treat with insatiable eyes, vicariously caressing that small pert rearend, before trailing down onto the sculpted curves of her finely-muscled legs, legs that lay carelessly sprawled apart so that from where we stood we could sight directly up along those converging lines to the dark tuft marking the vertex and the soft pouch of her half-hidden sex.

I called her name: "Pamela."

The girl turned to look over her shoulder, and pulled the sunglasses down her nose a little, to regard us from over the top of the frames. Her large dark eyes showed not the slightest surprise at our unexpected appearance. I beckoned her over.

Pamela stirred. Quite deliberately, she put aside the book, and pushed the glasses back up on her head. Then, moving with the tawny grace of a jungle cat, she got up on all fours before drawing herself up to her full height. With casual nonchalance, she sauntered over to where we stood waiting by the side of the path.

Pamela was perhaps in her mid-20s—a girl of medium height, with small, tight breasts and the wiry, athletic body of gymnast. Her slim torso tapered to a set of spare angular hips, marked by slight ridges. Her hair, a dark umber helmet of shiny straight layers, gently curved to form a soft bowel around her head; precisely-cut bangs falling evenly across her forehead. Her hair had been cropped to bare her neck, leaving the girl with a fresh, clean-cut appearance.

The dark silky hair was repeated below in a luxuriant bush, a fuzzy triangle of tiny curls which started as a sparse ridge low on her taut belly and thickened into a tuft as it spilled between her young thighs. My eyes followed her sleek curves to the compact hips, athletic, sinewy legs, and down to her trim ankles and pretty feet. Pamela's jaunty breasts were high-set, two tautly rounded, small globes that simply beckoned the hands. They were crowned with fleshy nipples were dark; the disks, of soft cocoa, slightly uptilted; the rubbery tips, small brown nubbins, extended hopefully.

As the girl stood before us, squinting up, with a slightly bemused look in her questioning eyes, I let my gaze take in that lean, tight-muscled body. Pleased at what I saw, I couldn't help smiling. And Pamela just stood there, letting herself be admired, waiting patiently, totally indifferent about presenting herself in the buff before two obviously appreciative males. I felt a definite surge in my loins as a wave of lust swept over me.

"Pamela, this is Mr. Edward," I said, introducing my companion by the honorific bestowed on all male guests at Ironwood.

The girl smiled in silent greeting and nodded her respects, lowering her gaze. Bedazzled, my guest opened his mouth to say something, but nothing came out. What the well-trained Ironwood girl did next left the gaping man even more astonished. Without a word, this marvelously submissive, naked girl lowered herself, falling to her knees before the male in the customary greeting of an Ironwood student.

Instinctively, Pamela assumed the familiar pose, sitting back on her heels, and lowering her head, while spreading her knees, letting her hands fall loosely to her sides, palms open as in offering. No one spoke.

I let a long moment go by, studying the shiny black crown of her respectfully bowed head. Then I reached out and carefully removed the uptilted glasses, letting one hand rest lightly on the silky strands.

"She's lovely, isn't she?" I said in a hushed voice.

Edward, struck speechless, could only manage a weak nod by way of response as he stood gaping at the kneeling girl.

"You see before you a well-trained Ironwood girl."

* * *

This was to become her new home, I explained to our captive.

She would be taken in and allowed to stay, but she had to earn acceptance in our little community. That would start with absolute obedience, and of course, self-discipline. She was an attractive young lady, I granted, and here I gave her a reassuring smile, which caused her to shudder and close her eyes. But she was one of those woman who used her prettiness as a weapon. Her pleasing good looks, her body, her tits, and her ass, and her cunt (I chose the words deliberately) were no longer hers to use in that perverse, manipulative way, I informed her dryly.

At this last the girl tightened her closed eyes, and a slight blush rose to her cheeks. I watched the front of her blouse. Her small, delicate breasts were rising and falling in ragged swells, as she held herself rigidly still, seething in anger, her eyes clamped rigidly shut, prepared to endure my words.

It was time to give substance to those words; time for this spoiled rich girl's first lesson in the ways of Ironwood. I nodded to the two girls who stood patiently waiting just behind her. Nikki, careful not to obstruct my view, reached over from behind the seated figure, and began undoing the buttons down the front of the girl's blouse.

It took a moment for Jane to grasp the significance of what was happening, but when she did, her big blue eyes registered her sudden alarm and she shook her head in vigorous protest, mewing her outrage from behind the hard rubber ball. I watched her knuckles whiten as she clutched the arms of the chair, straining upward in angry defiance.

Nikki, ignoring the muffled protests, worked unhurriedly, methodically undoing the blouse, exposing a gradually widening vee of satiny skin, a creamy upper chest, fine and smoothly textured. While Jane snapped her head from side to side, Nikki slipped the loosened blouse back over her shoulders, tugging it down her arms in back till it was bunched up against the leather straps binding her upper arms.

Now the terrified blonde's entire front was exposed to the waist. And in the process, my suspicions that our captive was quite flat-chested were unmistakably confirmed. The faintest outline of two slight swells could be discerned through the gauzy film of a buff-colored brassiere which, in her case, served no obvious function. The shallow cups, two curving triangles of filigreed satin edged in lace, covered the gentle contours of her supple chest, creating just the merest hint of cleavage where they met. Behind the snug press of the glossy fabric, the shadowy disks of her rosy aureoles were barely visible.

The wispy bra straps were peeled down each shoulder, eliciting a muffled cry of alarm from the frightened girl, whose fearful eyes begged me in mute supplication. Nikki slipped two fingers down the shallow cleavage, curled them around the joined cups, and yanked downward in single swift motion, suddenly exposing a darling pair of minimal breasts.

The straps were now caught up with the blouse around the girl's pinioned arms, and Nikki paused. She looked up at me quizzically. I nodded, and Jackie went off to get a pair of scissors. With a few strategic snips, the straps of the skimpy bra were severed. The mutilated undergarment tumbled into the seated girl's lap, leaving entirely free a pair of understated young breasts, two faintly circumscribed disks set high on her girlish chest. I noted that those modest rises were crowned with precisely made nipples; the tips, tiny nubs that protruded like miniature erasure stubs, all pink and promising.

I looked up to find a pair of hard blue eyes glaring back at me with implacable loathing. Bare-breasted and vulnerable though she might be, she still seethed with rage. For the moment, at least, cold hostility reigned where fear had once resided.

I met her hatred with a little smile, and let my eyes fall back down to those soft pink nipples which rose and fell with her ragged breathing. Fascinated by those small pancake tits with their delicately etched tips, my hand seemed to rise of its own accord, drawn irresistibly toward her sleek front.

Jane's eyebrows shot up, her eyes widening in renewed alarm. She brayed her protest with mounting urgency, snapping her head back and forth, shrinking back into the chair, desperately trying to avoid my touch. I couldn't help grinning when she flinched, shivering at the exact moment my extended index finger came into contact with the audacious tip of her left breast.

I kept my eyes on her face, closely studying her reactions as I pressed on that impudent nipple, as if that small round button were a doorbell. Jane clamped her eyes shut, holding herself rigidly, while my stiff finger pushed into the softly yielding flesh, indenting the dimpled aureole, till creases of pain shot across her brow and a tiny moan escaped from around the ballgag. At that, I released the steady pressure, intrigued to see the resilient flesh darken as the tip expanded, engorged now with the onrush of returning blood.

Immediately, the stiffness went out of the blonde's body and she slumped forward against her bonds. Her breathing was labored; she was snorting like a thoroughbred, her nostrils flaring, chest undulating in great heaves. Her blond head slumped forward, her half-lidded eyes downcast, carefully avoiding mine.

I noticed the rubbery nipple seemed to have grown just a little, the base widening, the tip hardening. Now, I delicately plucked the semi-rigid tip, pinching her lightly and rolling the tiny nubbin between thumb and forefinger, while Jane swung her lolling head from side to side, straightening up and craning back as I increased the pressure till I was pinching her viciously, my fingernail digging into the soft pliant flesh. Jane gurgled from behind her gag, throwing her head back, her face screwed up against the pain.

At that I opened my fingers a little, but kept the captive nipple loosely pinched between thumb and forefinger, so I could roll the engorged tip, pulling on it, stretching and twisting the elastic tittie-flesh till the blonde arched back and her muffled cries became louder and more urgent. When I released the tortured bud this time, it seemed to be throbbing angrily.

Awakened by this rough treatment, her nipples had blossomed forth expansively, the sensate tips stiffening with arousal till they jutted brazenly forward, rigid with desire. I couldn't resist the tempting invitation, and I leaned down and extended my tongue to lap the swollen, distended tip. Taking that sweet little nipple between my teeth, I tugged on it, biting very lightly, while the tormented blond squirmed and writhed in her fiery agitation.

Now I paused and took a moment to study the girl's passion-flushed face. I was surprised to find her looking down at me through narrowed eyes. A quiver shook her naked shoulders. Her highly-sensitive breasts were rising and falling in deep shuddering swells, the hardened nipples protruding in stiffened arousal, one still gleaming wetly with the smear of my saliva.

Now I spoke to her again, explaining that there were many things that she would have to learn during her stay at Ironwood. If she proved to be an obedient and willing pupil, things would go easier for her; if she proved difficult and obstinate, she would most certainly face the consequences, the way all naughty girls did. I explained all this to her in a voice that was dry and dispassionate. In a calm, business-like manner, I pointed out to our pretty captive that, at Ironwood, swift punishment would surely be meted out, for even the slightest infraction.

* * *

I managed to get there just a few minutes before the girls, and slipped into my chair to await their arrival. As the girls led her into the room, Jane looked up to find me sitting there, waiting for her. Instantly, she stiffened, struck with the sudden realization that she was to undergo yet another humiliation—to be brought before me clad in this sexy outfit. In her confusion, she half turned, shrinking back in the doorway, but her businesslike escorts, ignoring her obvious reluctance, merely tightened their grips on her upperarms and propelled her forward. Keeping her head rigidly down, her eyes fixed on the floor, the blond stumbled and was half-dragged across the carpet to be deposited on a spot directly in front of my chair.

Her attendants presented her to me now, as if for my approval, loosening their grip and stepping back to wait, deferential and expressionless. I eyed the obviously distressed blond up and down, taking my time, while she shifted uncomfortably, burning with embarrassment under my unwavering, and frankly lecherous, gaze.

I nodded, and the girls stepped forward to undo the silken belt, and peel back the thin wrapper, while the blond stiffened and shut her eyes tightly. They stripped the jacket off her pale torso and down her long arms to present me with a mouth-watering sight—the streamlined contours of the nearly naked blond. Nearly flat-chested, her darkened nipples seemed obscenely prominent. The narrow blond triangle tucked a little demurely between firmly contoured thighs, beckoned invitingly, as did the shiny black nylons encasing her attractive legs. And the wickedly gleaming high heels added the final erotic touch.

Jane's eyes remained tightly closed, and she was blushing furiously; resentful at being so openly displayed before me. But I knew something of the depths of her feelings at that moment. And I knew there was something else that stirred her, something more primordial. For this was a ritual that had performed many times before, and often the girls would confide in me later, when things had become much more frank between us, that they had been secretly thrilled when first presented in this highly erotic manner.

And so I kept her standing there, forcing her to endure my visual caress in silence while my openly admiring gaze freely roamed her lithe body, minutely examining every feature, before being drawn inevitably to her lightly-shaded sex, and there to dwell on that narrow, slightly-curved triangle, displayed just inches from my eyes. Driven beyond endurance by her humiliation, Jane suddenly lashed out.

"Stop it," she suddenly hissed with sudden vehemence, her eyes flashing, as she reacted reflexively, crossing her hands over her body in a protective gesture of girlish modesty. It was of course, a futile gesture; charming, yet hopelessly belated and, under the circumstances, rather ludicrous.

"Take your hands away," I ordered, in a matter-of-fact tone.

Sensing how foolish this silly attempt to conceal her feminine charms must have looked, Jane reluctantly removed the shielding hands from her pale blond delta and her right breast, and let her hands drop uselessly to her sides.

"Come closer." I pointed to a spot on the thick carpet just before my outstretched knees.

The open-toed sandals inched forward one small step, stopping just short of where I indicated I wanted her. She would obey, but grudgingly. For the moment, I would ignore the subtle challenge, as I felt a more immediate need to attend to the pair of attractive legs which beckoned irresistibly. My eyes relished those long coltish legs; attractive nylon-sheathed columns, so enticing that my hand seemed to move of its own accord, hypnotically drawn to sample those splendid limbs.

And so I reached out for her, leaning all the way down to touch her on the ankle, lightly running my fingertips, slowly, ever so slowly, up the outside curve of her left calve and tracing upward over those supple feminine contours up the entire length of her left leg till I got to the wide top band and beyond to the bare flesh, creamy smooth like fine marble.

Using just the pads of my fingertips I skated along the very top of her leg, around the fullness of her thigh, and down, following the inward curve to that hidden flesh high up between her legs. Jane clenched bared teeth and drew a shivering intake of breath. A quiver ran through her body at the intimacy of my bold touch.

For a moment I toyed with her there, slipping two finger as high as possible up between her legs, my fingernails just grazing through fine curls of wispy pussyfur, while I used the pads of my fingertips to make tiny circles on the band of silken flesh I found there. Jane gave out with a ragged gasp and closed her eyes, her face contorted against the rising flood of sensations. The first signs of her growing arousal spurred me on. In a heated rush my hands moved greedily, eager for more, determined to feel her up along every inch of those mouth-watering lengths.

With growing excitement, I shifted forward, cupping my hand, slipping it between her legs and curving it around her right thigh, savoring the incredible satiny smoothness of the innerflesh, feeling her heat, the sheen of moisture on her inner thigh. Gripping her firmly by the leg, I slid my hand downward onto the band of the sleek black stocking and down its length, relishing the feel of the slick slightly-damp, nylon; luxuriating in the inner firmness of her stocking-clad thigh, warm to the touch under the sheer smoky film. Thrilled by the sensual feel of her firmly-packed stocking, I traveled down those elegant feminine curves, exploring every inch till I got to the inside of her right ankle.

Here I paused to look up, sighting up along her swaying figure to find that the heat had risen in Jane's face, as she flushed with a renewed blush of arousal. I watched her minimal breasts undulating in growing swells, as her ragged breathing deepened. She exhaled a long shivering sigh through parted lips.

"On your knees." The most I could manage was a hushed whisper.

* * *

As she strode forward from the back of the room, the house lights were lowered while those over the platform were brought up. Wrapped around the gloved fingers of her left hand was a leash, and this was attached to the high collar encircling the throat of a familiar figure in a cream-colored Ironwood uniform who followed behind, her head lowered, eyes downcast. Although the rich auburn hair fell down in cowl along the sides of her face, partially masking her features, I recognized her instantly; Elsbeth placed a high-heeled sandal on the platform and took the step that brought her into the circle of light.

Madeleine urged her toward the center of the stage and there she stood, not moving, as Madeleine unclipped the leash from the collar that banded her lovely neck. Now, at a whispered word in her ear, the girl stiffened and came to attention. She shook her glorious hair back with a quick toss of the head, and drew back her shoulders to stand before us—shoulders back, tall and perfectly erect. She stood regarding us with that even curiously disquieting gaze of her, the light shining on that fine auburn hair that hung in even shimmering sheets.

She held herself rigidly stiff, as Madeleine stepped up behind her and reached around to lower the zipper down the front of her tunic jacket. The widening vee revealed first the high ridges of her collarbone, the gracefully sculpted contours of shoulders and upperchest, and then, as the zipper crept lower, the topslopes of her breasts, the modest cleavage, and finally coming into view, the full shapes of those charming crescent-shaped breasts; their perky little nipples, expectantly peeking up at us. Madeleine ran her hands down the girl's front, in a dry business-like manner. They never paused, but passed indifferently over the newly bared breasts to ease back the open sides of the loose jacket, slipping it off the girl's shoulders and down behind her, pulling it off her dangling arms. Throughout the undressing, Beth never moved, but stood like a manikin, her features, expressionless, simply letting herself be stripped.

And she never moved as Madeleine, kneeling down on one knee behind her, undid the side catch of her skirt, ran the zipper down, eased the loosened skirt down those slim-hipped loins and let it drop straight down Beth's rigid legs, till it collapsed in a soft heap ringing her ankles. Only when Madeleine urged her to lift each foot, did she stir, responding to the command, automatically lifting the foot, and all the while staring straight ahead, otherwise indifferent to her mistress who crouched at her feet, freeing the fallen skirt from her high-heels.

Now she stood before us, a vision of sheer loveliness, her lithe form essentially naked but for the cream-colored stockings, sheer and translucent that sheathed her gorgeous legs. I took in those sinuous lines and that narrow triangle of soft reddish fleece, and became painfully erect, aching with a throb of longing, to once more possess the girl with the mysterious green eyes. But that was not in the script of Victoria's carefully planned show.

Now a chair was brought forth and placed in the center of the platform. Small but wide, with a low curving back, it was upholstered in plush green velvet. Madeleine nodded curtly towards the chair. Beth took the assigned seat, placing her naked bottom on the seat cushion, there to sit erect, facing us, knees pressed together, wrapped in the regal indifference of a monarch, a naked queen wearing a slave collar, serenely enthroned above her subjects. I was struck by the cool remoteness of those seductive eyes as they looked right through me.

Madeleine tapped a knee with the riding crop, and Beth's thighs obediently swung open, to give us access to her splayed crotch and the plume of burnished pubic hair. Now at a murmured word of command, Beth slid down in the seat and simultaneously brought up her legs, folding them back till her crotch was open wide and her nyloned legs lay slatternly, hooked over the curving arms of the chair. It was a sluttish, wanton pose; the pose of a whore brazenly showing her pussy to the eager men seated just a few feet in front of her.

* * *

"Get undressed please." I tried to maintain a certain air of clinical detachment, even though my pulse was racing, and my mouth had gone dry.

It took a moment for the words to sink in.

"You mean here, right now?"

I looked up at her, meeting her beguiling eyes with mine, and in a dry, matter-of-fact voice, I slowly and deliberately repeated each word.

"Get undressed."

For a moment she stood there before me, staring down at me with those big dark eyes, lips parted as of to say something. But she appeared to think better of it. I watched her head drop in a mute nod of acquiescence. And she moved to obey. I smiled inwardly with a surge of immense satisfaction, watching as the young woman began to dutifully remove her clothes in front of me.

Amanda's hands rose up to slip into the lapels of her jacket, and peel it back off of her twisting shoulders. Under the jacket, Amanda wore a silky blouse of a softly pale yellow. With a high tunic collar and ruffled front, it had been tastefully selected to nicely complement the richer cream of the business suit. She looked around, suddenly at loose ends with her jacket in her hands. And when no assistance was forthcoming from me, she folded it neatly and placed it on the chair behind her. Then, with her eyes on the floor, she reached around behind her, to blindly fumble for the catch at the back of her skirt.

"Stop!"

She froze with hands in place behind her. Her eyes flickered up to find mine with an inquisitive look.

"I want you to look at me. It is important that you take your clothes off slowly, and keep your eyes on me all the while. Now, go on."

I held her eyes with mine as deft fingers worked open the

catch of her skirt, lowered the little zipper in back. Still looking down at me, she hooked her thumbs into the waistband of the loosened skirt and swiftly ran it down her legs, bending over, lifting each foot in turn to pull the skirt free, and all the while keeping her head raised, her eyes on mine as she disrobed.

Now she straightened up to stand in a peach-colored half-slip, with the shiny blouse hanging in straight lines from her wide, but narrow, shoulders. The pleasing sight induced a familiar stirring in my pants. I watched the girl remove the thin gold chains that circled her neck, setting them carefully aside on the seat of the chair. She gave me a fleeting smile as she reached up to the front of her high-banded collar to begin undoing her blouse.

I was fascinated, watching the long fingers work their way down the ruffled front, moving mechanically from button to button. The blouse fell open in a lengthening vee in the wake of those adept fingers, and my eyes flickered up to check the girl's face. She was still staring down at me, as she had been told. The look I saw there surprised me. For in those dark, wonderful eyes, I now saw the first glimmer of excitement. Did she find this stimulating? Was it arousing the woman to undress like this, to strip before an obviously appreciative male who sat watching her every move?

The ever widening vee drew my gaze back to the smoothly sculpted lines of the lovely woman's neck and upper chest, giving me my first view of a fulsome pair of hefty breasts, snugly ensconced in the lacy satin cups of a mocha-colored brassiere. Once the blouse hung open, she eased it back, twisting her shoulders free and arching up, thrusting out those taut, nicely rounded bulges that strained against their filigreed cups. She pulled the silky blouse down her arms. I saw the shadowy disks of large, puckered nipples, dimly visible as they pressed against the thin satin of those tightly packed holsters.

With the blouse disposed of, she proceeded to quickly deal with the half slip: slipping her thumbs into the band of thin elastic at her hips, bending forward to run the slip down her nyloned legs, lifting each knee in turn, stepping out of the collapsed silken sheath, the act performed as the woman watched me watching her.

Now the dark-haired girl stood before me, still wearing her heels, but otherwise reduced to her brassiere and a pair of honey-tinted pantyhose that molded the sensuous lines of her delectable loins. Through the snugly-fitted pantyhose, I could see her panties—the same milky coffee-color as the matching bra. The shoes would be the next to go, as she plopped her nylon encased rearend down on the edge of the desk, and looked down at each foot she raised while slipping off the sleek brown pumps. I was about to remind her of instructions, when she realized her mistake, and turned back to look at me. We were closer now, with her sitting on the very edge of my desk.

She was once again looking into my eyes, as her hands went to her hips and she started easing the pantyhose down, bunching them up, lifting her bottom up off the desk to peel the clingy web of nylon down her long white haunches. Tugging the stretching stockings off her feet, she gave them a toss in the general direction of the little pile of clothing without looking to see where they would land. Now she paused; suddenly at loose ends.

"Stand up," I ordered with growing impatience. I was tingling with excitement. "Go over there," I directed, pointing to place on the carpet several feet before center of the desk. Amanda did as she was told, taking up her appointed place to stand barefoot on the carpet, hands loosely at her sides, looking quite alluring in just her pretty underwear. The exciting promise of that bulging brassiere, the delicious smoothness of that taut midriff, framed with unexpectedly feminine lingerie, and the long, tapering lines of those bare close-set legs, all combined to make an inspiring picture—one that sent my cock uncoiling in a new rush of hopeful anticipation.

"Now the bra. Take it off." I managed to get out, struggling to keep my voice even and business-like.

She smiled down at me with a knowing grin. Did it give her a rush: to hear the obvious excitement in my voice? She seemed more sure of herself now, her old confidence returning as she saw the familiar power of her seductive allure reflected in my wondering eyes. She lowered her head, while bending forward and reaching up behind to undo the catch on the brassiere. The bra sprung open, to dangle uselessly from her shoulders, abruptly spilling its precious load right in front of my delighted eyes: a pair of generous breasts that, once freed of restraint, juddered heavily, settling into their natural lush shapes with just the slightest liquid quiver as their owner straightened up. A jolt of desire shot through me, stiffening the resolve in my already upright penis.

I kept her standing there, looking delicious in just her lacy little panties, while I took my time, leisurely admiring Amanda's impressive bosom, thoroughly enjoying the sight of those softly mounded tits: mature, womanly breasts with just the slightest bit of sag to them, somewhat flattened, with broad smiling undercurves, and big pinkish-brown nipples that sat there just out of reach, boldly audacious.

"Go on." I nodded my permission for the final act. She knew what was expected.

I watched Amanda's hands come to her slick satin underpants, and pause, just slightly. Then her fingers plucked the thin band of lacy elastic at her waist, and she slowly began to peel her panties down her hips, bending slightly, allowing those lush, generous breasts to loll forward, as she slipped her silken knickers down her legs. With one agile step she stepped free of the fallen underwear that ringed her ankles.

The mocha-colored underpants joined the growing pile of

feminine clothing draped over the chair, and lovely Amanda stood before me, for the first time, in all her naked glory, wearing nothing but (incongruously) her leather watchband, which seemed to have been overlooked in her ecydistic performance. Later, once her clothes were gathered up, I would have her surrender that watch. She wouldn't need a watch, not at Ironwood. Time meant nothing at Ironwood.

For now, I had her put her pumps back on, smiling, as she dutifully slipped her bare feet into the pair of rich brown heels. Next, I had her resume her designated place on the carpet just in front of my desk.

She stood with legs pressed tightly together, head lowered looking down at me, shoulders slumped forward, hands loosely covering her hairy sex. I ordered her to stand at attention: shoulders back, head held high, hands at her sides! And to my amazement, she promptly straightened, tossed back that glorious mane of shoulder length hair, and struck a pose, holding her chin high, shoulders pulled back to raise her proudly exposed breasts. And there she stood, with those wide brown eyes fixed on some distant horizen, splendidly naked, the first of the ladies who had been given over to me for training in the traditional ways of Ironwood.

* * *

I had taken my place behind the deeply rich mahogany desk, from where I could eye up the slightly-built girl who stood before me, avoiding my gaze; hands at her sides, nervous and unsure. Her face was pretty but her brow was knitted, the lines were tight, almost brittle, the lips thinly drawn. Chocolate brown eyes peered out at the world from behind glasses, wide rimless disks that she inevitably wore, giving the young woman a sober, studious look quite at contrast with the sexy outfit in which she was clad. Soft folds of auburn hair, sculpted in a short, stylish cut, were accented by a smooth swath of burnished brown that fell in a rakish slant across her brow.

The uncertain smile of the pretty girl was worlds away from the slyly confidant grin of the more mature and sexually experienced Amanda who had stood in that same spot when I conducted my very first interview. I took my time, letting her stand there in silence as I leisurely surveyed the girlish figure in the fetching wine-colored Ironwood uniform.

Her tunic was modestly zippered up almost to the neck; the twin bulges of two small mounded shapes pressed against the tight jacket: pert little breasts, high-set high and full of promise. Fitted at the waist, the tunic was drawn taut across her narrow torso, while below the flaring skirt hung not quite halfway down her youthful thighs, leaving a delicious view of her slim stockinged legs from the skirt's hem, to the pointed toes of her strapped sandals. Those lovely legs were clad in stockings of a dark royal purple. Deeply vibrant, the shimmering nyloned columns enticed the hand to indulge itself by gentle adoration of those seductively curved limbs.

I looked her up and down, before addressing the waiting girl in a calm, business-like manner.

"As you know Jillian, we shall have to insist on your full cooperation during your stay here. According to our records, there seems to be one minor matter that needs to be cleared up. It appears from what you've told us, that you've never experienced anal intercourse. Even more troubling is the sneering disdain you've expressed for the act itself. Such an attitude could create problems should a member wish to use that cute little butt of yours, as is sure to be the case. Naturally, we can't allow such reticence. Accordingly, we will take steps to see that you become more accommodating in that particular department."

Now I felt that familiar thrill that rippled up in me as it did each time I uttered those fateful words: "Get undressed."

Jillian didn't move; just looked down on me with uncertainty in her wide brown eyes. "Go on, take off your clothes," I insisted, my voice crackling with impatience that was more pretended than real.

I waited as the girl took off her glasses, folded them carefully, placed them before her on the desk. Then she reached up for the zipper at her throat and calmly rode the tab down, opening the front of the jacket to reveal her bare titties. Two small plump breasts with soft brown nipples, slightly uptilted, smiled out at me from between the open flaps of the jacket. I watched her newly freed breasts move as the girl pulled off the jacket and placed it on the desk. The bare-breasted girl dutifully continued to remove her clothes, looking down at her fingers as they undid the catch at the side of her skirt and let the loosened skirt fall straight down her slender legs to collapse in a soft pile around her ankles. She stepped free of the skirt and as she bent over to retrieve it her youthful breasts shifted forward to hang tautly before me for one enticing moment. I couldn't resist jumping to my feet and stopping her from straightening up with a sharp command.

I kept her frozen in place, bending over the desk, while I sampled her left breast. Sliding the shallow cup of my fingers under that delicate pendant, I gathered up the silky smoothness and rolled it in my palm as I slowly closed my fingers on that softly yielding tittie-flesh. For a moment I held the bending girl by the captive breast, fondling her, squeezing, pumping that little tit, while she squirmed and twisted her shoulders. Letting the delicate weight rest lightly in my cradling palm, I rubbed a thumb over a rubbery nipple, all the while I looking into the girl's big brown eyes. Jillian kept her eyes on mine as she had been trained to do, and her lips opened, though not a sound came out. We stared into each other's eyes. The moment passed, and I released her, and let her pick up the skirt, fold it, and place it with the jacket.

Jillian had not yet acquired the ease in her nudity that was the hallmark of an Ironwood girl and now, as she stood in nothing but her stockings and heels, she placed her hands in front of her sex, fingers loosely linked. The attempt at modesty shielded her pussy from my obvious male interest. That annoyed me.

"Hands at your side. Stand at attention!" I growled. She shifted and straightened as her hands moved away, exposing her pale dusky-furred pubes to my eyes.

"Turn around."

The young woman turned in place, offering me the smooth graceful curve of her tapering back and an enticing taut, high-set buttocks. My stiffening cock surged with the power of desperate longing to lay into this choice piece. If at all possible I meant to reserve for myself the exquisite pleasure of being the first to take Jillian's virgin ass. But that was not on today's agenda; the Commander had been very explicit on that. My role was simply to prepare the girl. I got out of my chair and came around to stand behind the tense nude.

"You have a lovely little bottom, my dear," I murmured, giving her a friendly pat on that solid little rump. "One simply meant to be enjoyed. Are you sure you've never been fucked in the ass?"

* * *

"You seem to be quite well suited for a position here at Ironwood, Mona. But first, I shall have to examine you. Please take your clothes off."

It always fascinated me to see how each new girl would respond to this, the first order she was given at Ironwood. The abrupt command didn't faze this seasoned professional in the slightest. She was used to stripping for men. She simply stood up and went to work on the front of her jacket. She smiled down at me, while elegant, red-tipped fingers made their way down the line of buttons, opening the front of the jacket to answer my unspoken question: under the jacket she wore nothing but a bra. I was now greeted by the delightful sight of a pair of small, compact breasts, snugly nestled in the soft gauzy cups of the lacy black brassiere that banded her lithe chest.

Mona in her bra was an awesome sight! Thin ribbons of

black silk looped her shoulders and suspended in place, high on her chest, the lace-edged demi-cups of that feminine lingerie. Dusky nipples pressed against the thin curved film of those translucent cups, softly cradling the delicate flattened swells. As I sat admiring the splendid sight, Mona reached up behind her back to unhook the flimsy black brassiere. Brushing off the shoulder straps, she leaned forward to let the loosened bra fall from her, releasing her charming little breasts and scooping up the discarded bra in one hand. Now freed from the confines of the their thin satin pouches, I was able to get a good view of those small, but exquisitely made, breasts as she straightened up: twin crescent shapes defined by smiling undercurves, the flattened pendants hung low on her long torso, sporting dusky nipples that protruding slightly from their small disks of crinkled flesh. My eyes lingered on that lithe torso, the streamlined, long-waisted form of the bare-breasted girl who stands proudly before me.

"You have lovely breasts, my dear," I breathed, in a tone of honest admiration. "And I love those darling little nipples of yours. Can you get them to stick out for me?"

"I can try." The girl smiled readily, flashing me her best sexy grin.

"Good. And it's 'Yes, Sir.' Say it now."

"Yes, Sir."

"Good! Now go on. Play with them a bit. Make them stick out."

Mona brought up those elegant, long-fingered hands to lightly cup those delicate weights. The bright red fingertips nosed up over the small slopes as she lifted those soft little titties in the palms of her hands. She gave herself a gentle squeeze, two or three times, then released the taut little mounds. I watched their liquid quiver as the jiggling tits settled back into their natural shapes. Then she cupped herself again, curving her fingers under her breasts. Looking down on me, she used the pads of her extended thumbs to brush lightly back and forth across the stubby nipples, teasing the nipples into greater prominence.

Fascinated, I watched her bring a hand to her lips, sticking two fingers in her mouth to moisten them. She did the same with the other hand, then went back to her nipples to pinch them between her fingers and tug on the little stems. She plucked the pliant nipples out, stretching them, rolling the rubbery tips between thumb and forefinger. Her eyes were half-lidded and I saw her curl her lower lip and she bit down on it with a row of even white teeth, indenting her tautly-drawn lower lips. The self pleasuring was obviously having its effects on her. She tugged on the elastic flesh of those nipples and when she released them and they snapped back into place, I could see they were darker, throbbing, pointing out, saucy and defiant, the tips having hardened into two hard pebbles.

"Lovely. Now you may proceed. Take off the rest of your clothes."

Mona took a deep breath, and shook her shoulders, like a spirited filly after a workout.

Wasting no time now, she reached behind her to find the catch of her short narrow skirt, run down the zipper, and ride the black sheath down to her ankles. Stepping out of the puddled skirt, she straightened up, to let me see her in her heels and pantyhose. A sexy pair of skimpy black panties banded those svelte hips, their outline clearly visible through the dark mist of a pair of smoky pantyhose.

Mona stepped back to sit on the edge of the chair, and raise each foot in turn, reaching down to slip off her pumps. She hooked her thumbs in the waistband of the pantyhose, and worked the clingy nylon down over her hips, pulling the stretching stockings down her long legs and off her feet. Her hands went to her briefs, but at that point I stopped her. I wanted that pleasure of taking down the girl's panties, all to myself.

I had her slip her heels back on, then get to her feet. Then I ordered her to come around the desk to stand close before me.

I looked up at those rangy shoulders; those long supple arms. The long-waisted torso tapered subtly before flaring out to form a pair of long narrow hips. The low-slung breasts were boldly presented, softly rounded shapes that hung appealingly. My eyes dwelt on those delicate pendants, taking pleasure in finding that the excited nipples were still tightened, two stiff points protruding from tautly drawn aureoles. My eyes adored the flattened belly, the tightly stretched panties that spanned those prominent hipbones. The low-riding panties were thin and translucent like the bra, with a wedge shaped center of opaque satin. The slick gusset was drawn tight up in the crotch, snugly molding her pouting vulva, while the high arching legbands left bare the delicious lengths of those smooth haunches and tall, beautiful legs.

I reached out for the girl, clamping those narrow hips with my hands. Mona didn't move, though she swayed slightly as I closed my curling fingers on those solid, panty-clad hips. With thumb and forefinger, I delicately plucked the thin elastic waistband at either hip, and slowly peeled down those lacy black panties exposing Mona's pussy, shadowed with a thin haze of soft brown pubic hair that darkened and thickened into a riot of tiny curls as it spilled down between her naked thighs.

Under the haze pale brown pubic hair, I could see the soft bulge of the girl's pussylips, and the pinkish brown cleft neatly tucked between them. The lacy panties were twisted inside out, spanning her knees; I shoved them the rest of the way down, to leave them ringing her ankles. Then I reached down to tap an ankle, and she obediently lifted each foot in turn while I pulled her skimpy panties free. Bent over as I was, my face was even with Mona's sex, and I couldn't help leaning closer to bring my lips to that proffered pussy and lightly plant a kiss right on the center of her furry love mound. Mona's long body swayed like a reed in the wind, as I held her by the hips and buried my nose in the puff of tiny curls. My senses were overwhelmed as I drank in the intoxicating smell, the distinctive musky scent of a woman in heat.

Pressing my face between her silken thighs, I licked her briefly, tracing up over the folded tuck and drawing a sharp gasp from the woman who quivered and tottered on her high heels. I drew back, intent on exploring her pussy, sending two fingers into her crotch, probing the soft furry folds of the girl's vulva, pressing up into the yielding softness of Mona's moistening pussy. The tall girl stiffened and arched back as I fingered her sex, sampling the wet slickness by wedging a finger in between the tightly closed pussylips, while Mona sucked in a long shivering breath of air and swayed like a sapling in the wind. I pulled my scent-impregnated fingers and brought them to my nose, savoring once more the earthy, pungent smell, as I looked up at the naked girl who stood watching me through lowered lashes. Once more I held her by the naked hips as I informed the new girl that I wanted to see the way she moved. It was to be a sort of screen test, I explained.

"Go on now. Walk around for me," I ordered.

Mona smiled at me, and swung on her heel to stroll around that elegant, well-appointed room wearing nothing but her black pumps and her best professional smile.

* * *

But it was Allison who truly arrested his progress. The tall blonde stood almost even with his eyes, as he took in the exquisite lines of her face, the high cheekbones and those haughty blue eyes. For a moment they stood staring at each other. His eyes sparkled at the challenge they saw there. White, a man who seemed use to command, never doubted he would win the battle with the cold blue eyes that looked back at his, still he was intrigued by the challenge he saw there. Although she was uniformed and her status made plain by the tagged collar she wore, this girl did not defer to him, nor did she lower her head respectfully as she had been told to when introduced. She seemed much more likely to offer to shake his hand, as though he were a business partner, and might have done so had not Renata instilled at least a modicum of respect into her.

"A spirited filly, I'd venture," White said in an aside, whispered for my ears only. I nodded and allowed as how that was so. Then, as he stood looking her up and down, admiring those glacile curves of that tall blonde in that form-flattering Ironwood outfit, he continued aloud.

"I wonder," he mused, "might it be possible to have her show us her panties?" He turned to me with a eyebrow cocked inquisitively. "If it's not too much trouble?"

"But of course, Sir. No trouble at all."

I turned to the waiting girl.

"Lift up your skirt, Miss."

There was just the slightest pause, a hint of hesitation that caused me to wonder. Then Allison's fingers dutifully gathered up the hem, raising the loose pleated skirt, sliding it up all the way to uncover the lacy tops of stockings that banded her legs and left exposed several inches of succulent thighflesh, and a pair of peach-colored underpants. White was delighted! His fingers extended out to touch the front of Allison's panties, feeling the puff of fine pubic hairs through the thin satin, before sliding a little lower to find, with satisfaction, that the tightly-drawn gusset was slippery and slightly moist. He pressed firmly, fingering the delicate contours of the girl's pussy through the slick fabric, while Allison bit down on her curled lower lip.

* * *

Supper that evening found our guests seated, with the ladies who had been invited to join us, around the ornate table in the main dining room. The Commander took his seat at the head of the table, I sat on his right and Renata, dressed all in black, sat at the far end of the table. Members were interspersed with the girls and I found myself opposite the superbly composed Mona. No doubt inspired by the brief taste of feminine pulchritude he had sampled in the hallway, it was White who suggested that it might be quite amusing to have the girls dine *sans* top coverings, a suggestion that was eagerly adopted by the enthusiastic male contingent. When they were told that they were to dine topless, these well-trained Ironwood girls did us proud. They never missed a beat, readily sloughing off tunics, stripping with complete indifference, running down zippers, freeing their swaying breasts to eager male eyes with all the equanimity of coolly detached professional models. And so now seven women sat at the elegantly appointed table wearing identical black velvet ribbons around their throats, lovely breasts left nonchalantly exposed, while their randy male companions took their places at the table much more formally attired in dinner jackets and white ties.

Unique Arrangements

WHILE URSULA WAS almost as tall as Jackie, the differences between their naked forms were striking. The lithe brunette's body was pale and slim, a smooth contoured form of polished alabaster that seemed cool and hard, and strangely unapproachable. By contrast, the healthy young blonde was lightly-tanned all over, her skin was warm to the touch, and it had the silky feel of fine velvet. The young woman's dusky body seemed to glow, radiating a sexual allure that reached out to touch even the most jaded men in the audience.

For a moment they stood there together, like two sisters posing for a picture for the family album: standing side by side, their hips barely touching, their arms loosely slung around each other's shoulders. Then they turned to face one another and embraced, clasping each other and squirming till their naked young bodies fused together while their eager mouths found each other's in a deep soulful kiss. And they maintained that kiss while they sank slowly to their knees, all the while clutched in writhing embrace. When at last they broke their kiss, it was to ease themselves down, collapsing till they were sprawled on the floor, limbs intertwined, needy pussies rubbing urgently against restless thighs, soft breasts pressing into soft breasts.

Now, the wiry dark-haired girl clambered on top of the languid blonde. Placing a knee on either side of her supine form, she straddled her Sapphic partner and leaned over to impart a gentle kiss. With little fluttering kisses she teased over the blonde's mumbling lips and down her chin and neck, licking a wet trail along the narrow path between the twin flattened mounds of her maidenly breasts. Throughout this adoration, the blonde lay perfectly still, her eyes closed as her amorous playmate tenderly, and most lovingly, cupped a gently mounded tit, squeezing it to force the tip up towards her straining mouth. Jackie rolled her head from side to side, her eyes half-lidded in dreamy reverie, her hips twitching restlessly. She sucked in a sharp gasp of breath as the captive nipple was drawn into the hot damp cavern, to be thoroughly worked over by greedy lips and lively tongue.

Ursula worried that burgeoning nipple, lightly clamping the stiffening bud between her teeth and shaking her head from side to side like a playful puppy gently tugging on the sensate tip. The blonde let out a strangled groan and strained upward. And when the wet tip plopped free, we could see that the glistening nipple was now protruding, hard, taut, and saucily erect.

With loving adoration her tender lover slid slow hands up over the blonde's sensual body, over ribcage and on down the long flanks of the writhing nude. The caressing hands sought to savor every inch of the undulating body before seeking and finding the lightly-furred vulva. Jackie opened her scissoring thighs to encourage the intimate caress, instinctively welcoming the exploring fingers, urging her friend on with little whimpers of pleasure uttered through tightly pressed lips.

Ursula palmed the mounded pubis, pressing hard, rubbing deeply, till she had the passion-driven blonde moaning helplessly. Then it was that she inserted a single finger up the other's cunt; then two joined fingers; then three. Jackie's eyes clenched tight, her brow knitting with the sudden intensity of an abrupt flood of sensations as the adept female deftly caressed her sex, fingering her friend, penetrating, exploring her inner recesses. Jackie's lips parted in a long, drawn-out sigh of deep animal satisfaction. Her obvious flush of arousal spurred her eager young friend on to even greater heights, and soon Ursula was vigorously thrusting her stiffened fingers in and out of the blonde's churning cunt.

The rhythmic squishing sounds broke the stillness of the room. The passion-soaked blonde was squirming in sensual abandon now, tossing her head from side to side, driven by lust; flailing the carpet with her long silken strands. Through moans and sighs she would urge her lesbian lover on, till she was responding to the frenzied finger-fucking by a series of high pitched "nooos", repeated with mounting urgency. Then, with a sharp cry, we saw her thrashing body stop, her limbs stiffened and she arched up, suddenly rigid from head to toes, as she clung there, poised on the ragged edge of a rampaging orgasm.

Ursula, with exquisite timing, plunged her stiffened fingers up the straining cunt, burying them as deeply as she could till she was palming the girl's underarch at the precise moment the straining blonde hit her peak. Jackie moaned; her body trembled and then, with a tiny whimper, she slipped almost imperceptibly over the top to collapse in a spent heap.

Now, as the lissome blonde basked in the afterglow, Ursula leaned over to whisper in her ear. The blond head nodded weakly and, in a moment, she stirred herself, pulling herself to her knees, while the agile brunette took her place, laying flat on the carpet, her arms at her sides. Next, the blonde swung a leg over the reclining form, to kneel straddling the other girl's narrow hips, facing her feet. Then Jackie let herself fall forward onto all fours and backed up, squatting slightly to bring the soft, dew-moistened folds of her love pouch right down on the pretty face of the supine brunette. Falling down onto her elbows, she ducked her head till her pursed lips grazed the proffered tangle of ebony curls below her. Now in the position of mutual love, the girls began to pleasure each other, lapping cunt with obviously practiced skill.

I saw Jackie's tongue slither out to lovingly lap the perimeter of her sister's triangle. The blond head ducked down to burrow deep between thrashing legs, sampling the smooth flesh of the innerthighs, licking greedily while silky strands of blond hair spilled down over the pale clenching thighs. She placed eager hands on each thigh, prying open her lover still further, increasing the other girl's vulnerability to her intimate probing of the half-hidden labia.

Now she switched tactics, flattening her tongue, and wetly lapping up and down the ragged slot in long broad strokes, till she had Ursula whimpering and making little squeals of delight.

Swollen and distended, the yawning cuntlips had darkened with infused passion, and to those heavenly gates Jackie now turned her entire attention. Ursula's hips bucked up in instinctive reaction as she strained to force the tantalizing tongue in deeper. Meanwhile, Jackie had stiffened that tongue and was ducking her head, bobbing up and down in a flurry of action.

Ursula responded by arching upward and clamping her spasming thighs on the attractive blond face, seeking to draw her even deeper into her hot welcoming womanhood. Both young women were moaning now, their involuntary cries muffled as mouths burrowed into opened cunts. Ursula's thighs were quivering, the tendons straining rigidly as they tightened on the blond head. Then, with hips bucking furiously and legs thrashing, the reedy brunette bounded to a roaring climax.

Slowly, gasping for breath in mighty heaves, Jackie drew herself up on her elbows and sat back to reveal a face glistening with love juices. As she straightened, her hands went to her dangling tits. She held herself and inched backward on her knees till she could perch with her wet sex pressed squarely on the brunette's face. She let her half-lidded eyes slide closed, and she slowly began to fondle herself. I saw a smile broaden over her blissful countenance and her hard-working partner, half smothered, struggled to bring her to a second shattering orgasm. This time, when the sinewy blonde came, her rigid body arched up and backwards, and a massive quiver ran through her shoulders. Then she tumbled forward and the two young women, thoroughly depleted, lay in an exhausted heap, their breath coming in ragged gasps as warm waves of pleasure slowly receded.

* * *

It was a warm summer's night in late August. Cora and I were naked, perched on the edge of the bed, side by side, while before us stood our little playmate for the evening, a sultry sloe-eyed lass named Kimberly. She waited with head demurely lowered, her eyes on the floor, the light shining on the crown of her helmet of straight black hair. I followed the supple lines of her slender body up from her finely-made feet and ankles along the slight tapering curves of her girlish legs to her slim hips and beyond, up her svelte torso to her gently sloping shoulders, finally pausing to settle on her small tits—two tight mounded disks with precise brown buttons at their exact centers.

My eyes swept back down, drawn magnetically to the shading of fine jet-black fleece marking the girl's pubescent sex. The dim outline of her pursed labia was dimly visible through a soft puff of pubic curls. She stood submissively before us, waiting to be called upon, to serve at our pleasure. I felt myself stiffening with arousal at the very thought of such a prospect, and allowed myself to devour this young naked beauty with rapacious eyes.

Cora, for the most part, ignored the waiting girl. She

seemed more intent on watching me, studying my face with interest. I felt her hand slide along my thigh to boldly grab my semi-hard penis and give me a playful tug. She kept her hand on my thickening manhood, holding me in a loose grip, as she leaned over to kiss my cheek. Her heavy breast swayed and brushed against my arm; the scent of her perfume was strong and intoxicating—heady stuff. Then, with an affectionate pat on my rising cock, she got to her feet, abandoning me for the moment. to pad off somewhere without a word. I watched her pad off, leaving the room, with an easy sway of that full, shapely behind of hers.

In a minute or so Cora returned; in her hand—two paddles. She resumed her seat on the bed beside me, and with a knowing grin, handed me one of them. These paddles were the short-handled types, like those used in table tennis, the wide flat blade were faced with a thin layer of rubber which, grooved with tiny ridges, would insure a stinging bite.

Through this all, Cora paid not the slightest attention to the patiently waiting Ironwood girl. Now she turned to her, and brusquely ordered her down on all fours, forcing the young woman to crawl toward us as we sat on the bed, and, in the process, providing us a nice view of her darling little breasts. The narrow titties hung taut beneath her slender torso, as the slim girl crept forward like a big cat.

Kimberly knew what was wanted of her. She closed in on us till she got almost to our knees. Cora and I obligingly shifted apart, opening a gap between so she could ease up to rest her breasts on the satiny sheets, bringing her cute young bottom well into range. Kimberly, turned her head, resting her cheek on folded arms, closed her eyes and waited.

I couldn't resist reaching down to cup one of those tempting satiny mounds. I gripped a solid rearcheek firmly, sliding my curved hand up and down the rounded contour. Kimberly's delicious bottom was smooth and warm. Hers was an ass designed to entice the hand, to invite a soft, adoring caress. But tonight we had other plans for that appealing little behind.

Cora was well-practiced at this sort of thing. A proper spanking should be done with short, decisive strokes, not too hard, yet laid on briskly, she assured me with authority. We should begin with a set of ten. She would concentrate on the right cheek; I, on the left.

We raised our paddles and, as Cora began a crisp staccato count, we simultaneously spanked those twin domes, lightly tapping out a steady beat on the girl's well-placed and totally vulnerable butt. Kimberly gave out with little tight-lipped yelps, as she recoiled forward. Soon she was twitching and writhing frantically under the relentless rain of short, choppy whacks. I watched as each hit flattened the left hemisphere with a splat, biting into the solid rubbery cheek, sending the resilient mound wobbling delightfully.

At the count of ten, we abruptly drew back. Kimberly's hands flew behind her as she grabbed her hurting bottom and rubbed frantically to ease the fiery sting. She was sniffling; tears welling up in her dark eyes. Cora didn't stop her from trying to rub away the sting. She just sat there with the grin of Cheshire cat, perfectly content to give our victim this brief respite.

Then abruptly, she grabbed the girl by the wrist, warning her in her best Headmistress' tone that her punishment was far from over. Another set of ten was on the agenda. At this the girl gave out with a plaintive whimper, but once again, she was ignored. We waited while she set herself, stiffening and clawing at the sheets, clutching two handfuls of satin and holding on with white-knuckled determination, trying her best to harden herself to receive the additional spanking her mistress had decreed.

Again, Cora gave a brisk nod, and again the count. We started in on her. With a smart snap of the wrist I sent the devilish blade biting into the proffered behind, sending the little mound dancing merrily. The resounding echoes of twin paddles smacking the juddering cheeks soon began to mingle with little Kimberly's high-pitched yelps.

I stole a glance at my collaborator. Cora's face was sheened with sweat, her blond features set in a look of grim determination, as she bent to the business at hand with surprising vengeance. Her obvious excitement, stirred me to new heights of arousal, and I determinedly attacked my target with renewed vigor, matching my smacks with Cora's in a steady rapid tattoo.

The reddened flesh rebounded, wobbling loosely with each impact. Kimberly was howling now, and between ragged gasps of breath, she managed to babble a plea for mercy. The desperate girl was unable to keep still, and in her agitated squirming I noticed she began clenching her fearful rearcheeks spasmodically under the continuing assault. By the time we paused for the second time, she was crying openly, gasping for breath between great heaving sobs, while rubbing furiously at her tender behind, in a frenetic effort to ease the permeating sting.

We sat motionless, fascinated by the girl's frantic gyrations and the sounds of her gradually subsiding sniffling in the quiet of the room. And when Cora turned to me, I saw she had been powerfully moved. There was a peculiar gleam in her eye, and as I watched, her lips widened and curled in an a wicked smile of triumph.

Watching that self-satisfied, smug grin it occurred to me that it might be amusing to have the proud headmistress of Ironwood soothe our little victim's chastised behind, comforting her with soft tongue and tender lips.

I had Cora get off the bed and told her to take up a position behind Kimberly who I ordered down onto her elbows. Cora looked at me with a glint of steel in her eyes, and for just a fleeting moment she seemed about to protest. I waited, my gaze locked on hers. The moment passed and, with a resigned shrug, the big blonde let herself slide off the bed and onto her knees. She crawled forward bringing her face near the jutting butt of her erstwhile victim. She looked up at me; I nodded.

"Go on, make it up to Kimberly," I urged softly.

Cora did as she was told, pursing her lips, imparting a single kiss to the freshly-punished mounds.

She turned to look up at me.

"Better than that! Go on, kiss her. Kiss her ass!"

Dutifully, the humbled Mistress of Ironwood turned back to task at hand, planting light fluttery kisses up and down the lush contours of that warm, throbbing buttocks while little Kimberly whimpered through tightly pressed lips.

"Keep going," I ordered tersely.

Obediently, Cora extended her long wet tongue and began to lave the rounded curves, while Kimberly exhaled a long contented sigh of deep pleasure. I kept the older woman at it, licking up and down the slopes, probing between them, sending her tongue deep into the girl's narrow crack while the electrified lass wiggled with delight. I could only imagine what went through her head as she felt the tongue of the imperious Mistress of Ironwood licking her ass, thoroughly lapping each pert cheek, trailing down the slopes to trace the smiling undercurves. By the time she was finished, Kimberly's tight little butt was gleaming, shiny wet from her lesbian lover's tireless efforts. The girl stirred sensuously, her eyes closed in dreamy repose, head resting on folded arms. I saw the trace of smile curl her thin lips as she sighed contentedly, luxuriating in the experience of her mistress' obsequious devotion.

* * *

Now I settled in to watch as, with tender solicitude, the serving girls helped their charge to step into a large square onyx tub, gently easing her down into the warm water till her bottom came to rest on the built-in cornerstep. She was totally spent from her recent tribulations and now, lulled by the warmth of the scented water, the leggy blond let herself sprawl languidly back, half-propped up on her elbows, her legs loosely parted, perfectly content to offer up her sleek front to the tender ministrations of her dutiful handmaidens.

As she let herself slide into a dreamy reverie, Jane's eyes slowly narrowed, the lashes fluttered, and the lids slid closed. Her pretty features slackened as Nikki took up a position kneeling behind her and began hypnotically kneading the soft muscles of her shoulders. Meanwhile, Jackie, peeling off her damply transparent tunic, climbed in to join Jane in the generous tub. Kneeling between the long outstretched legs, Jackie slid her warm soapy hands up the girl's front until they rested directly on Jane's barely-perceptible breasts, and then she began easing the flattened mounds around in a slow circular massage.

Jane lolled back, sunk in blissful lethargy, giving herself up to the magic hands and the warm irradiating waves of deep pleasure they induced. She watched them through heavy-lidded eyes, barely stirring when their small flattened palms slid up the wet sheen of her front; eager fingers seeking her nipples. And when they closed on those delicate little tips, her thin shoulders quivered, and her lips parted in a long, shivering gasp. And now they played with her, the impudent fingers scissoring the swollen buds, audaciously plucking and tweaking the distended nubs, till she clenched her eyes and moaned in half-distracted torment at the exquisite sensations.

Now Nikki, following Jackie's lead, unbelted her own sopping wet tunic, and pulled the clinging garment up over her head, stripping her nubile young body with one quick motion. Eagerly, she climbed into the commodious tub so the two girls could join forces to cover the entire front of the sprawling blonde's streamlined torso with a milky film of slick lather. Working together as a team, they soaped their way across to the ridges of her hips, and back and forth over the smooth even plane of her belly, edging lower, ever closer to the slight swell of her mounded pubis, which sat posed just above the waterline. They skirted the topmost edge of her pristine triangle, but went no further.

The girls had their instructions and they were quite skilled at their work. For their job was to gradually awaken the new girl's passions, to arouse her lust and keep the fires simmering; but they were to go no further. Their task was to tease, to titillate, to sharpen the edge of the blonde's erotic appetite, till her healthy young body was resonating, fully alive and tingling with vibrant desire.

And so they did their job, soaping her methodically, covering every inch of flesh. Clever fingers thoroughly explored every inch of flesh, sliding along smooth feminine contours; playful fingers sought every curve and crevice, save that most sensitive place—just between the legs. Occasionally, an audacious hand might slip into that forbidden valley, but as soon as the aroused girl stirred in quickened response, reflexively clamping her needy thighs to capture the impudent intruder, the foraging hand would slither quickly away.

The new girl was to be comforted, petted and stroked. And she would be allowed to find what pleasures she could in the roving girlish hands, but for now, ultimate release was to be denied to her. Her body was to be tuned like a fine instrument, so that in time, she could be brought to climax by the slightest means: a fluttering kiss along the nape of the neck, a touch on the ankle, the casual brush of tentative fingertips over an understated breast, the press of a hip against her skirted thigh, as she sat in some restaurant, a furtive hand cupping her skirted butt in a crowded elevator. All these things alone would thrill her, firing her newly heightened sensitivities with an aching intensity. Such gestures would be enough to induce in her a ragging lust, a mindless pleasure that would drive her to shattering paroxysms of ecstatic delight.

* * *

Madeleine tugged on the leash, causing the girl to stumble in her heels as she was forced to take one more reluctant step that would bring her closer to an encounter she quite obviously would rather avoid. Diane stood before Victoria with head bowed, her body held rigid, fists clenched at her side. She never moved a muscle as Madeleine reached around to undo her tunic and peel it back to expose the girl's front to her seated mistress.

Since Diane stood facing Victoria, her back was to the audience, and so we could see the appreciative gleam in Victoria's eyes as the zipper descended, and the reassuring nod she gave the girl as Diane's taut, youthful breasts came into view.

Now Madeleine's deft hand were at the girl's hips, efficiently undoing the little skirt, starting its downward journey with a tug over the hips, and letting gravity take over so that the skirt dropped down Diane's coltish legs to collapse in a folded heap. The girl held herself erect as her skirt was taken from her. One hand went out so she could brace herself on the shoulder of her crouching assistant as she raised each foot to step out of the fallen skirt.

As she presented herself, naked before her mistress, we could now fully savor the back view: the shoulders, slight, with a gentle slope, the narrow back, a smooth-muscled even expanse, the smoothness broken by the traces of angular shoulder bones and the faint ridge of the spine, the shallow dip of the lowerback sweeping up to form a pair of narrow buttocks, slightly elongated and perfectly symmetrical, accented by a deep thin crack, and well-defined, plump undercurves. Her slim hips flowed smoothly into slender, tapering thighs, banded half way up their lengths with the snug elastic bands of the stockingtops. I sighed in admiration at those wonderful legs, molded as they were by the slick gleaming nylons, so lithe and slim, yet contoured with feminine elegance.

Victoria's encouraging smile brightened; she motioned the nude girl forward. With a prodding nudge from Madeleine, Diane moved. The stockinged feet in their high heels took two small steps to bring the girl's willowy body within reach of her admiring mistress.

Almost reverently, Victoria brought up a hand to follow the sinuous lines of one flank, tracing down over the graceful curve of the hip like an art connoisseur admiring a classic piece of sculpture, her curved palm following the gentle taper over the ridge of the elastic band and down the slender column till she curled her fingers digging into the meaty firmness of the thigh just below the topband of the stocking. Gripping the young woman with one hand like that, she drew Diane's loins even closer, all the while letting her eyes play over that lithe young body.

Diane arched back in her mistress' grip, her hips bowed forward, swaying slightly. When Victoria released her it was to raise a single finger to describe a little circle in the air. Diane obeyed the silent command, pivoting in place, to afford her mistress the back view while we were treated to what the censors like to call 'full frontal nudity'.

The girl was clearly nervous now, embarrassed to stand naked under the gaze of her mistress and the crowd of hungry men whom she was now made to face. There was a slight flush to her delicate cheekbones, a look of unease on those pretty features. From under the fringe of her bangs, her hazel eyes, which had been enhanced by the judicious use of liner and a sepia shadow, darted here and there, unsure. She moistened her thin lips nervously as she stood fidgeting under our gaze.

Although not as tall as the statuesque Annie, Diane was only slightly shorter than Madeleine. Her narrow shouldered frame and long slender lines were all pleasingly proportioned. Her breasts were small and pointy; the nipples surprisingly large; richly brown, succulent tips. The taut skin of her smooth torso was flawless, sleek and inviting; narrow lines tapering to the slight cradle of her angular hips.

Boldly prominent, Diane's sex was richly furred with curlings of dark pubic hair that defined the narrow triangle of her gently mounded vulva. Her coltish legs, encased in the vibrant blue sheaths, were slender columns with an agreeable taper to her elegant thighs.

Her lashes fluttered nervously, and I saw her work the fists she held stiffly at her sides, The blush was rising in her face as she stood there for what must have seemed an eternity to her, displaying her vulnerable feminine charms to the raunchy men in the darkened audience while her mistress, seated behind her, casually inspected her naked bottom.

At a gesture from Victoria, Madeleine moved up to the rigid girl, and whispered something in her ear. Gradually, like a beautiful automaton moving in slow motion, the girl turned and lowered herself, obediently getting to her knees, kneeling before the black-stockinged legs of her mistress, undoubtedly grateful to have her back to the audience once more. Madeleine unclipped the lead, and surreptitiously shifted the riding crop to her right hand, signaling her readiness to use the instructive wand should it become necessary. Now, with a light warning tap on Diane's bare behind, she urged the girl forward, towards the crossed legs of her mistress.

Diane moved up on her knees, her eyes on those attractive legs, and the stockinged foot that swung idly before her. The Mistress of Ironwood slowly raised that foot, and held her rigid leg out, the pointed toes aimed straight at her naked love slave. Diane hesitated, suddenly unsure, wavering as though unable to continue what had been started. Madeleine, on the alert for just such a sign of reticence, leaned over to hiss a harsh command in the girl's ear as she drew the tip of the riding crop menacingly up the eloquent curvature of Diane's tense butt which tightened instinctively at the deadly hint.

The threat was real enough. Diane submitted, moving to do as she was told. She reached out and took the proffered foot in her hands, unbuckling the thin straps that held the sandal in place, and slipping the loose shoe off the stockinged foot. Then, without pause, she leaned over, bending down to bring her lips into contact with the toes of her mistress, bestowing a kiss through the veil of black nylon; the perverse thrill made those toes curl with pleasure.

Now she kissed the top of the foot, then looked up hesitantly at Madeleine who stood over her, arms akimbo, watching her progress with a critical eye. Madeleine nodded, and Diane proceeded to kiss her way up to the ankle, kissing, moving her lips, nibbling her way up.

"Lick it!" Madeleine's insistent hiss was loud enough to be heard where we sat.

Obediently, Diane extended her tongue and began to lap up that sleek, nyloned length. Victoria's eyes lidded over as she sunk back into idle bliss, warmed by the pleasures of her personal love slave who paid this mindless, obsequious devotion to her elegantly curved legs. The girl was dutifully kissing and licking a wet trail up the leg to the knee, then shuffling closer at a tap on the bare bottom from her mentor, she brought her face up to her mistress' lap, there to offer her kisses along the top surface of the curving thigh.

Victoria looked down on the girl, watching her ministrations through hooded eyes, and she stirred sensuously, slowly, liquidly moving her hips, uncrossing her elegant legs. We heard the rasp of nylon in the silence of that expectant room as those long legs scissored languidly, then fell loosely apart in negligent, offering what they held between them in wanton abandon.

Madeleine brought the riding crop into play, using the end to raise the slippery gown the last few inches, uncovering Victoria's thickly fleeced vulva. She pointed to an inner thigh, and Diane's lips submissively followed the pointer paying tribute to the graceful contours of those inner thighs, wetting the inner surfaces as she slowly made her way up along the sheer nylon and across the shaded elastic topbands. Madeleine had her trace the arching line of the upper ridge of the topband and soon had the girl licking avidly at the silky smooth flesh of the innerthigh. And when her devoted tongue found that sensitive band of flesh, Victoria drew in a sharp shivering breath and brought her hands up to lay them on the back of the burrowing head.

As Diane licked along the very tops of her legs, Victoria let out a low rumbling moan and her head fell back on the pillows, her mane of radiant black hair spilling back around her. Feebly, her hands groped for the head ensconced between her restless thighs; the fingers twisting the soft brown hair tightened as she held the girl in place. Deliberately, she pulled the girl in, guiding those obsequious lips closer to her needy sex, forcing the girl to bend her neck till her lank collar length hair fell forward along the face that was buried in Victoria's superheated crotch. Victoria squirmed, grinding her pubic arch against the helpless girl's mouth and chin, smothering her in the intoxicating smell, pressing her face into the slick folds of her hot wet cunt.

At last Victoria released her and Diane, breathing heavily, came up for air. She tossed her hair back and we could see her lips and chin glistened, smeared with copious love juices. Victoria's hand played with a lock of Diane's hair, rubbing the tress between her fingers as she smiled beneficently down and muttered something only the two lovers could hear.

In response Diane brought up her hands and to finger the pouting cuntlips that waited before her, embedded in that hairy crotch. Experimentally, she plucked at the ragged folds, rubbing the pliant lips between thumb and forefinger. Victoria tensed, and held herself perfectly still as, with delicate precision, Diane ran her thumbs down along the swollen labia and pressed open that passion flower, revealing the gleaming innerfolds, a salmon pink blossom that flushed outward from the darkened opening.

And now we waited, tense with anticipation, as the girl brought her lips closer to the forbidden fruit, summoning up her courage for her first deliberate taste of another woman's cunt. The very thought of performing oral sex on another woman would have been inconceivable to a girl like Diane only a few short weeks before. But here at Ironwood, reality often took dramatic and sudden turns. And so the cautious and careful girl, who kept sex confined to a narrow and closely watched channel, now found herself facing a throbbing vibrant cunt, her nostrils flaring with the scent of the thoroughly aroused woman who squirmed impatiently before her.

We saw that narrow pink tongue peek out and then extend boldly, stiffening, as the girl leaned closer, bringing the tip of that tongue to the slick, fleshy folds. And we also saw the delicious shiver that ran through the long legged brunette at that first thrilling contact, as a helpless moan escaped her lips. Now, still holding that cunt splayed open with her pressing thumbs, Diane brought her tongue straight up the center, lapping in a single broad stroke and getting a breathy sigh of satisfaction from the pleasured woman.

I wondered what thoughts went through her head as she learned to first use her tongue to give indescribable pleasures to another woman. Had she read about this, saw the forbidden films perhaps kidding with some boyfriend, as they watched a porno actress perform? Had she wondered what it would be like, to do it with another woman? And now here she was—a lusty cuntlapper!

* * *

Burning to get at each other, the eager lovers didn't bother with shoes and socks, but fell into each arms, pressing their naked bodies together, suddenly hungry for more. It was as if a dam had burst, and their burgeoning passions become fully inflamed. Margo's firm cones were squashed to bulge out between their hard pressed bodies; hard nipples bored into the shallow chested Whitney's flattened rises. They were locked in a passionate kiss, a kiss that was long and hard, with flickering tongues that pushed their way into opened mouths. The two bare-breasted women were squirming in heat, rubbing their tits together, savoring the warm softness of malleable tittie flesh crushed between their wriggling torsos.

I heard a movement across the room, and turned to see my raven-haired assistant leaning back in her chair, shoulders pressed back into the curving cushion. She had one hand jammed down the front of her black twill pants. She was breathing hard, her gleaming eyes fixed on the steamy lesbian action, while the hand buried in her pants was slowly moving, palming her mounded vulva in a deep languid caress. Before her eyes the two lovers lay absorbed in each other, limbs intertwined. The smaller girl lay on her back, slowly moving her hips, while her older sister covered her body, writhing in agitated passion, pressing her tight breasts against the modest disks of her smaller companion.

As Whitney lay down along the couch, Margo crawled up along her outstretched figure, and now it was the younger girl who seemed intent on pleasuring her friend by attending to those taut conical tits with tight hardened nipples that were being brushed up to tease along her sprawled body. As those swaying breasts were brought forward, she opened her lips to accept the right nipple into her mouth, even as her hand came up to cradle and test the resiliency of the dangling left tit. Now it was Margo's turn to close her eyes. She raised herself up on extended arms and let her breasts dangle over the girl's mouth; as the thin blonde paid tribute to her jutting breasts, she arched her back in sensual pleasure.

Whitney lapped that large expanded nipple with a broad stroke of her flattened tongue, then sucked it in between her teeth, while its owner tossed her head and whimpered like a hurt kitten.

Margo fell on her and the excited women rubbed their naked bodies together, squirming in heat on that green velvet couch. Excited hands were everywhere, hot and feverish, exploring each others writhing body. Margo played her companion like a instrument: sliding wondering fingers over that nubile chest, following the shallow contours of the upper chest, then moving hotly down along her flanks, skimming once more over those dimly circumscribed breasts, lightly grazing the fully-erected nipples. Driven crazy with lust, young Whitney was flinging her head from side to side, the pony-tail whipping the plush pillow. She shook vigorously; a long shivering moan escaped her lips.

Her dominant lover managed to insert a hand down between their tightly-pressed bodies to cup Whitney's womanhood, digging curving fingers into the soft fleshy underarch. The young girl's loins twisted up in lustful response and her arms flew up to wrap around her lover's bare back and squeeze her even more tightly to her own needy body.

Margo pulled back abruptly leaving Whitney's upraised arms to close on nothing but air. Moving with frenzied lust, she grabbed the girl's narrow shoulders and threw her back against the cushions. Then while Whitney wriggled in heat on the velvet couch, Margo started working her way down the girl's front. This time she paid only perfunctory attention to those thoroughly aroused breasts, lapping the upstanding nipples in passing as she grazed lower, licking and kissing that hot writhing body, moving down toward the puckered navel, kissing along the indentations of each jutting hipbone, lapping her way back and forth across the taut plane of the girl's quivering belly with broad, wet strokes that ended up edging along the soft pale down at the very top of that blond Venusmound. And when she kissed her friend there, and pressed her tongue in hard, right between the legs, Whitney was electrified. Her head shot up and arched back; her hands flew down to clutch the burrowing head.

We heard her whimper as her head fell weakly back on the pillow, and her lushes flutter down, as she gave herself up to the warm wonderful waves of pleasure generated by that restless tongue of a lover determined to pay her obsequious devotion.

Margo was clearly in charge. She moved smoothly and languidly, ducking between those slender young legs, bringing her hands up to spread the girl's loose thighs, urging open her lissome lover up to show her what was between her legs, so she might better get at the small mounded sex. She gave a tickling lick along the inner thighs, than advanced once more to the lightly fleeced vagina, licking her way up between the girl's legs, following the delicate folds of the vagina, then up the center slit in a long lapping stroke. Whitney moaned, as the older woman, with single minded devotion, licked her way along the very crest of the pubis, nosing into the puff of fine curlings as she followed the gently-sloping mound of young Whitney's blond-furred sex.

Trembling with excitement, Margo slid her hands under the girl's hips and eased her naked loins to the front edge of the couch. Then she went down before the thin blonde, moved up between the dangling legs and encouraged those slack thighs to open wide as she dove in, burying her nose in the spongy mat of soft hair, her nostrils flaring with the full woman smell, the tangy musk of arousal, that was warm and moist. The blond head nuzzled into the pale curlings impregnated with love-dew oozing from the passion-swollen lips; the tongue probed deeply, tasting the deeply flushed petals that protruded, slick and swollen, between the held-opened thighs. Margo slid her hands into the splayed thighs. Extended thumbs pried open the blond pussy, pressed back the fleshy lips; Margo rammed her flattened tongue straight up the slick insides of her young friend's pulsating core, causing the passion-soaked blonde to whimper a plea, to mumble and toss her head from side to side in hot delirium.

I heard an answering grunt come from across the room, deep throated and tight, and I turned to see Renata rubbing herself off with fiery urgency. The hand jammed down the front of her pants was palming her grinding cunt, while her hips bucked in lewd response. Whitney's moan brought me back to the enthusiastic cunt-lapping, the squishy sounds of which were audible in that quiet room. Margo's face was deep in the younger woman's crotch, nose and lips pressed into the spread netherlips, face buried in the wet warm folds of soft pussyflesh. Whitney's sinewy legs came up to close on that blond head, and tighten clamped around Margo's ears.

Whitney's lithe body arched back and she let out a screech of ecstatic delight. The girl was skating on the edge of a ragged orgasm. The bare legs tightened, squeezing that burrowing head; her small butt was clenched, as her hips rose up, straining high off the seat cushion. Her lover with unerring timing, took advantage of the moment to stiffen her tongue and stab repeatedly into those pulsating depths.

The slender blond body tightened into a long bowed arch, her loins came up to teeter at an impossibly curved apex, and the girl strained upward and let out a long series of tiny yelps, a high pitched crescendo that ended when a tremendous convulsion shook her. She flailed about wildly, grabbing and holding that blonde head that sought her core, grinding her friend's face into her slick, sopping wet pussy, while she let out a long wavering moan.

CLASSICAL PIECES

As she recounted her feelings, her hand moved slowly creeping up my naked thigh, and I gave her an affectionate squeeze in response. Abruptly, she sat up on her knees, and brightly proposed doing something equally good for me as I had done for her. Always eager to try the new games this inventive little sex kitten came up with, I smiled in agreement. She urged me down to lay flat on the bed and then rolled me over onto my belly. I watched her out of the corner of my eye as she grabbed the bottle of champagne.

I closed my eyes as my fun-loving playmate poured a stream of the lively liquid onto my back, letting it trickle down into my rearcrack. My butt cheeks clenched instinctively against the cold splash of the bubbly, and my hips jerked forward in excited response. I realized I was hard again when I felt my manhood rub against the sheet as I slid forward. I felt her steadying hand on the small of my back, and my hips twitched, as a second stream of champagne was poured into my hidden valley.

I waited with eyes closed, tense and expectant. Now I felt the faint tickle of the fine ends of that silky hair being drawn across the backs of my thighs. My cock jumped, electrified by the tickling thrill.

Then an even greater thrill powered through me with the first touch of Nikki's sweet tongue as it slid wetly into my crack, probing, licking and lapping up the runny liquid. My butt clamped in instinctive reaction to the electric thrill, but she placed her small hands on my buttocks and pried me apart, holding me open so she could dive right in. The feel of her nose and lips in my ass, her wet tongue sliding up my rear crack was absolutely exquisite, and I heard myself moan and quiver with pleasure. Busy Nikki spent some time there, slowly trailing up and down, making little slurping sounds, while I twisted my hips and squirmed in wild excitement, driven wild by the heavenly feel of that agile tongue that sent repeated jolts of pleasure through me and had my painfully erect prick once again throbbing with lust.

A single blinding thrill shot through me as her wet agile tongue found my anus, and the devilish vixen inserted her stiffened tongue, stabbing at that clenching target repeatedly, then sticking her tongue flatly on my asshole and pressing, probing my spasming asshole. I groaned in helpless abandon, as wave after wave of ecstatic delight swept over me.

A small hand snaked under my body searching for, and finding, my iron-hard prick. And the electric touch those girlish fingers gripping my cock, combined with the exquisite feel of that slithering tongue in my crack, set me off, and I came with an earth-shaking explosion. I came with groan, rubbing my pulsating prick on the sheets, as I exploded in a powerful climax. And as I lay in the sticky cum, depleted, and gasping for breath, my playful bedmate bent down to kiss my butt. Then, snuggling lower, she lay her head on my ass, using it as a pillow. Totally drained, I slipped into the warmth of well-deserved sleep. And the last thing I remember was the whispered:

"Welcome home, Mr. James."

* * *

Through half-lidded eyes I looked down on that bowed head, and watched as this most apt pupil used just the pads of her fingertips to lightly trace up and down my swollen length, outlining my male equipment from the crown of my prick down to my balls. And when she tenderly cupped my hairy scrotum, and fondled me with a light, deft touch, an even more powerful rush of pleasure shot through me. Once again, I fought the demanding surge of pleasure down as a helpless groan escaped my lips.

With shaking hands I reached out for her, curving my hands around the girl's small head, running my fingers into the silken mass, digging into that hair till I clasped her by the head and pulled her forward. And I held her there, my curled finger in her hair, clamping her small head so her face was pressed to me, buried between the cradle of my hips, her silken hair spilling across my loins. I could feel the warmth of her breath on me, and I twisted my hips, rubbing my tumescent manhood all over her pretty face, letting her feel my urgency, my need, my desire.

I eased back a little to give her room to work me over. Her mouth found me and her lips began moving up and down my swollen prick. I heard my own whimpers coming as from a distance as delicious waves of pure pleasure welled up in me, drowning out all else. And Robin continued her obsequious devotion, methodically covering every inch, working me over with avid lips and agile tongue, until she had me squirming helplessly, uncontrollably, driven to distraction by the exquisite feel of that unrelenting tongue action.

Now she extended her talented tongue until the very tip touched the sensitive underside just below the crown. I clenched my fists and groaned, craning back at the piercing thrill generated by the feel of that wet, tantalizing tongue as it lightly fluttered along the underside of my straining manhood.

Instantly, she switched tactics, flattening her tongue and laving with broad wet strokes, lapping up the length, swirling around the ridge of the crown then slithering down to the base. And there she would lightly nibble at the root of the shaft, soaking my pubic hair. Her velvety tongue slid wetly, lavishly, all over my scrotum, till she reached the perineum and once there she crouched down and stretched up awkwardly to bury her face between my thighs, electrifying me with jolting thrills as she pressed nose and lips to my crotch.

I couldn't stand the maddening ticklish pleasure any longer, and my hands reached out to extract her burrowing head. When she came up for air, it was to immediately go back to my erect penis, lightly holding it in both hands and greedily licking it all over like a kid with a lollipop, broadly lapping along its length till my upstanding cock was glistening with the sheen of her saliva.

Then the tickling play of her lively tongue stopped, and when I looked down at her through half-lidded eyes, it was to see her reach out to grab me, and tilt the rigid shaft towards her as she bent down to slowly take my cock in her mouth.

Inch by inch, she took me in, sliding the taut ring of her lips down the swollen shaft, ducking her head to go down on me. Looking down on her through slitted eyes I watched the top of her small head as she bobbed up and down.

Now this expert cocksucker was working hard, her cheeks hollowing out, head bobbing up and down in measured rhythms, as she vacuumed me with single-minded determination. I groaned at the exquisite agony, and clamped my hands on her naked shoulders and held on, tightening my grip, clenching my teeth as the most excruciating waves of pleasure rocketed through me. Then the enthusiastic brunette tried something new, she continued that slow even sucking but now she added a delicious twirl of her tongue each time she raised her head. The novel sensation instantly drove me to the ragged edge of pleasure, it was a pleasure that was almost painful, unbearable, straining my endurance to its absolute limits as I held on, arching my rigid hips up off the seat, clinging to my sanity.

The last shreds of control were evaporating at an alarming rate under the sheer intensity of the repeated thrills, thrills which rocketed through me, escalating wildly, till I felt myself careening towards the supreme moment of climax. The powerful upsurge in my loins told me I could hold out no longer. My last conscious act was to push the dark-haired girl back, extracting my cock, and aiming it right at her face. At that exact moment I exploded in a tremendous climax sending a powerful surge of cum erupting from the pulsating prick to hit her squarely in the face. Then I was coming with furious urgency, thick wads of cream jetting out to splatter on that lovely countenance, painting her pretty features with sticky ropes of cum in pulsating explosions that seemed to go on, and on, and on.

* * *

I ordered her back onto the bed, and awkwardly, for her arms were tied behind her, she climbed up to once more assume the submissive pose—on her knees, with head and shoulders lowered, her brow pressed against the pillow. Kitteridge's freshly-chastised rump stuck out prominently, the taut skin flushed, warm, and suffused with a rosy pink blush. Once more, I scrambled up to kneel behind her. I couldn't resist running a hand down over the jutting mounds, causing her to flinch and whimper at my touch on her tenderized mounds.

The spanking had the desired salutary effect, for when I now applied for entrance, there was only a token, instinctual tightening, before her resistance softened and I was able to force the tip of my finger into the tiny gate as the sphincter muscle gradually yielded to my determined advance. Once through the portal I worked my greased finger further up into her, inch by inch, up the hot tight channel, getting tight little grunts from behind the ballgag with each inch I gained.

Kit uttered an urgent whimper and tossed her head from side to side as I wiggled my finger up her tight little ass. Her muted cries became one long tremulous moan as I slowly withdrew the offending digit, watching the clinging asshole distend as I made my retreat. But the retreat was only a tactical one, made till I could sally forth again, this time to assault the gate with my rock hard prick!

Placing the head squarely on my vulnerable target, I pressed inward until the tight ring of rubbery flesh yielded and the crown of my cock forced its way right up young Kitteridge's bottom. Slowly I eased myself in, with Kit whimpering every inch of the way as I forced my cock right up the tight-fitting channel until I was about halfway in. Then, with a furious thrust I lunged, burying myself up to the hilt, and getting a sharp strangled cry from the impaled female who shook and writhed in agitated fury.

I clutched her dangling tits, holding onto her as I pulled back and lunged with my hips, driving all the way in. She squirmed helplessly, and gave out with a passionate moan, smothered by the ball gag. Her sensual writhing only fired my excitement and I pounded into her, grinding my churning hips against her solid mounds and letting her get the feel of my prick up her ass. Her tight little anus spasmed, clenching my prick, sending delicious sensations coursing through my body. I felt her shudder with pleasure, moaning softly as I draped myself over her and squeezed her tits, holding on to them as I fucked the girl's ass, and skidded towards an exploding climax that had me pumping wads of come into Miss Kitteridge's churning buttocks.

Kit collapsed onto the bed and I fell draped over her trembling form. My cheek lay pressed against her smooth sweaty back, the cradle of my hips snugly fitted against her nicely warmed rearmounds. My softened cock, depleted and shrunken was expelled from her spasming anus which still twitched with the quivers that ran through her body in tiny aftershocks, the remnants of her own powerful orgasm.

Taking pity on her, tied as she was, I released her wrists. And the grateful girl fell forward, flinging out her arms and flopping on her belly, her head turned to one side. She lay with eyes closed, shoulders heaving, slowly coming back down to earth.

* * **

Most women are fumbling amateurs when it comes to cocksucking. And while many of them are well-intentioned, it's not surprising that they should be so inept, considering that that most exquisite feminine skill is one their mothers never taught them. Left to their own devices, they learn by trial and error. Of course there are those fortunate few who seem to instinctively grasp the essence of using mouth and lips and tongue and hands to pleasure the male and bring him to the ultimate heights of ecstatic delight.

At Ironwood, these skills were systematically taught and rigorously practiced till even the most inexperienced and inhibited of our novices was able to lavishly tease and titillate until, working with the consummate skill of a professional call girl, they would induce a cascade of soul-piercing thrills in wave after long delicious wave. And only then would they allow the long-tantalized male the unsurpassed pleasure of ultimate orgasmic release. They would learn the many creative variations on this theme, till like practiced courtesans, their moves became entirely instinctive, an extension of their very being found in pleasuring an other.

These thoughts flashed through my mind as I stood up, towering over her, looking down on the docile blond head poised just inches from my erect prick. I slipped out of my shoes, opened my belt, and shoved my slacks down my legs. Then I quickly skimmed down my briefs and stepped out of the tangle of discarded clothing. Naked from the waist down, my semi-rigid prick extending straight out, swaying obscenely and pointed right toward her pretty face, I took a small step forward.

"You will begin between my legs. Get your face in there, right up . . . all the way . . . into my crotch . . . now lick! Go on, do it!" I commanded in voice that would brook no further delay.

To do as I ordered, Jane was forced to crouch down, ducking her head between my legs, while she placed a hand on the front of my thigh to support herself. Then twisting awkwardly and craning back, she tilted her head back and strained upward to bury her face between my thighs, her nose pressed up against my scrotum, so she could do my bidding, seeking the sensitive flesh of the perineum. At the first tentative probe of her tongue in that secret place, a perverse electric thrill surged through me, and I shivered with involuntary delight. Shifting my weight, I widened my stance to allow even greater access to the burrowing blond head. The maddening tickle of her lively tongue in that secret crevice soon had me wriggling and squirming in wild excitement, dancing in sweet agony that I knew I couldn't tolerate for much longer.

"Enough," I gasped, gripping her by the short silky hair at the back of the neck, and yanking her head roughly back out from between my legs. "Now, my balls . . . lick them," I managed to get out in a strained voice.

The docile blond dove in to lap at the underside of my scrotum, sliding her tongue in long, broad strokes, soaking the tiny hairs and coating the crinkled sac with a sheen of her saliva. I closed my eyes to savor the pure bliss of her sweet, velvety tongue as it slid wetly over my balls.

"Now the rest . . . go on . . . lick my cock!" I hissed with mounting urgency.

Jane seemed to be getting into the spirit of things now, for she no longer needed my encouragement. In fact she was now pursuing her task with an eagerness I found quite surprising.

With long delicious strokes she ran her agile tongue up along the side of my stiff shaft, swirling around the crown before slithering back down the other side. Now she reached up to grab my swaying cock and she held me loosely in her delicate cool hand while she hungrily lapped my manhood, running her tongue along the underside and sending tiny spasms of pure pleasure pulsing repeatedly through me.

Suddenly, feeling my control slipping, I desperately reached down to grab her head and pull her back to relieve the exquisite torment for a few brief seconds. When I released my grip, my eager cocksucker, by now warming up to her task quite well, attacked the vulnerable underside once again, this time flicking her tongue and stabbing at the sensitive flesh just under the ridge of the crown. I clenched my teeth and gasped, shivering when the relentless tongue slithered up to thoroughly lave the turgid knob.

Then she was working me over with lips and gums and tongue, nibbling and licking avidly, till I could stand no more of the sweet torture. With feverish haste, I clamped both hands on the sides of her face and pulled her mouth down over my aching phallus, forcing her to accept my entire length into that warm moist cavern.

"Suck it!" I croaked.

And suck it she did. Curling her lips protectively over the ridge of her teeth and sliding her rimmed lips up and down my length, she bobbed her head, vacuuming me with mounting enthusiasm, till I had to grip her shoulders to hold on. I no longer knew or cared if this was a natural talent or one she had learned somewhere, but it was obvious that this delightfully surprising woman knew a thing or two about giving an incredible blowjob.

Her energetic efforts soon had me bucking my hips in involuntary answer, thrusting deep into the enfolding depths, fucking her mouth, while I tightened my grip on her naked shoulders, fighting desperately to hold on to my rapidly melting control. Thrill after thrill pounded through me as I was inevitably driven to the very edge. And there I struggled to hold on, teetering on the brink for a long, excruciating eternity, before finally yielding to the irresistible surge of a monstrous eruption.

At the exact moment of climax, I pulled out, erupting in a brilliant mind-blasting explosion of energy. Slapping a hand on the back of her head, I shoved her forward, so I could rub my pulsating prick all over her pretty face, letting the erupting jets of cum spurt forth to spatter her fine aristocratic features, decorating her forehead, trailing down her closed eyelids, along her nose, and down one cheek, painting her lovely face with thick ropy gobs of sperm. The creamy residue soaked the edge of her hair, and dribbled down over her lips and chin.

Suddenly drained of all passion, my knees weakened and my legs turned rubbery as I clutched the shoulders of the kneeling female for support. Through narrowed eyes I looked down to see her reach up to wipe my dripping issue from her face. I couldn't help feeling that we had reached a new level of understanding, Jane and I.

* * *

I grabbed my prick and pulled once or twice, reassuring my needy prick of the satisfaction to come. Then I scrambled down to the foot of the bed, to release her ankles. Helga stirred languidly, scissoring her freed legs on the silk. Still groggy, she raised her head and shoulders to look down at me through half-lidded eyes where I knelt on the bed. I lifted her slack legs up, ran my hands up the backs of those stockinged columns, and forced them apart to fully expose her wet, gaping pussy.

Half crazed with lust I fell on her, impaling her, plunging my painfully swollen cock into the warm sanctuary of lovely Helga's slick, spasming cunt. I luxuriated in the delicious feeling of having my prick slide so smoothly up the silken walls of her enfolding womanhood. Immediately, the long-legged beauty threw her exquisite limbs around my hips, welcoming me joyfully, embracing me with a fiery urgency.

Her sinewy thighs tightened, and the thrill of those nylon-encased columns encircling my loins drove me wild, sending my passions skyrocketing, while the lusty blond spurred me, with urgent pleas whispered in my ear. Our fucking was at first, wildly erratic, but we soon settled into an even cadence. Resting on splayed elbows, I watched her face as with eyes closed she absorbed each powerful thrust. I was pumping into the girl with slow, measured strokes, while she was thumping my butt with her heels and meeting each plunge with her own bounding pelvic upthrust. In this way we rode to a gallop, my hips rocking furiously, her loins gyrating, and bouncing off the mattress, all the while her lips were babbling heated words of lust, desperate pleases to be fucked even more.

I could feel the tension rising in her body before the first convulsive shudder racked her thin frame, sending me careening over the edge at the same time. I surrendered to the inevitable, and came with a violent tremor, crushing my groin against her furry vulva, erupting deep inside her, flooding her innards with my sperm in deep rutting thrusts, holding myself there, buried to the hilt, while a spasm of pure delight electrified me and obliterated all in a single flash of blinding pleasure.

Measure for Measure

I CAUTIOUSLY OPENED the rear door to Gretchen's classroom, and slipped unobserved into one of the hard wooden seat at the very back of the room. Gretchen saw me enter, but she was the only one who did. Since the class sat with their backs to the door, I was able to take my seat without disturbing the lesson in progress. I was eager to see classroom discipline meted out at first hand.

I didn't have long to wait, since considering the number of rules and the spirited nature of some of our students, it was only a matter of time till one of the girls ran afoul of some regulation, and incurred the wrath of their stern teacher.

The class was being called upon for recitations, and it became painfully obvious that an impetuous young blonde named Maggie had not properly prepared her assignment. The young woman was of indeterminate age, but she had the body of a leggy adolescent and her more juvenile appearance was enhanced by the way she wore her hair, drawn to either side to form two youthful angel wings, twin hanks of blond silk that flanked her freshly-scrubbed face.

Gretchen ordered Maggie to her feet, and pointed decisively

to the glass-fronted cabinet. It was a classroom rule that a girl about to be punished must personally fetch the proper instrument of discipline. The choices the poor girl encountered were few; none of them very appealing. The young blonde hesitated, then reluctantly selected a wicked-looking paddle, turning to offer it to her stern mistress with a look of definite unease. The paddle was as long as a cricketer's bat with a sizable broad blade and an eighteen-inch haft; a weapon substantial enough to be gripped with both hands. Gretchen nodded her approval; Maggie dutifully handed it over.

Without a word, Maggie turned on her heel and, with lowered head, made her way to the front of the room, there to belly up to the teacher's desk till the front edge of the desk top pressed against her thighs. Slowly, she leaned over the desk, bending at the hips and stretching down along the sides of the desk, reaching for the conveniently-placed handholds which had been ingeniously worked into the filigreed ironwork decorating the sides. I watched the leggy blonde clench her eyes shut, and tighten her white-knuckled grip, grimly steeling herself to receive the impending spanking.

But she would be made to wait, for her mistress was not yet entirely pleased with the arrangements. Gretchen stepped up behind the anxious girl and pinched the hem of the brief, pleated skirt between thumb and forefinger, delicately lifting the skirt up and neatly folding the soft wool fabric over the bent girl's back. The unveiling revealed Maggie's pantied behind, the rearcheeks clenching fearfully, cowering in dread anticipation of the harsh attention they were about to receive. I was pleased to see that the bending girl's thin white underpants, drawn taut over the twin curves, had ridden up behind so that the her chubby bottomcheeks peeked out impertinently from below the overarching legbands.

Gretchen, with a decidedly wicked grin, now surprised me by turning to offer the lethal paddle to *me!* Thrilled at the opportunity fate presented to me, I graciously accepted the proffered haft. I took the weight of the weapon in my hand, hefting it a bit. Having already learned much from Cora on the value of anticipation, I had no intention of starting right in on the waiting girl. First, I meant to amuse myself by savoring that cute, tight-cheeked young bottom.

I tucked the paddle under my arm and stepping up behind the bending female, I clamped my cupped hands firmly on her jutting mounds. Taken by surprise, the girl recoiled, jerking up off the desk. I tightened my grip; forced her back down. She squirmed a bit but lowered her shoulders submissively, coming to rest once again on the desktop, her head turned to one side, eyes closed tightly. This was not the type of treatment she had set herself to receive!

Now I kneaded those taut little mounds, pressing my fingers into their firm resiliency, palming them, wobbling them, rubbing the thin slippery panties all over the pert domes of Maggie's little rump. The tantalized girl couldn't help squirming in mounting agitation.

After playing with that delightful girlish bottom in this way for a several moments, I crouched down behind the bending girl, eager to conduct a more thorough inspection. My eyes were only inches from her crotch as I studied the delicious undercurves that met at the juncture where the gusset of the panties had been pulled into a taut crease caught up between her legs. Extending a single stiff finger I poked the silken strip even deeper into her cleft, getting a startled whoop and a bounding recoil from the electrified girl.

On a perverse whim, I clutched the waistband of her panties, hauling them up stretching them till the narrow gusset was firmly embedded between her pussylips, while Maggie grunted and shifted uneasily. I paused to admire the neat *cache-sexe* I had arranged, snugly moulding her pubis, the narrow strip of twisted nylon all but disappeared between the rearcheeks, leaving the girl's saucy little mounds pertly exposed.

The mouth-watering sight fired my lust and, with tingling

palms I grabbed her hips, sliding my hands around to curl my fingers in the thin elastic waistband. Clutching handfuls of panty I eased her drawers lower, baring the perfectly symmetrical domes with their tight crack, and then bringing into view the tiny wisps of pale blond fleece marking the half-hidden vulva—a pouch tucked up between her tightly-pressed legs. I left the twisted nylon at half-mast, displaced underpants encircling her agile young thighs. Slowly, I got to my feet. And then, with my eyes on the newly-bared bottom, I reached for the paddle.

Tapping her heel lightly, I urged Maggie to widen her stance. She shifted her weight, obediently if reluctantly, spreading her legs and setting her stance while she renewed her white-knuckled grip on the iron handholds. Her bent body went rigid with anticipation as she waited, tense, hardly daring to breathe. I stepped back and raised the paddle, tentatively tapping my rounded target to size up the distance. I smiled to see her vulnerable rearcheeks clench anxiously at the first delicate kiss of the smooth wooden blade.

Without further ado, I hauled back and struck, landing a satisfyingly solid smack which sent a resounding echo through the hushed room.

THWACK!

The crisp smack jolted my victim so that she bounded up on her toes and gave out with a tiny, high-pitched yelp. Immediately, an angry red welt began to form across her juddering rearmounds. Taking careful aim, I whacked her ass again, and again, flattening the resilient softness of that gyrating butt with two quick shots fired in rapid succession, sending Maggie bounding up on her toes with each well placed slap.

THWACK!.... THWACK!

Maggie gave out with a tight-lipped whimper and wiggled her throbbing rearend as though to shake off the sting. I watched the pinkish blush spread across the twin domes, as the bending girl worked her butt muscles spasmodically, the cheeks clenching, the sides hollowing in rapid spasms, then tightening in fearful anticipation, as she hardened herself to receive my next shot. But I was in no hurry. I decided to wait for her to relax, the hardened muscles to uncoil. At Ironwood, brute force was frowned upon; timing and finesse were everything.

She must have been surprised when, instead of the dreaded paddle, it was a pair of comforting masculine hands she felt touch her inflamed butt. At first, her cowering cheeks flinched at my touch, but soon they slackened, and then she was actually shoving her jutting bottom back into my cupped hands in lewd, obscene movements, squirming her hips like a little whore, and sighing in pure sensual delight. I savored the warmth of those lush contours, caressing their silky smoothness for a several minutes, and gradually lulling the girl into dreamy contentment.

Swiftly, I stepped back and struck, this time adding just a flick of the wrist. Catching my victim completely off guard.

THWACK!

Maggie jerked upright and yelped at the top of her lungs. Her hands flew back, and she rubbed her ass in a frantic effort to ease the sting. She had, of course, broken the rules by failing to maintain the proper position. And she knew it!

There was no need for me to admonish her. In docile resignation, Maggie bent stiffly down. I watched her take a deep breath, tightly clenching the iron handles, and biting down on her lowerlip, setting herself to receive what she knew would be inevitable.

As a result of her agitated squirming, the skirt had fallen back into place, and I now peeled it back as I had seen Gretchen do. Confronted with the throbbing, reddened bottomcheeks of her well-punished behind, I suddenly took pity on the bending girl, and quickly finished her off with a single light slap.

Her punishment over, the chastised female straightened up stiffly, her brief skirt falling back into place. She was sniffling a little, and I noticed tears in the corners of her eyes. She had a flushed and slightly-bedraggled look, yet she was none the worse for wear. The distraught young woman started to hitch up her displaced panties, but Gretchen stopped her. She was made to leave her underpants lowered, spanning her knees, while resuming her seat, to attend to her lessons sitting erect and bare-bottomed on the hard wood bench.

* * *

The first girl was to be given five strokes. She was a short in stature but pleasingly curved, with plump little tits and a nicely-rounded bottom. Ringlets of auburn curls framed her broad face, falling to tease her shoulders, and a rich tangle of reddish-brown pubic hair was clearly visible through the wet front of her coral-tinted panties.

Monique had already selected a suitable weapon, one of the short-handled, wide bladed paddles much favored for use by the overseers of Ironwood. This paddle was a bit larger than the type used for table tennis, with a pliable thin blade coated in rubber on the business side. The rubber facing was grooved to assure a stinging bite.

The girl strained to look back behind her, her eyes wide with apprehension as mistress Van Daam approached, the paddle at the ready. Monique stood for a moment regarding the upturned buttocks encased in those damp underpants. Of course the thin panties offered little protection, yet at Ironwood it was a rule that paddling must be administered on bare bottoms, a predilection more symbolic than anything else, Cora had once confided in me.

And so Monique prepared her victim by plucking the waistband and peeling down the wet clinging nylon, lowering the silken scrap to a place halfway down the thighs, to leave the displaced underwear there, hobbling the girl just above her knees.

One more the pleasing shape of that cute naked behind was exposed to our eyes, while the upended girl waited anxiously for the swift kiss of the dreaded paddle. Monique took a moment to size up her target, testing the paddle in a half swing that stopped an inch or so short. Then she hauled back and delivered a crisp stinging blow.

THWACK!. . . . went the solid sound of wood, splattering the soft fleshy mounds; and the little girl bounded up on her toes at the juddering impact.

And before the girl could recover, the wicked paddle struck her wobbling rearmounds again, and again.

THWACK!. . . . THWACK!. . . . THWACK! Three crisp solid smacks were delivered with an extra snap of the wrist that sent the wooden paddle blade into those soft cringing bottomcheeks.

There was a pause, and you could see the tense anticipation in the girl's thighs, the tightening of her butt muscles as she steeled herself to receive the next slap. Monique took her time, trying out a swing that would bring her wrist up in a deep arc. Abruptly, she whacked that pert bare ass with a single vicious cut. The girl yelped and sprung up on her toes, squirming her burning bottom, but she managed to hold her place, her fists tightening on the lower bar. Pleased at her obedience, Monique released her charge and ordered her to take her seat, which the relieved girl did, sitting down quite gingerly.

* * *

We talked about Venice, and about her business, about her plans for the future. She teased me about what she assured me was my "wicked reputation," and smiled when she made some allusion to "meeting, the wolf in his lair"—this in the same lighthearted teasing manner. I noticed a distinctly licentious gleam had crept into her merry gaze.

Somewhat bemused, I smiled back, and waited. Once again I found myself captivated by the woman's charm, her confident feminine pride, her darkly eloquent eyes. As my eyes found hers, I felt suddenly self-conscious, acutely aware of the woman's sexuality, and of some deeper purpose here, something unspoken that was eluding me.

In time, our conversation trailed off, and we found ourselves staring at each other, during one of those "pregnant pauses." Then Victoria seemed to make up her mind about the thing that hung in the air unsaid. Her eyes dropped to the floor, and she spent some time studying the rug in front of my chair. Then, as I waited, she took a breath and began.

"James," she began haltingly, "the moment I saw you I knew you were the strong and masterful type. My type of man. And from what I hear about Ironwood, you're also quite the disciplinarian? Rumor has it that it is you who personally administers the spankings to the naughty little girls you train here."

I said nothing, waiting with bated breath to see where this going. The dark eyes looked up at me searchingly while a tentative, half smile played across her rich full lips.

I nodded, smiling back at her, vaguely puzzled, my mind racing with a thousand possibilities. Now, in a burst of sudden determination, the pretty brunette continued.

"The thing is, James, I was wondering if . . . well, would you demonstrate your technique for me?" she managed to blurt out in a throaty whisper.

"You want me to watch while I paddle one of our girls?" I asked. The request did not seem so outrageous to me; no more than we would do for any of our more voyeuristic clients, the ones who enjoyed watching a little show from time to time.

"No. no . . . not exactly; not some girl of yours. I want you to do it to *me,*" she breathed, biting down on her curled lower lip and studying me with that devilish gleam in her eyes.

"You want me to spank *you?*" I asked carefully.

Still looking me in the eye, she nodded her pretty head.

I managed to keep my smile plastered on my face, not showing my incredulity at this astonishing good luck. I waited, still not sure I could believe my ears. But one look at the intensity in her silent eyes was enough to convince me. The woman was perfectly serious!

"Of course. How? I mean when?"

"Why not here? Now?" she whispered in a heated rush. With her eyes averted to the floor, I saw that this elegant, well-dressed lady was actually blushing like a schoolgirl. I found it charming. And I knew just what she wanted. I would immediately take charge.

"Stand up! And take off that jacket," I ordered, tight-lipped, swallowing down a knot of wildly rising excitement.

Her tongue peeked out to nervously pass over her set lips as she got to her feet and without hesitation undid the buttons of the suit jacket. With the jacket removed she waited before me in blouse and skirt, her dark eyes expectant, watching as I stood up, opened up the desk drawer and extracted a long thin ruler. Eighteen inches long, the narrow wooden strip would be ideal to whap that most appealing bottom. Her eyes followed the menacing ruler I held loosely in my hand as I came around the desk toward her.

Tucking the ruler under my arm, I reached out and placed my curved hands on the cradle of her hips so as to gently maneuver the big woman into place facing the desk. Sliding up behind her I whispered my next command into her ear.

"Belly up to the front of the desk. And bend over," I instructed

Victoria inched up, positioning herself so that the edge of the desk crossed just below her hips. Then she bent down to rest on her propped elbows. Tossing back her mane, she turned to look over her shoulder at me, like a schoolgirl seeking approval. The position was good, but not quite right.

"Reach across the desk. And hold on," I warned her.

As her hands gripped the far side of the desktop, she was

forced to lower herself further down, turning her face to the side so that one cheek rested on the padded blotter at the center of the desk. I placed a flattened palm squarely between her shoulder blades and pressed down firmly, forcing Victoria to arch her back even further and raise her behind most invitingly.

Using the ruler, I lightly tapped her ankles.

"Spread 'em," I muttered.

And Victoria spread her legs stretching the narrow skirt to its limits as she set her high heels in a widened stance.

Now, I was satisfied, at least for the time being. Victoria was nicely in place, presenting her skirted bottom to me, while I stood behind her sporting a very solid erection. Tingling with excitement, I leaned over the bending woman and brought my lips close to her ear.

"So you're one of those girls that enjoys having her ass warmed up a bit, eh?" I teased.

The dark-haired head moved in just the slightest nod.

"Say it!" I hissed.

"Yes, I like it."

"You like being spanked?" I prompted her.

"Yes, yes . . . I like being . . . sp . . . spanked," she breathed.

"And you want me to spank that pretty ass of yours, right now, don't you? Well?!"

"Yes, I want you to spank me!"

"Then you must ask nicely," I purred. "Go on, say it. Ask me to spank your pretty ass!"

"Yes, yes, spank me, James," she breathed in a voice gone suddenly husky.

"No! Say please, please spank my pretty ass, Sir," I taunted her.

"Spank my ass, Sir. Please, spank pretty my ass," the words tumbled out in a heated rush.

I couldn't help smiling to myself.

"Reach back . . . and lift up your skirt . . . all the way," I ordered.

I watched Victoria's narrow elegant hands reach behind to

clutch at the expensive fabric, grabbing handfuls and bunching it up as she hoisted the narrow skirt up to her waist uncovering a pantied rearend encased in the gauzy nylon of her sheer pantyhose.

"Not quite right," I opined critically. "A proper spanking must be administered on the bare butt to be fully appreciated," I informed her primly.

Reaching up I hooked my fingers in the thin elastic waistband grabbing panties and pantyhose in one handful, and yanked her undies down, exposing in one fell swoop the delectable twin contours of Victoria Ginacola's eminently-spankable bottom to the warm air. What I had laid out before me was a most splendid ass, not the hard girlish butt of a young woman of Ironwood, but the voluptuous, ripe curves of a mature, womanly behind. Hers was a substantial, rich and shapely ass. One simply made for spanking. I would take a great deal of delight in doing so!

I tugged the clinging nylon a few more inches down her thighs, exposing the bulge of her furry vulva, before leaving it twisted in place, spanning her arcuate legs. My hand was drawn to caress those perfectly shaped mounds, and I couldn't resist cupping those choice satiny contours, lightly squeezing, pressing curled fingers into the firm resiliency of those delightful twin domes.

Stepping back I admired the perfectly lewd invitation the bending woman presented: an attractive brunette, bare-assed, tail up and head down, waiting with growing impatience for me to warm her naked bottom. The pale sunlight coming through the tall windows fell on that perfectly rounded ass and the backs of her smooth white thighs, imparting a shimmering glint to her taut nylon-encased calves their sleek muscles strained by the demanding pose. With the skirt out of the way, it was now possible for her to widen her stance even more.

"Now spread your legs a little more . . . and hold on," I cautioned.

Victoria shifted her weight, spreading her heels even further apart, stretching the twisted nylon that still hobbled her at mid-thigh. Her knuckles tightened and her body tensed as she steeled herself to receive the kiss of the pliant ruler.

I hefted the whippy rod, slapping it against my palm, so she could hear the crisp smack. My pulse was racing as I was thrilled beyond belief by the at the sight of this sophisticated worldly businesswoman holding the humiliating pose of a naughty schoolgirl, simply begging to be spanked.

Taking my place behind and to the left of those jutting rear-mounds, I widened my stance and took aim. I hauled back and gave a smart snap to the flick of my wrist sending the wicked lath singing squarely across those vulnerable cheeks with a resounding Thwack!

Victoria let out a tight-lipped whimper, and her butt clamped tight. The curving sides hollowed out; the crack narrowed to a thin slit as the butt muscles coiled down instinctively. I didn't give her time to recover. Reaching back I whapped her clenching cheeks again, delivering a more solid whack this time, one which jarred her and propelled her forward against the massive desk.

"THWACK!

This time she recoiled and grunted; a short tight grunt that barely escaped her tightly-pressed lips. Now, it was time to pause, giving her some time to recover.

Victoria shifted uneasily, stepping in place, before setting her stance once again, and planting her heels with renewed determination. Then she looked over her shoulder at me. Her eyes were hard and bright with excitement. She curled her lower lip, biting down on it with white even teeth as she set herself to receive even more of the throbbing ache of perverse pleasure that she desperately craved. At last, she took a deep breath and signaled her readiness by a brief nod of the head.

By now the disheveled skirt had slipped to angle down, partially covering the proffered rump. I delicately lifted the fine fabric, folding it back to bare her rich womanly ass once more as I carefully adjusted the layered skirt across her waist.

Then, stepping back, I struck again, sending the whippy rod biting into soft, cringing flesh, as the lady jerked up and yelped, wiggling her ass as though to shake off the sting.

THWACK!

Now I laid it on, not hard but methodically, spanking her first directly across the center of those quivering domes, then on the firmer topslopes, and finally smacking the wobbly undercurves, leaving not a single inch of Victoria's hot, squirming bottom untouched by the stinging wooden lath.

THWACK! . . . THWACK! THWACK! THWACK! THWACK! THWACK!

Each smart slap produced a tiny ouch.

"You love it, when I warm your ass for you, don't you, Victoria?" I asked, punctuating each word with a precisely measured whack of the thin wooden ruler.

"Oh . . . yes . . . yes . . . yes . . ." she babbled deliriously.

"Tell me about it. I want to know how it feels!" I demanded harshly.

"It hurts," she managed to get out, in a deep guttural grunt.

"But it's *your* kind of hurt. And you love it."

"Oh God, yes, yes, I *love* it. I love the hurt," she hissed through clenched teeth.

Her heated whisper drove me on, till I was whipping her quivering asscheeks again and again, watching the wild dance of those juddering rearmounds as they darkened with an angry pink blush that spread all over the curved surfaces beneath the steady beat of the punishing ruler.

Her tiny yelps grew into one long passionate moan, low and earthy, and I held my hand, while she squirmed furiously, shaking her hips in a rush of secret delight. The excited woman was trying to catch her breath, her shoulders heaving as she shifted her weight from foot to foot, dancing in fiery agitation. I waited, letting the ruler drop from my hand. In time, Victoria settled down, her ragged breathing subsided, and she slowly dragged herself up onto her elbows, although she remained bent over the desk, somewhat bedraggled, skirt still rucked up around her waist. I couldn't resist any longer.

I quickly fell to my knees behind the bent-over woman and reached up to lightly caress that well-spanked bottom. She flinched at the first touch, but she stayed in place, as I skated the pads of my fingers over the silken contours of those throbbing rearcheeks. They were so soft, deeply firm, and still warm to the touch; Victoria let out a low throaty moan. Almost reverently, I leaned forward to plant a single loving kiss on Victoria's recently-chastised ass, and as I did I heard a deep sigh of profound satisfaction come from the lady who wiggled her bottom in perverse delight.

***

"Down!"

The last shreds of resistance crumbled. The defeated blonde closed her eyes and obediently lowered herself to one knee, then the other, assuming the subservient position, kneeling erect between my open thighs, her blond head tilted in abject surrender.

"Look at me!" I ordered.

But there was no response from our captive. She held herself rigidly still, kneeling erect before me, eyes riveted on the floor. I studied the top of her bowed head, the shock of ash-blond hair slanting rakishly across her forehead, the sides close-cropped in that stylish boyish cut, the subtle slope of her thin huddled shoulders, the lean proportions of her naked torso, the supple bare arms, and the delicate circular ridges of her small pancake boobs, young adolescent breasts that beckoned temptingly, rising and falling in barely restrained rhythms.

Leaning forward in my chair, I reached out to touch her, bringing a cupped hand up under her chin, raising her head to force eye contact. Her steel blue eyes held the hard glint of angry defiance; a smoldering defiance just waiting to erupt. I let my fingers trail down over her chin, while she kept her gaze steady, her eyes locked on mine in a silent battle of wills.

Using just the pads of my fingertips, I traced the lines of her neck and upperchest, gliding up the faint swell of her right breast, to graze the rubbery little nipple, before following the slight undercurve. The blond girl flinched, and curled her lip, biting down to keep from crying out. I let my fingertips slide down her satiny midriff. I watched her closely as my teasing fingers dipped down, moving inexorably towards her silvery blond sex. Her breathing quickened when I first touched her pussy; she gasped sharply, her eyes widening at the piercing thrill of first contact. With my eyes still on her face, I lightly skated over the pale trace of down that marked the slightly mounded curve of her vulva.

Shifting forward, I leaned over, bringing my face to within inches of hers as my hand slipped lower to explore the secrets of her delicate cleft. Looking her straight in the eye, I blindly felt my way along the ridge of her swollen cuntlips, pressing inward into the softness. The blond resonated to the intimacy of my touch, her naked shoulders quivering, electric thrills ricocheting in quick succession straight through her thin frame. I watched her fine lashes flutter as she struggled to hold on, until, under this relentless stimulation, she finally yielded, her eyelids slid dreamily closed and she exhaled, a long shuddering hiss through slightly parted lips.

"No! Keep your eyes open. Look at me!" I commanded, as I continued toying with her now-moistening pussylips. Her eyes snapped open, immediately alert, the pale blue fires flaring once more in blazing defiance.

Blindly fumbling with two fingers, I pressed open the labia, forcing back the butterfly petals of her opening flower. In this way I played with her cunt, all the while studying her face with intense interest, keen to observe her every reaction. In time, I saw those blue eyes soften, glazing over as the rolling waves of mindless pleasure flooded through her. Her delicate lashes fluttered in nervous agitation as she fought the temptation to shut out the world and let herself slip once more into the dreamy sensuality stirred by my caressing hand.

Now, I cupped my palm, crooking my middle finger to insert it right up her yawning cunt, and getting a tight-lipped grunt at the viciousness of the abrupt stab. Jane's eyes gradually narrowed into two slits of smoldering passion while I jiggled my finger deep inside her. I soon had her squirming uncontrollably, her hips bucking in answer to my tiny thrusts.

Next, I began finger fucking her, pistoning in and out in a frenetic blur, while the impaled blond grunted and writhed in sweet agony, twisting sensuously and craning back and upwards, the tendons in her neck jutting out as she clenched her jaws, determined to hang onto her slipping control.

But things had already gone too far for that. By now her hips were bucking in lusty abandon, and a tortured moan slipped out from between her tightly-pressed lips. At that, I abruptly yanked my hand away and shot to my feet. The dazed girl, panting heavily, slowly raised her face up. Her half-lidded eyes seemed drugged with passion.

My fingers were wet and sticky now, impregnated with the telltale spendings from the rapidly moistening cunt of the healthy, thoroughly aroused young woman. Bringing my fingertips to her nose, I offered her a whiff of her own feminine fragrance. And when she turned away from that lewd offering in obvious disgust, I laughed and rubbed my fingers under her nose, leaving her lips and chin glistening with the sticky residue of her own juices. Then I pressed my fingers between her clenched lips, forcing her lips apart.

"Lick them," I hissed insistently, pressing until she yielded and opened her mouth wide enough for me to slip my fingers over the tiny ridge of her front teeth and into her mouth.

"Suck them, lick them, taste yourself," I demanded in a furious whisper.

The painful memories of her earlier punishment must have been still fresh in her mind, because the implied threat in my voice brought the ready compliance.

For the moment, at least, it looked like she was willing to obey, for now she accepted my crooked fingers into her mouth and began working them over with lips and wet velvety tongue. I let her stay at it for a few minutes licking my fingers clean of her sexual spendings, before removing my hand and giving her an affectionate pat on the cheek.

Slowly, she tilted back her face to look up at me, a silent question in those big blue eyes. I smiled down at her.

"Nikki, the collar," I ordered.

And my little assistant handed me the thick strap of three-inch wide raw leather which would serve as Jane's slave collar. Her eyes widened when she saw what I intended to do, but she said not a word. Without being told, she docilely lowered her head, offering me the nape of her neck, that soft white column with the wispy tendrils of fine blond hair, so strangely vulnerable.

I looped the strap around her pretty neck, buckling it in place. The collar might occasionally prove useful, but its real purpose was symbolic, a constant reminder of the novice's servitude, one she would see each time she caught sight of her image in any of the numerous mirrors which decorated the walls of the Manor house. And whenever she reached up to touch the raw leather, fingering the encircling band, she would inevitably reflect on its meaning. This was the import of the collaring ceremony I now concluded by buckling the band around Jane's lovely neck.

* * *

All business-like now, I stepped to one side and hefted the paddle in my right hand. Tonight, I had chosen a medium-sized paddle, perhaps two feet in length and most of that composed of the thin wooden blade, six-inches wide. It was quite effective, although one could not deliver a blow with the authority of the longer handled variety, the kind that might be wielded with both hands. But for that, the victim had to be properly restrained and braced, and that meant its use was necessarily confined to the punishment chamber. Here, the smaller variety would serve my needs quite well.

For my purpose was not so much to punish the girl, as to provide a sharp reminder of things to come, should she persist in her recalcitrance. Accordingly, I brought my hand back only part way, and when I swung it was with a restrained, but definite crack, using an expert snap of the wrist at the end to provide an added sting.

The solid "thwack!" echoed in the bare room like a gunshot, sending my victim lurching forward, her cheeks juddering. Jane jerked upright, yelping and clutching at her hurting bottom.

I didn't say anything, but held my hand, waiting to see if, when she settled down, she would resume the position on her own. Now, as she rubbed her behind furiously, she looked over her shoulder at me, giving me the reproachful look of a naughty schoolgirl wrongly chastised. One look at my face must have been enough to remind her of the mandated position she had thoughtlessly abandoned, for she quickly bent back down to renew her grip on her ankles.

Now I watched the girl's butt muscles clench, the sleek sides of her tight young ass hollowing out as she cringed in nervous anticipation of the next blow. Again I swung, snapping the blade straight across those cowering rearcheeks, biting into the lovely softness and rebounding from the contact with the underlying firm resiliency of her twin pillows. Again, the girl shrieked. Her head and shoulders jerked forward, she tottered, but this time she managed to hold the pose. I paused, giving her a moment to recover, letting the anticipation of the final assault slowly built.

I gave her time to renew her grip on her ankles. Then I saw

her buttocks tighten once more, as the shallow indentations at the sides hollowed out and she clamped her butt fearfully, prepared to receive the final blow. But I let her wait, bending low, her eyes clenched tight, her grip white-knuckled as she braced herself against the coming onslaught.

And I kept waiting until eventually I saw the taut muscles of her butt begin to slacken, and then, winding up, I spanked her decisively, sending a smart crack straight across the reddened cheeks with a loud retort, and setting the wobbly mounds to dancing one more time. The shock reverberated right through her thin frame, sending the blond reeling, stumbling forward to come to rest on hands and knees with the sharp cry of a hurt animal.

And there she stayed, her head hung low, shoulders heaving as she struggled to catch her breath, gasping raggedly, and sniffling from the fiery sting blazing in her ass. I waited for her to regain her equilibrium, and then I said in a low, matter-of-fact tone:

"Assume the position."

It was enough. Slowly, painfully, the sobbing blonde got back to her feet and bent over, folding her supple body at the hips, stretching down, to once more grip her ankles with her trembling hands. She cringed in anticipation, but I had no intention of punishing her further. Three had been promised, and three had been delivered, and, as any of our girls could have told her, I was nothing if not a man of my word. And so, once I was sure she would obey, I released her.

* * *

At a nod from Madeleine, she was dragged kicking and hollering over to the waiting horse, but instead of trying to mount the wildly gyrating female (a task that would have almost impossible without some degree of cooperation), they pulled her over to the horse. There ensued a brief struggle just on the other side of our viewing glass, an interlude which allowed me to fully appreciate young Kitteridge's sinewy limbs, her spare clean lines and the dim shadowy haze of wispy puff of pubic hair, dimly visible through the thin folds of the skimpy skirt.

We witnessed the girl's silent struggle as she twisted and turned in a frantic attempt to free herself. But she was inevitably overpowered and in one quick motion spun around and pressed belly-up against the horse's side. Caldwell swiftly retracted the dildo while his compatriot, restraining their captive with a half-nelson, one arm locked behind her back, forced the girl to bend down from the hips, lowering head and shoulders down the far side till her supple form lay draped over the leather saddle.

Now we were treated to a delightful view of Kitteridge's naked haunches as all was revealed, the little skirt having ridden up in back to expose her tight-cheeked young bottom.

Caldwell dropped to one knee and clamping a wrist, pulled down on a dangling arm, while his teammate held the squirming girl over the saddle, a large hand flattened on the small of her back keeping the girl firmly pinned in place. Kit flailed her legs in protest, kicking up her heels, but Phillips stepped back with surprising agility for so big a man, and the heavy hand that pressed against her back never wavered.

Caldwell was working with swift efficiency now, banding the wrists with leather cuffs, clipping them together, and running a line from the girl's joined wrists to a convenient iron staple set in the wooden floor to serve as an anchoring point. Taking up the slack in the line had the effect of drawing the girl still further across the saddle till her tightly-pressed legs hung straight down on the near side, toes straining to touch the floor.

Now that she was secured in place, Phillips eased up on his hand and the two assistants turned to the mistress of discipline, who gave them a curt nod of approval; then dismissed them with an airy wave of the hand.

Madeleine approached the miscreant with an evil smirk. She bent down to whisper something in the ear of the inverted head, words which caused her victim to twist and kick up her heels. The poor girl could do no more in her strained circumstances. But Madeleine ignored her protests and stood eyeing the squirming behind, lightly tapping her palm with the paddle that she held in her right hand. This was the kind most widely used at Ironwood: the short-handled variety with a wide flat blade, it looked like those used in table tennis, although at Ironwood they were used for a very different indoor sport.

Now Madeleine took up her position behind and just to the left of the dangling legs, running a hand down over the wiggling ass as though sizing up her target. We saw her set her heels, widening her stance, and draw back her hand as she tightened her grip on the paddle.

THWACK!

The muffled smack was clearly audible from where we stood on the other side of the glass wall as the wooden blade splattered those pliant mounds, and the girl jacked up in her bonds, and simultaneously kicked up her heels.

Now Madeleine settled in to an easy cadence, spanking her wiggling victim, not hard, but with short choppy strokes, rapidly administered, until she had the juddery rearmounds wobbling under a peppering rain of slaps. Even in the next room we could hear the high-pitched yelps coming from the inverted head of her victim, who shook her hips and writhed across the saddle shifting her loins in agitated fury, desperately trying to shake off the relentless spanking.

Now Madeleine slowed the pace, giving her victim a slight pause between each decisive slap.

THWACK! The firmly resilient rearcheeks flattened under the impact and bounded back. A red imprint left across the twin curves. THWACK!.... the blade bit once more into the spongy mounds.... THWACK!.... a firm, decisive stroke, all quite methodical.

We watched the punished cheeks clench, sides hollowing out as the girl steeled herself to meet the next attack. The buttocks contracted in fear, coiling down, tightening to harden the rearmounds and constrict the crack to a tight slit.

THWACK! Madeleine smacked the hardened butt squarely across the twin contours with a sharp swat, delivered with a crisp snap of the wrist. We heard Kit's howl of outrage clearly, even through the mirrored wall, as the frantic girl kicked up her heels, legs flailing, bare feet flying up in a furious blur.

Now the stern disciplinarian paused and knelt down to bring her face near to that of her inverted victim. She was checking to see if the girl had learned her lesson and was ready to be more cooperative, fully prepared to continue the steady spanking till she had beat her victim into submission. But that wasn't necessary, as Kit's answer apparently pleased her, and she ordered the girl to be released.

* * *

Approaching the proffered behind, I clamped my curved hands on that pert little ass, dug my thumbs in the hidden valley and pried open her rearmounds, exposing the tallow strip at the very center and the deeply embedded rosette to my avid gaze. Ignoring Kit's muffled protest, I held her open with the splayed fingers of one hand while I dabbed a glob of gel right on that dimpled grommet, smiling to myself, as I watched it tighten in instinctive reaction to my impertinent probing.

Now I pressed with greater determination, but the harder I pressed, the more her resistance stiffened, and a garbled protest issued forth from behind the ballgag. The tiny gate remained locked, stoutly resisting my persistent finger, while her butt muscles strained to clamp shut, and a wavering bray of protest rose in pitch from behind her gag. Fed up with this renewed flare of defiance, I reached back and delivered a stinging slap to her hardened butt.

WHACK!

Kitteridge shrieked her outrage as I grabbed her by the hair, and hauled her to her feet, propelling her over to a hard wooden chair before she could react. I sat down and yanked her forward, spilling the struggling girl over my naked thighs. She squirmed hotly on my lap, kicking up her heels, and making what I could only consider was a screeching protest into the stoppering gag. I brought a hand up to the back of her shoulders, pinning her in place and held her down, while I spent a few minutes leisurely contemplating that well-proportioned behind, setting my hand on the pleasing curve and following the neat symmetry of those twin domes. Curving my fingers around the left rearcheek, I squeezed and fondled that silky smooth mound till I heard a low gurgle of pleasure come from the inverted head of my playmate. Playing with her ass had gotten Kitteridge worked up. She was excited in spite of herself, and she wriggled her hips, squirming on my lap, one solid haunch pressing up against my fully-erected prick.

I clutched a small rearcheek, digging into the meaty flesh, raking my fingernail over the taut contour, smiling down at Kitteridge's perfect little bottom. I shifted a bit, widening my knees to better balance the dead weight of that limp body that lay draped over my thighs, legs angled down to the floor. Steadying her with the heel of my flattened hand pressed between her shoulders, I hauled back, bringing my cupped hand down across Kit's butt with decisive authority.

WHACK!

I heard the muffled howl of indignation as Kit's head shot up and she kicked up her heels, flailing the air with her scissoring legs. I struck again . . . and again . . . and again, landing one solid whack after another squarely across Kit's bounding bottom, delighting in the bouncy resiliency of those solid little mounds as they juddered and danced under my rhythmic hand.

WHACK!. . . . WHACK!. . . . WHACK!. . . . WHACK!

My victim was struggling frantically now, kicking and squirming so furiously that she threatened to wriggle off of my lap. I held her in place more firmly, pinning the floundering female across my widened thighs while I spanked her, not hard, but methodically, delivering a series of crisp glancing slaps that ricocheted off her upturned bottom and sent the twin mounds wobbling.

WHACK!. . . . WHACK!. . . . WHACK!

My hand was stinging and I slowed down, settling into a slow, even cadence, solidly smacking Kit's ass till the quivering mounds began to redden under the unrelenting slaps.

After a few more minutes, her struggling began to subside, till finally she lay inert, passively accepting her punishment; her only movements the sudden jerk upward of head and shoulders with each slap, the tiny muffled grunts, and the reflexive tightening of her buttocks as she steeled herself to receive further punishment.

I watched fascinated as she clenched her taut rearcheeks, hollowing their sides, narrowing the tight crack into a thin dark slit, as she tensed up instinctively in anticipation of the next smack.

And that smack came. And another as I walloped her ass repeatedly, spanking her till those lovely swells of her upturned bottom were throbbing angrily, the rounded contours blushing a fiery crimson. By now all shreds of resistance had melted away and Kit had totally surrendered, letting herself go limp, beaten into submission.

I paused and let my gaze travel down her long naked form, as she lay passive and quiescent, inert across my legs, her only movement the ragged heaving of her shoulders as she struggled to catch her breath. With my palm throbbing and my arm aching, I decided it was time to quit.

For a moment I let her rest there, then gently lifting her head by the limp pony tail, I urged the chastised girl to her feet.

* * *

With a look of grim determination on her face, she stood poised like a hawk waiting to pounce. Her firm, hard-muscled body was taut with anticipation; the smooth whiteness of her lanky shoulders starkly contrasted against the sleek black bustier that molded her lean torso. One gloved hand was set on her hip, while from the other she let the paddle dangle loosely at her side. You could feel the coiled power building, as she tapped the paddle lightly against her booted calve, and then slowly brought her hand back, tightening her grip on the handle.

THWACK!

The resounding smack rang out like a gun shot in the quiet of that tense room as the paddle came swinging down to flatten the twin mounds. Charli screeched her outrage into the gag with the sudden shock of the solid impact. Immediately, the first smack was followed by another, swiftly delivered so that wood contacted the resilient mounds, flattening them again, just as they bounced back.

THWACK!. . . . THWACK! THWACK! THWACK!

A series of rapid fire shots which had the girl mewing urgently into the leather stopper.

Madeleine held her hand, giving her victim a few seconds of respite. An angry pink blush had formed across the jutting bottom, and poor Charli couldn't help shaking her tail, as if trying to shake off the sting.

Madeleine's thin smile widened into a truly evil grin as she saw the butt muscles coil down, as the girl hardened her self to review the next slap. The poised butt was tense, the skin taut, the sides hollowed out and the centerline a narrowed slit, as her victim held herself tensely waiting for the slap she knew would come. Madeleine let the anticipation grow and then she struck, whacking those hard little rearcheeks with an extra snap of the wrist.

Now Madeleine was spanking her victim with slow deliberation, not terribly hard but with steady methodical strokes, pulling her hand back only halfway, but giving a little snap to the wrist as the wooden blade bit into the cringing mounds, and the blonde threw back her head and brayed in protest.

Watching Charli getting spanked sent my excitement soaring; my rock-hard prick ached with desire. Wildly passionate, my eager hands were greedily fondling Kitteridge's choice loins. I fitted my hand to the sweet curvature of her tempting little butt and squeezed, digging my fingers into the meaty mounds till I had her writhing uncontrollably, and whimpering with passion. Then, I began to spank the girl, lightly smacking her taut little rearcheeks, then pausing to caress the object of my affections, stroking the blushing mounds with the cupped palm of my hand. I kept alternating between these two approaches, caressing her, and punishing her, teasing her with mixed feelings till I got a soft moan of pleasure from her inverted head. A shiver of desire rippled through her shoulders, followed by a little wiggle of the hips that told me the girl was hot, savoring the feel of my masculine hand as it warmed her bottom.

I dipped a hand between her legs and slipped it up into her cleft, there to hold her between my fingers, feeling her heat and the wetness of her needy pussy. Kit breathed a long sigh of pleasure at the feel of my fingers as I idly toyed with the soft folds of her slick cunt.

I'm not sure that poor Charli was as delighted with the attention that was being paid to *her* posterior, however. The insatiable Madeleine quickly became obsessed, driven to deliver a series of shot choppy strokes, alternately smacking both cheeks of the squirming behind. As she watched the wobbly mounds dancing under the relentless slaps, her eyes narrowed into gleaming slits, Her lips were drew back, and her jaw was set as she attacked the girl's agitated rump with almost maniacal fury. Muffled grunts, at first interspersed with the solid thunk of the wooden paddle splattering the fleshy mounds, quickly escalated into high-pitched keening cries, effectively muffled, but shrilly insistent.

Madeleine had worked herself up into a frenzy and I was becoming alarmed, for I had seen her when she raged out of control, driven by perverse sexual demons. But just as I was about to intervene, Victoria beat me to it. She had been sitting quietly in the shadows throughout the whole performance, and now she jumped up behind her assistant, reaching down to clamp the swinging wrist as it came forward, staying the punishing paddle in mid-air. Madeleine spun around in surprise. Her face was flushed with excitement and she stared wild eyed at the woman who held her by the wrist. She stood regarding Victoria for a moment, and gradually her eyes came into focus. She lowered her gaze and nodded, as though she recognized how close she had gotten to losing all control. Victoria released her grip, and Madeleine let her hand fall weakly to her side.

* * *

I took my place in the sturdy armless chair, and summoning the willowy lass to me I took her hand, and drew her down, tugging her by the hand till she was forced to stumble forward in her heels, and finally end up sprawled awkwardly across my lap. I adjusted her the way I wanted her, shifting her weight, easing her forward, till I had her properly stretched out over my widespread thighs, shoulders over one side, inverted head dangling down, while stockinged legs angled down the other side till the pointed toes of her high heels dug into the thick carpet. Shifting her hips with a final, nudging adjustment, I looked down on her, well-satisfied. I now had our pretty maid in the classic spanking position: her delightful young bottom nicely served up over my right thigh. As she lay down, the mischievous skirt had promptly flipped upwards, exposing the layers of stiff petticoats underneath as well as a pair of tightly-packed, black lace panties which now came into view to greet my smiling eyes. It was a perfectly charming picture she presented: the extended lengths of her outstretched legs sheathed in those long black hose, the bands of smooth white thigh-flesh that lay exposed between the stockingtops and underpants, and Jennifer's tight-cheeked young bottom encased in a taut pair of black satin panties that strained to cover her pert reardomes, the lacy legbands having ridden up into her underarch to leave exposed the smiling undercurves.

I brought my left hand up to slide it up along the back of the satin dress following her curving spine to a place right between her shoulder blades, where I let it rest lightly. Meanwhile, the right hand slid up to cup her right hip and explore the length of a streamlined nylon-sheathed leg, before coming to rest, comfortably fitted to the elegant curve of her outer thigh. Holding her loosely on my lap, I savored the pleasant feel of the warm smoothness of that solidly-packed nyloned column.

I leisurely stroked the lissome girl in a slow, lazy caress, letting my hand pass repeatedly up and down the sinuous lines of that slim leg, following the delicious contours, sliding up the gradual backslope of a taut-muscled thigh to the pertly rounded prominence of a tempting rearcheek, rubbing the thin panties over the crest of that little hillock with my fingertips, then trailing back down again, this time to slip up between her slack legs to explore the silken flesh of the inner thigh exposed at the top of the wide elastic bands of her stockings, then going beyond, to seek the crotch of her panties. I found the silky fabric warm and slightly damp. I held her there, cupping the wet crotch of her slippery panties in my palm. Pressing an extended thumb into her bottom-crack through the thin layer of nylon, I tightened my hand, squeezing and kneading the soft folds of pussy flesh, till Jennifer wiggled her hips, shifting excitedly in my lap. From her inverted head I heard a little tight-lipped whimper. I couldn't resist bending down to kiss that pantied ass, and then follow that up by running my flattened tongue over a pert curve through the thin layer of slick nylon. I heard a low earthy hum of contentment coming from somewhere deep in the girl's throat.

"Ah yes, you like this don't you Miss? But we mustn't forget ourselves by this little dalliance, however pleasing it may be for the moment. And you do have the most pleasing little ass," I assured her magnanimously. "Positively delightful! Still, you're not in this position in order that you might enjoy yourself," I said, all business-like. "Let me remind you Miss, that pretty little ass is here to be punished. And punished it shall be!"

Now I slipped my wet fingers from the soft folds of her damp underarch to follow the shadowy line that divided her cheeks, caressing and kneading Jennifer's wonderfully pliant rearend through the slick seat of her silken panties. Sighing at the sheer beauty of the splendid sight before me, I delicately fussed with her panties, smoothening them out, tidying up the elastic legbands, restoring them to their rightful place—the neat symmetry of two curving lines that snugly contained the twin curves of those tight little asscheeks. I laid my firm possessive hand squarely on Jennifer's small round bottom, and patted it lightly as I explained things to her.

"Now, let's begin, shall we? I'm going to prepare you for your real punishment by first spanking you on the seat of your panties. Just five smacks I think, as a bit of a warm-up. Please be so good as to count them out for me."

So saying I took a deep breath, raised my cupped hand, and swung, bringing it down in a single decisive slap, a crisp smack smartly delivered to that neatly-poised, pantied ass.

SMACK!

Jennifer's head shot up and her body tightened into a straight line in startled reaction.

"Count Miss, or you'll get twice as many." I shouted the threatening reminder.

"Ooo, One," she yelped, twisting in my lap.

I spanked her again.

SMACK!

"Yeeouch. Two."

And so it went, through three more precise, regularly administered smacks, each squarely on those bouncy mounds, each getting a tiny yelp from the poor girl before she was able to squeak out the required number.

After the requisite five had been delivered, I paused to admire the results of my handiwork, while Jennifer let her rigid body go slack across my lap.

"I'm afraid these panties will have to go. They offer far too much protection," I sighed. "In the end, only a spanking on the bare bottom will do."

My prick was incredibly hard, and I felt an ever greater rush of excitement that rose up to form a lump in my throat, a dryness in my mouth, as I reached for the waistband of her taut-stretched knickers and took them for their downward journey. I eased them down in back, peeling them down over the little domes of Jennifer's bare ass. Raising one knee, I shifted her dead weight to reach under her body and tug her knickers down in front. Once freed in front, they could be more easily be worked down her hips, and then stripped down her thighs with a final quick yank, so they ended up bunched up just above the hollows at the back of her knees. With her bottom bared, panties lowered ominously, Jennifer could do no more than wait in anxious expectation, holding herself stiff against the punishment that was sure to come.

I smiled down, contemplating with pleasure the enchanting sight of young Jennifer's naked ass, as an intense throb of lust powered through me. I couldn't resist playing with her. Feeling devilish, I poked a pointed finger deep into the girl's rear valley and watched her hips jerk and her cheeks clench instinctively at the intrusion. Next, I laid a flattened hand across her plump bottom, relishing the silky smoothness of those taut mounds. Easily spanning her rearcheeks with my splayed hand, I tightened my hand, clasping them together, squeezing while Jennifer whimpered and twisted in my lap. I released the rubbery mounds, patted her ass lightly, affectionately. The small cheeks clumped fearfully at the teasing touch of the single finger I ran up and over a choice curve.

Slowly I hauled back my flattened hand, and then whacked her solidly, right across the twin domes with a single stinging smack. Jennifer's head shot up and her body arched back; I spanked her again and again, with glancing slaps that sent those bouncy mounds wobbling. I slapped the center of the rounded domes, the sweeping tops, the fleshy bottoms, walloping her bounding ass in a methodical spanking that soon had my victim kicking up her heels and squirming hotly in my lap. Placing my left hand flatly on the small of her back to pin her in place, I whomped that squirming, agitated bottom two or three more times, admiring the dance of her bouncy rearcheeks under the rain of stinging smacks as she wriggled her hips in fiery torment.

SMACK!. . . . SMACK!. . . . SMACK! . . . SMACK! SMACK!

Jennifer yelped and bounded up in recoil, as I whacked the quivering mounds of flesh, slapping again and again, not hard but with precise determination, each spank getting a tiny "ouch" from the anguished girl, as her legs shot up reflexively. Then, just as unexpectedly as the spanking had begun, I once again held my hand, and listened to her sniveling in the quiet that followed. Jennifer was gasping for air, sniffling, and no doubt immensely grateful for the chance to catch her breath.

I held my hand as I smiled down to consider the object of my affections, appreciating the blush of pink that was spreading across the taut skin of her punished behind. I watched as Jennifer's cowering cheeks clench in repeated spasms. And my smile broadened when I saw them tighten up as she held herself in anticipation of the next set. She waited, shallow indentations at the sides of her cheeks hollowing out as she clamped her buttocks fearfully, steeling herself for what was to come. I let her wait a little longer, letting the dread anticipation build. And when I laid a gentle hand on her reddened throbbing behind, she cringed under it.

Suddenly I felt an overpowering surge of passion, deeply stirred by the sight of those choice impertinent mounds just begging to be punished. I attacked with gusto, delivering a hard spanking that she wouldn't soon forget, slapping in a furious rain that soon had the young woman squirming and yelping, stockinged legs flying up in back to scissor the air, kicking up her heels in a wild frenzy. It was only when my palm was throbbing with an unbearable sting that I finally held my hand.

Flushed with arousal, I sat with my incredibly hard penis straining up against the press of the girl's solid hip. I looked down on her well-punished bottom, panting heavily from the exertion. I brought my tingling hand down to lay it on the heaving reddened mounds of Jennifer's ass, savoring the delicious feel of those warm smooth mounds, rubbing her hurting behind in a slow deliberate massage, while a thoroughly chastised Jennifer wiggled her hips in sensual delight and gave out with a contented, dreamy moan.

* * *

Renata, who thoroughly enjoyed the anticipation of what she was about to do, crouched down before the blonde's dangling face was to show her the wicked paddle, smacking her palm with it, while she grinned at her helpless captive. I watched her take up her stance, behind and just to one side of the exposed buttocks; careful not to block the view of the camera. She lightly tapped those solid mounds with the wooden blade, and I saw them cringe in dread anticipation, tightening down as the girl steeled herself for her ordeal. Renata raised her arm and swung, snapping her wrist at the last second to send the wicked blade biting into the clenched buttocks with a vicious sting. Allison's head shot up and she must have let out a howl of protest, though I was sure the gag would have effectively muffled any such outburst. I watched the thin wood strike the tightly-drawn swells of Allison's asscheeks, bounce back and leave them shaking, as a pink blush began to form across the twin curves. Almost immediately, Renata struck again, hard and crisp. And then she set up a fast rhythm that had her captive wiggling in a vain attempt to escape the stinging whack of that peppering paddle. Once again I had cause to regret the lack of audio, disappointed that I couldn't hear the satisfying "THUNK" of the hard wood blade as it splattered Allison's solid fleshy mounds.

My new assistant was clearly enjoying herself. I zoomed in to study her face. Under the loose bangs, her brow was sheened with perspiration; her lips curled in that wicked grin as she concentrated on the task at hand, smacking that vulnerable butt with glancing slaps that sent the little mounds wobbling, letting them subside, their pink blush deepening as she paused, before striking again, settling into a slow steady rhythm, smacking not too hard, with dull regularity. As for her victim, the blond head was raised, the loose mane shaking furiously, while the girl's hips squirmed and wiggled as the relentless spanking went on and on. Finally, with a parting and particularly nasty swing, her tormentor stopped. Renata's eyes were shinning; her face flushed and sweating profusely now, although whether it was from her exertions or her burgeoning excitement, it was hard to tell. Her shoulders were heaving and she was panting through open lips, as she let the paddle slip from her gloved fingers. It was obvious that she had been profoundly turned on by the pretty blonde's distress, for now she did a strange thing.

She stepped right up to that freshly-chastised ass, reached around to clutch her captive by those svelte hips, and pulled her back while she herself pressed forward, mashing those hurting mounds against her strong, leather-clad loins, grinding her hips against her victim's soft tenderized ass while she threw back her head and closed her eyes to wallow in her own kind of perverse heavenly bliss.

DOMINANT CHORDS

NIKKI LAY STRETCHED out on her back on the silken sheets of my bed. She was totally naked except for leather straps at her throat, wrists and ankles. She lay spread-eagled, arms and legs tied to anchoring rings set in the corner posts. The muscles of her lithe body were tense with the strain of being stretched out by the taut leather straps. The girl had been blindfolded. I don't know how long she had been there, stretched out like that, and waiting for me there in that darkened room.

I went to the bathroom, leisurely stripped, then slipped on a short silk kimono. Moving very stealthily, I crept to where the unsuspecting young woman lay on the bed waiting for me. I stood beside the bed, scarcely breathing, gazing down on that stretched-out wiry body, hardly daring to breathe. Her dark hair, tucked in by the blindfold's strap, had fanned out on the silken sheet between her splayed arms. The tightly-stretched skin of her reedy torso was marked with the finely etched lines of her articulated ribcage, pulled taut to a form a shallow indentation at the belly, the jutting hipbones prominently marking the cradle of her trim hips.

My eyes dwelled on the girl's slightly-mounded breasts:

two gentle swells, barely rising softly from her nubile chest. The modest, flattened mounds were tipped with delicate nipples: little brownish nubbins that nestled in quiet repose in the crinkled flesh of dusky aureoles. I paid silent tribute to the loveliness displayed before me, before letting my eyes fall down the shallow depression of her belly to the dark thatch marking her furry little vulva. The pose exposed the dusky pink furrow; the delicate pink pussylips distended, kept slightly agape by the open angle of her legs.

So far, I had been content to merely caress her with my eyes, but now the growing desire to sample her taut young body was proving irresistible. My hand was drawn to her left breast, which I brushed with two fingertips, just lightly glancing over the dormant nipple. Caught by surprise, the blindfolded girl gurgled and flinched in startled reflex, jerking her bonds and sending the soft mounded flesh wobbling. I snatched my hand back, and stood still, waiting for her startled agitation to subside. Beneath the blindfold, I saw her lips part, and she exhaled in a long shivering sigh. I wondered what might be going on in the head of my blindfolded playmate at that moment.

When stillness returned to that out-stretched figure, I would touch her again, but this time the touch would not be so intimate. A little foreplay seemed in order!

And so I placed my fingertips on the palm of her delicate hand, weaving little circles on that fleshy pad. Her hand trembled in confusion, and she clenched her small fist, capturing my teasing fingers. Patiently, I waited for her to release me, and when she unclenched that little hand, I traced over her palm and down across the wide strap banding her slim wrist. Now, following a delicate blue vein, I glided down the smooth flesh on her inner arm to curve over her shoulder and slip into the moist hollow of her exposed armpit, lightly sampling the faint black stubble that grew there.

I spent only a few seconds in that most sensitive area, since my delicate touch sent Nikki's hips immediately bouncing;

her fists clenching spasmodically. I decided to spare her the sweet torment of my friendly tickling and moved on, down her side and along the fine-boned ribcage till I came to rest on a solid jutting hip.

The dark-haired girl's breathing was more labored now, her chest heaving in ragged escalating swells. She tensed with excitement. My teasing fingertips were driving her wild. I traced a single line from hipbone to hipbone, straight across her flattened belly which flinched at my light touch. Then I moved upward into the slight hollow, and on, up to her chest along the shallow cleavage between her gently-mounded breasts. Now I used both hands, placing one on each tit, and leisurely playing with those small sexy tits, sliding my hands over the pliant masses, kneading the pretty slopes, testing the resiliency of the soft skin with its underlying firmness, squeezing her delightful breasts with gentle urgency.

After a few minutes of this more or less constant stimulation, Nikki's responsive nipples began to awaken, the little disks swelling, the crinkled buds unfolding to peek out, the tips hardening in saucy semi-erect impudence. Fascinated by her reactions, I looked to her blindfolded face to find that her cheeks were flushed, moist lips parted, her breath coming in quick ragged gasps.

The girl was helplessly rolling her head from side to side as my circular massage deepened with steady firmness. Now, she was emitting urgent little whimpers, half-moans, half-pleas, the plaintive sounds escaping her lips as she arched up, offering up her boobs to my loving ministrations. I would tantalize her, waiting till she strained up to meet me, only to suddenly withdraw, eliciting a disappointed little "oooh" from the tethered female. Her tongue flickered out to rim her lips restlessly. I watched her heaving chest begin to subside, inordinately pleased to see that her alert nipples were proudly upstanding, hardened with the full blush of growing passion. Feeling a rutting surge of lust, I started in on her again.

This time, I clamped my hands squarely on those satiny

mounds, grasping her decisively by the tits, and clenching my cupped hands so that the soft flesh bulged between my tightening fingers. Nikki threw back her head, clenched her jaw and grunted, the stiff tendons along her neck sticking out as she arched upward, desperately pressing her small, hard nipples into my palms. She gave out with a rapid series of escalating "ooohs" which led to a high-pitched whimper as a minor convulsion seized her tautly-stretched body. She shuddered and gave out with a long sigh, then her head fell forward and she lay perfectly still, the only movement the rapid undulations of her roughly handled breasts.

Giving her a brief respite, I got up to fix myself as drink. At Ironwood each bedroom contained a well-stocked bar. I dumped some ice in glass, poured in a generous helping of scotch, splashed in a little soda, and sat down to feast my eyes on the girl as I thought over my next move.

When a quarter of an hour had passed, I got up and walked to the foot of the bed, my glass still in hand. Surreptitiously, I dug out an icecube and moved my hand close to my blindfolded captive.

When the cold shock was applied to the underarch of her foot, Nikki exploded in a wild frenzy, whooping and yelping in surprise. Quickly, clasping her ankle, I held her foot steady while I tickled her toes with the dripping cube, hearing her whimper, watching the toes curl reflexively. Then I glided the wet cube up the arch and around to the top of her foot, over the leather cuff at her ankle, and on upward along a tightly-muscled calve. A glistening trail of moisture marked my path up the long elegant curve of her leg and across to the smooth silken flesh inside of her straining thighs.

Now, my crazed playmate was gyrating frantically, twisting, wriggling, and squirming under the relentless advance of the little cube. I thoroughly coated every inch of her inner thighs with a thin sheen, and then couldn't resist leaning down to touch the tip of my tongue to the wet softness. I lapped up and down that satiny surface until I had her whimpering in delight, her whole body quivering, racked with sensual pleasure.

Next, I reached back into my glass, this time extracting two icecubes. With the cubes nestled in my palm, I brought my hand up in a sudden smack, cupping her lovemound, the cubes pressed firmly against her splayed-open sex. Nikki yelped at the sudden frigid shock, and tried to twist away, but I held my hand in place, the ice pressing hard against the soft folds of flesh, while her heat melted the cubes. Then I pinched a cube between thumb and forefinger and used it to outline her gaping pussylips, while she wriggled helplessly, shivering and shaking, mumbling incoherently.

Nikki, tormented to distraction, was yelping like a little puppy, but she was in for an even bigger surprise when I pried open her gaping vagina and inserted a cube right up her cunt, poking it in with an extended finger. Now her little moans turned into a single long, quivering "noooo." She shivered and quaked, her thighs quivering, her hips bucking maniacally, as I fumbled to make her gaping sex accept the second cube.

I ignored her mumbled pleas, determined to wait till her inner warmth melted the ice lodged deep in her core. Then I would take her! The tormented girl lay there, moaning softly and occasionally tossing her head to beat the bed with her silken strands while her hips moved sensuously as she responded to the novel sensations emanating from her stimulated womanhood.

Watching her writhing and squirming on the sheets had brought my own excitement soaring to a fever pitch, my eager prick seemed close to exploding. Eagerly, I scrambled up onto the bed and tore open the straps holding her ankles and wrists. Then I fell on her, plunging my painfully stiffened cock right up into her wet gaping pussy.

I luxuriated in the delicious feel of my prick sliding easily right up young Nikki's tight satiny cunt. I savored the odd mixture of feelings, the coolness of the spasming vagina, the heat of the girl's inner depths. Immediately, she flung her arms and legs around me, wrapping me up, clasping me to her tightly, welcoming me with a fiery urgency. Her small feverish hands were exploring the muscles of my back, her sinewy thighs clamping my hips as she spurred me on with urgent pleas whispered in my ear.

Our fucking became more rhythmic, smoother as it evened out; she was thumping my butt with her small heels and meeting each plunge with her own bouncing pelvic thrust. In this way I rode the dark-haired girl to new heights, her hips bouncing wildly, her lips babbling in incoherent mumbles. I could feel the tension rising in her body before the first convulsive shudder racked her thin frame, sending me careening over the edge at almost the very same moment. I came with a violent tremor, crushing my groin against the damp fur of her bucking mound, pressing myself deeply into her core till I was erupting, flooding her innards with pulsating gobs of cum in a delirium of wild rutting lust.

* * *

The other unforgettable scene in that gracious dining room holds at its center a burning image of sensual, dark-eyed Pauline. On that occasion her cool beauty was again to grace our table, but this time instead of being a diner, her pale young body arranged to serve as our centerpiece.

Dinner that evening was a private one, just for members of the Ironwood Sporting Society. Periodically we would make it a point to dine together enjoying the easy camaraderie of our male company. That night, as we entered the darkened room, we were stopped short in the doorway by the dramatic tableau we saw before us. The table had been set for the five of us, gilt-edged china and gleaming silver sparkling in the muted glow of the candlelight. But what drew our eyes to the center of the table was a single nude figure, kneeling there on the table, lit from a spotlight placed directly over her.

The hard white beauty of raven-haired Pauline had been displayed for us in stark relief; an erotic centerpiece whose feminine contours were sharply etched by the shadows from the overhead light. She was naked but for shiny black straps that banded wrists, thighs, and ankles. The wrist straps had been clipped together in front and then her arms drawn high over her head and pulled slightly backwards so that she was held in place with back arched, chest thrown out. A taut line ran from her wrists to a hook in the ceiling holding the kneeling girl in place.

Another set of black straps, somewhat wider than the wristbands, snugly banded her thighs just above the spread knees. A "spreader bar," some eighteen inches long, was clipped in place between thigh straps, keeping the girl from closing her legs, and thus assuring that the young woman's sex would be always accessible. Behind her, her ankles had been crossed and tied together. As a final touch, Pauline had been blindfolded with a black of padded silk. I don't know how long she had knelt there, silently waiting for the entrance of the dinner party.

Fascinated, we moved up to take our seats, unable to take our eyes off the breathtaking centerpiece. Even though her features were masked, I knew instantly who she was as that willowy body and short shiny black hair were pleasingly familiar. I knew well those memorable tits, small and sexy, with the neatly-etched nipples. With her arms stretched high overhead, her slender body seemed elongated, streamlined from her bound hands down to the gentle curves of her narrow waist and slight hips. Between her legs, the slight mound of her pubis was marked by a hazy shading of black puffy curls that darkened and thickened toward the apex of her triangle. The girl's pussy was stretched open by the way her thighs were held wide apart: a thin slit of pastel pink exposed between the ragged cuntlips that were boldly displayed within the tangle of black pubic curls.

We took our seats and our dinner was served by two pretty

students who had been assigned serving duty. Throughout the meal we found our attention inevitable drawn to the taut female figure placed only inches from our plates. She became, of course, the subject of conversation; we openly discussed the girl's obvious charms.

I paid little attention to the food that night, drawn as I was to the sculpted contours of those choice young thighs, spread open before me, tendons quivering as the straining muscles were stretched by the pose she was forced to maintain. Placed as she was, the naked girl was within reach of any of us seated at the table. I couldn't resist reaching out to sample the taut satiny skin along the inner contour, the silky smooth band of flesh inside her upperthigh which led me to the wispy bush of her pubis, and there I dallied, taking a little tuft of hair between thumb and forefinger, rubbing it, tugging gently, before moving on to run a single finger along the gaping outer lips, and get a sharp intake of breath from the blindfolded girl.

* * *

Then, with my eyes never leaving her, I got to my feet and stepped closer, entranced, drawn hypnotically to her unspeakable beauty. My hand seemed to have a life of its own as it came up to clasp a trim ankle and gently shift one leg, opening her up more fully to my view. I let the hand that rested on her ankle begin to move, and it glided along the subtle feminine contour, up over the gentle swelling calve, and beyond to the satiny-smooth flesh of the inner thigh, which twitched faintly as my fingertips touched her there. The blonde stirred, shifting her hips, and scissoring her legs sensuously. She opened her thighs to encourage my probing fingers, seeking to entice them deeper into her warm, moist essence.

I ran my fingers along the seam of her lovepouch, lightly tracing the outline of her labia. But as soon as she began to squirm in delight, I pulled my teasing hand away. There would be time for that later. But for now, I had a few other things in mind for the sultry blonde.

From a nearby chest of drawers, I fetched a pair of metal wrist bands. These were two-inch wide bands of polished steel, the insides lined with padded leather. I had Justine roll over and, without a word, she offered me her wrists. I clamped the steel bracelets in place. Next I looped a leather strap through the D-ring that was attached to each cuff. Then, moving to the top of the bench, I grabbed her left wrist and pulled her arm up and outward, before pulling the line taut and tying the other end of the strap to the leg of the bench. Justine let herself become a rag doll, limp and passively submissive. After repeating the procedure with her right arm, I tightened down the lines, stretching the young woman out before me.

Kneeling on the floor at her feet, I clamped another set of cuffs around her ankles. Tightening the lower bonds, I stretched her legs out towards the corners; thigh muscles stood out hard, the sinews drawn taut. The girl gave a tiny grunt through clenched teeth, as I tugged on the last strap and tied it down. Otherwise, she bore it all in silence.

Now I had her lean body spread-eagled, drawn into an elongated X, limbs tautly outstretched. Her stomach muscles were stretched tight as a drum; the belly, flattened and pulled into a slight indentation; hip bones jutting out prominently; haunches elongated; breasts pulled into two flattened mounds; pert nipples upstanding.

Standing beside the laid-out girl, I reached down to sample a conveniently placed nipple, plucking the jutting nub, rolling it between thumb and forefinger. I gave her a pinch and the pinioned blonde winced and gave a faint gasp, a quick, a sharp intake of breath through slightly parted lips. The thought struck me: would it be possible to bring the girl off, with nothing more than a bit of breast stimulation? I was eager to try the experiment.

Placing my hand over the thickened disk, I began to massage the soft mounded flesh with a light circular motion. Justine closed her eyes and sighed. I rubbed my palm up onto the mound and pressed more firmly, palming her bosom deeply into her chest as she threw back her head and stiffened in her bonds. Between my splayed fingers, the crinkled tip was swelling, the nipple unfolding with the healthy young woman's growing sexual arousal.

Once again I turned my attention to those sensate nipples, teasing, plucking the semi-erect nubbins, pulling on the elastic tittie flesh, stretching it out, and twisting the distended shape. The blonde moaned through tightly-pressed lips, clamped her eyes shut, and arched her back, arching up to offer her precious breasts for even more of my rough play.

I worried the swollen bud, toying with it, rolling it between thumb and forefinger, flicking it with a fingernail, and all the while listening to her moaning—tiny mewing sounds she was emitting that rose in pitch with increasing intensity. The fully aroused girl was arching up as far as her restraints would allow. I watched her work her fists, digging her nails into her palms with white-knuckled urgency.

"Oh, yes, . . . fuck me . . . fuck me . . . fuck me," she mumbled, whipping her blond hair from side to side between her outstretched arms.

It was an invitation no red-blooded male could possibly resist.

* * *

When first meeting Allison one was struck by two things: her crisp precise beauty, and her cool insolence. The girl was a proud beauty with finely-chiseled features, an slight arrogance in the way she curled her lips in a kind of smirking smile, and dark eyes that most often appeared to be impossibly bored. Her chestnut hair was swept back, cropped short in the modern style, the neat haircut giving her the appearance of a very pretty boy. The young woman sat stiffly, rather disdainfully, sipping her tea in a thin cotton dress of pale yellow. The summer-weight dress was scoop-necked and sleeveless, leaving bare her nicely tanned arms and shoulders, and a hint of cleavage between her small snuggling breasts. From time to time she would cross her legs, and the hem would ride up to reveal a pair of attractive legs clad in sheer beige nylons. She made no attempt to hide the fact that she was bored with the staid tea ceremony. Allison saw herself as a thoroughly modern young woman, defiant of authority, a rebel who with her good looks and money could afford to be disdainful of tradition. We would disabuse her of such foolish notions.

Cora had, of course, had seen to it that the young lady's tea was liberally laced with a novel drug we sometimes found useful. We had to tolerate her disrespectful attitude for no more than twenty minutes when its first effects became evident.

I was closely watching the girl's face as she sipped her tea, waiting for the first signs. I noticed she blinked several times, long lashes fluttering. When she went to set the cup down, her hand trembled. She started to get up, but her legs folded under her and she promptly collapsed to the carpet without uttering a word. We looked at each other, then down at the crumpled figure in the yellow dress. We assured her alarmed guardian that the young lady would be fine after a little nap, and we ushered the aunt outside to her waiting car. The older woman seemed a bit reluctant, but basically she was grateful to place the burden of her niece's further education entirely in our hands, and once outside she beat a hasty retreat.

On returning to the room I grabbed our guest under the arms, while Cora picked up her loose legs, holding her by the ankles. The girl was limp as a rag doll; we carried her slack form down the stairs to the Discipline Hall.

We dragged the unconscious female over to one of the sturdy trestles which were bolted to the floor at the far end of the room. This wooden support resembled a carpenter's sawhorse with the sturdy crossbar set at waist height. Propping her up, with belly against the padded crossbar, we folded the girl's supple body in half over the bar, letting her head and arms dangle down the far side.

Cora handed me the leather wristbands, thick serviceable straps that we fastened around the limp wrists and cinched tightly in place. Next, we pulled the girl's arms down to attach the D-rings in the cuffs to the iron staples set in the floor at either corner of the trestle. Once she was stretched over the bar and secured in place, Cora left the drugged female entirely in my hands. I decided to have a closer look at what our captive had to offer under her dress.

I circled behind the bent-over figure and lowered myself to kneel with my face only inches from her behind. First, I removed the open-strapped sandals from her dangling feet. Then, I placed a hand on each leg just below the hem of the thin summer dress she wore. Slowly, I slid my hands up the outside contours of her nyloned legs and on up her sleek haunches till the thin cotton dress was rucked up around her waist.

The girl's nether regions were sheathed in honey-tinted pantyhose, the nylon encasing her slim, attractive legs in a dusky haze—smooth and silken to the touch. Under the sheer pantyhose were a clearly outlined pair of bikini panties, bronze-tinted panties whose high-arching legbands narrowed to a thin strip at each hip, while in back the high cut left bare the undercurves of two saucy rearcheeks that peeked out from beneath the upriding elastic arches.

I worked the billowy dress up, gripping her by the hips to shift her inert form back a little so that I could wedge the crumpled fabric against the crossbar to keep it pulled up out of the way. Then, squatting down behind her, I crooked my fingers into the waistband of the pantyhose and began to lower that nylon barrier, peeling down the clinging film over her narrow hips, unveiling the pantied behind.

I worked the pantyhose lower baring the gentle contours of her nicely-rounded thighs, leaving them to span her parted legs just above her knees. I couldn't wait to caress her naked thighs.

Eagerly, I clamped my feverish hands on those firm rounded columns, and leaned forward to peer between her legs, catching a whiff of feminine musk, a raw, slightly tangy odor which impregnated the moisture on her innerthighs. The narrow gusset of the panties, a thin metallic strip tucked up in the cleft between her legs, had allowed a few wispy pussy-hairs to escape. I slipped a hand in, high up between her legs, to savor the satiny smooth flesh of the girl's innerthighs. Then I thoroughly enjoyed that young ass, palming our captive's pantied rearcheeks, massaging the firm mounds through the tightly packed seat of those slick metallic panties, pressing into their bouncy resiliency. Allison had a delectable ass: an ass simply *made* for fucking!

On a whim, I delicately plucked at an arching legband, peeling it back and twisting the nylon into a little roll between my thumb and forefinger. I carefully rubbed the roll of fabric up and over the dome of one small dome. Then I did the same with the other legband. Next, twining the silky strands together at the center, I poked the remainder into the narrow crack between her cheeks. By gripping the waistband and tugging upward I was able to stretch the fabric, embedding it in her crevice, and creating a delightful *cache-sex* which left bare her taut boyish buttocks.

I paused to admire my efforts. In this pose, the girl's tight-cheeked young bottom was bared to my hungry gaze, a naked rump nicely presented in lascivious display; the jutting mounds, hard and smooth, were starkly white in dramatic contrast to the sleek tanned body and dusky legs. My hands were drawn irresistibly to those small, perfectly-shaped domes, so pert and saucy. And so I allowed myself a few leisurely moments playing with her, squeezing and fondling and thoroughly enjoying Allison's delectable young bottom.

This pleasant activity soon had my burgeoning lust raised to a fever pitch, and I was trembling with impatience. Even my hands were shaking with excitement as I unceremoniously clutched the girl's underpants and yanked them down her legs in one swoop. Leaving the silken underwear twisted between her thighs, I clamped my hands on her behind, splaying my fingers to span her taut globes, thumbs pressing inward along the crack. As I slipped my curled thumbs into the deep valley, I pried her open so as to get a good look at her tiny rosette. As I stared at the small dusky ring of rubbery flesh, the thought crossed my mind that hers might well be a virgin asshole! It raised intriguing possibilities.

For now, I continued my intimate inspection of that secret place, lowering my head and twisting a little to get a good look at her love pouch. I traced the short seam between her asshole and her cunt and saw an unmistakable quiver shoot through her inner thighs. I wondered if the effects of the soporific were wearing off.

Deciding to test her a little, I held the soft folds of her hairy pussy open with the fingers of my left hand while I cupped the pouch with my right, crooking my middle finger and slipping it up her cunt. She was hot but dry. As I diddled her I heard a tiny gasp come from the other end of my captive. I rotated my finger against the silky walls of her sheath; this time getting an unmistakable moan from the semi-conscious female.

I thought how amusing it would be to have our most recent acquisition awakened by a welcoming poke in the ass. It was the sort of gesture that would, in no uncertain terms, impress on her her place in the scheme of things in our little world.

* * *

Thoughts of my early days at Ironwood bring on a flood of images that threaten to overwhelm me. Images of nubile young women, dancing and cavorting in uninhibited play, moving with the youthful grace of ballerinas; restrained in the most provocative manner so as to invitingly display and present their firm, young and eager bodies; being severely disciplined even while they were being teased in that delicate balance that kept them in a constant state of sexual arousal. It was arranged that the Ironwood girl would be constantly reminded of her sexuality. Exhibitionism was encouraged. A well-trained student would feel a thrill of pride when put on display, finding herself excited by arousing those who like to watch.

Erika was such an exhibitionist. I saw her now, laid out on the high table, eyes closed, wearing nothing but a brief pair of peach-colored panties stretched low across her prominent hip bones. Arms loosely at her sides, head and shoulders propped up by pillows, the big blonde lay passive, limp as a rag doll, letting two of the girls arrange her supple body according to instructions.

First, a blindfold was used, the ends tied around her head imprisoning the silky blond hair. She was spread open, her knees bent back steepling those long folded legs, till her thighs were drawn back, almost touching her softly mounded breasts. Once in this vulnerable position the wrist cuffs were clipped to her ankle bands. Next they rolled the helpless girl back onto her shoulders, raising her bottom and thus serving up her panty-covered cunt. Displayed as she was, the prominent crotch of the slick panties was drawn into a taut strip of silk, pulled tight into the groin between her thighs. At the front the slick fabric was tightly fitted to the upturned bulge of her gently-mounded vulva.

And that was the way they left her, on display: an inspiring decoration, an interesting conversation piece set just at the entrance to the ballroom. Passing guests could admire Erika's supple form. She would be fondled shamelessly, or her vulnerable pussy rubbed through the moistening crotch of her panties. Guests masturbated her to the ragged edge of orgasm, as they lingered in the entranceway. As the evening wore on an ever-widening stain spread across the wet nylon plastering it to her crevice, while Erika whimpered in frustration. Her little mewing pleas rose and fell in intensity under the unrelenting caress of the curious hands of strangers that roamed freely over her restrained body, gliding over the sopping wet panties, shamelessly fondling her damp, upturned, pussy, teasing the poor girl unmercifully as they kept her simmering in sexual torment.

* * *

I climbed on the bed to sit beside Helga, admiring that sleek narrow butt. My hands ached to explore the sinuous lines of that long, streamlined body. I reached down to place a hand on her left foot, lightly touching her ankle. The stockinged toes curled with pleasure when I drew my fingertips along the curve of the instep, over the knob of her heel, and beyond, up the back of taut-muscled calve. I followed the firm contour through the slight hollow behind the knee and up the back of a smoothly sloping thigh.

Helga hummed with contentment, wriggling her hips. Her legs opened invitingly as I traced a line right up to the wide band of elastic at the top of her stocking. Following the elastic ridge of that stocking top, I savored the smooth silky feeling of that warm nyloned-encased leg as my fingertips dipped between those loosely parted thighs.

Helga's low purr grew to a moan as my fingertips sampled the silken band of flesh along her inner thigh. I traveled a few inches higher sending inquisitive fingers to explore the soft purse of the big Dane's pussylips. I pressed along her furry vulva, feeling my way along the rubbery, slick lips, testing her wetness, and getting a soft shuddering moan of pleasure from the blonde, before I ran my teasing finger up the perineum and then drew it along the narrow crack while the girl wiggled with a simmering excitement that was driving her crazy. I spent a few leisurely moments, delighting in the warm satiny feel of that adorable, upturned bottom. While Helga sighed with pleasure, I lavishy fondled those slim, taut mounds. Her narrow rearcheeks were so neatly symmetrical, so smooth and soft to the touch, yet so deeply firm and bouncily resilient. Helga's splendid, mouth-watering ass was simply irresistible. I cupped my hand, and gave it a crisp whack, delivering a playful slap to flatten that taut-cheeked behind, and happily test its bouncy resiliency.

SMACK!

Helga jacked up and her heels flew up in shocked reflex to the sudden shock. But I calmed her by laying my flattened hand on the small of her back, and moving it in a slow caress up the sweeping slopes to clutch a single meaty cheek and give her a reassuring squeeze. And so I played with Helga's superb bottom, feeling her up, mauling, kneading those twin mounds to my heart's content, while the tall blonde squirmed in rising sensual heat.

With a reluctant sigh, I decided to give up this pleasant dalliance, for I was feeling the mounting urgency to get on with the main pursuit. For what I had planned, I would have my playmate on her back. I leaned down, and breathed in her ear, coaxing her to turn over.

Helga complied, and once on her back, looked up at me from under the fringe of her bangs, her pale blue eyes shining with excitement. Without a word, this marvelously compliant young woman, silently raised her arms up over her head, as if in loving surrender. She knew exactly what was wanted of her, and the very thought thrilled her to the core.

Sitting on the edge of the bed, I lifted a proffered wrist, and carefully banded it with a leather cuff formed from a 4" wide strap. A slip lock allowed the strap to be buckled in place snugly, but not too tight; a D-ring sewn into each cuff, provided a convenient anchoring point for restraints to be attached. I preferred elastic strapping for the restraints, running it to the ring set in the corner post, tightening it down, so that the supple arm was pulled taut. I found the strapping better than cords or chains, since it is strong enough to hold the arm outstretched, yet it also allowed a bit of slack should the girl thrash about, as I knew from experience that Helga was wont to do, once caught in the throes of a ragging orgasm.

As I banded the other wrist, I looked down at her to find Helga's big blue eyes on me, watching me with interest; a little smile grew on her lips. She said not a word, but I knew she was powerfully aroused, for Helga, a strong independent woman, found the helplessness of bondage to be a powerful turn-on. She could get wet with an ache of longing, just thinking about being tied up! I secured the wrist to the other cornerpost, and took up the slack, stretching her extended arm so that both arms were now raised and angled outward over her head. I paused to admire the neat symmetry of the vee, and the way the silken strands of her pale blond hair had fanned out on the sheet between her outstretched limbs.

Now with Helga's eyes following my every movement, I came around the bed to stand at the foot, with the second set of straps in my hands. I contemplated those loosely parted legs, and Helga obligingly opened them up even further for me. I sat on the corner of the bed. I studied her a long narrow foot, ran a hand down over it to clasp her ankle, and adjust the slack leg so that it pointed towards the corner of the bed. Although I was burning with impatience, I forced myself to take my time, carefully banding the left ankle, and then the right, attaching the restraints and tightening them down, so that her long tapering legs were extended to the corners of the bed, her thighs held well parted, her blond pussy gaping, open and vulnerable.

Spread-eagled and totally naked, but for the high collar encircling her throat, and the black leather straps banding wrists and ankles, the statuesque blonde was a mouth-watering sight. A mighty surge of lust powered through me; my prick throbbed with a vibrant ache of desire.

Every fiber of that long, streamlined body was pulled taut by the restraints. The sinews of her arms and legs took much of the strain, drawing taut her sleek torso and stretching her tits into two elongated, slightly flattened, swells; the bottom ridge of her ribcage was dimly visible under the tightly stretched skin, and below that a slight hollow had been formed as the skin of her belly was pulled taut as a drum between the jutting points of her prominent hipbones. My eyes were drawn to the splay of pale silvery pussyfur that crested the softly mounded pubis.

I slid an arm under her, gathering up her loins to stuff a pillow under her bottom. Now Helga's blond sex was on prominent display. I didn't touch her, but I contemplated that vulnerable pussy, thought of slipping my fingers between her outstretched legs and palming her upraised mound, heating up the sensual Dane till she pleaded for mercy. The thought sent my rigid penis throbbing with excitement.

I looked up to Helga's face and found her watching me through half-lidded eyes. I saw her tongue peek out to quickly rim her lips in an anxious flicker.

As I sat beside her on the bed, I reached out to touch her cheek. At my gentle touch she turned to kiss my hand, nuzzling into my palm and extending her tongue to slavishly lick. I rubbed my fingers over her lips and then traced the lines of her face, the curve of a soft cheek, and on down her chin to her throat, pausing there to finger the supple leather of the high collar. I continued my explorations across the ridge of her collarbone, around the shoulder and along the sensitive flesh of the underside to sample the soft underarm with its trace of blond stubble, while Helga's shoulders jerked from the light tickle of my teasing fingertips, and she uttered a barely suppressed whimper of delight.

Now I followed the route from underarm to hip, admiring the gentle sweep of curving sideflesh that tapered down and then swept back up to the flaring cradle of her hips. Helga's hips twitched in her growing agitation, as my fingers explored her outstretched body, tracing over an angular hipbone to circle her navel, pressing on the dimple before I drew that single finger up the narrow path between her distended breasts.

The tense blonde closed her eyes; I saw her throat muscles working as she swallowed, once, twice. Then her lips fell open in long shivering hiss of breath while my fingers splayed out to ride up the slopes of her tautly-drawn breasts. I passed my hand lightly over both breasts and then pressed my finger on the fleshy nub of her left nipple, embedded in the soft pink crinked flesh of her thickened auerola. I worried the nipple a bit, indenting it, sampling the little nubbin between thumb and forefinger, tugging on the pliant tittie-flesh, while the helpless Dane whimpered like a hurt puppy, arching up and uttering tiny urgent moans through tightly-drawn lips.

I watched the sensitive tips swelling with passion; the disks of her aureoles expanding, nipples stiffening with excitement, as I played with the girl's modest tits, first one, then the other. I looked up at her face as she craned back in feline pleasure. Her breathing was ragged, the breath coming through slightly parted, moistened lips; those nipples, tense and excited now stood up in full blossom. The young woman was twisting and rolling her blond head from side to side, arching up with eyes clenched tight, luxuriating in sensual delight.

I edged closer to her. My upstanding prick brushed against her naked hip sending a wild electric thrill racing through me, causing me to jerk my hips back even as I leaned over her. Primed and ready, I knew the slightest touch might well send me off, firing off gobs of cum to splatter that writhing, naked body. And I didn't want that . . . not just yet, anyway.

And so I drew my hips back as I slid my hand down her belly to protectively cup her lightly-furred pubis. Helga let out a long sigh of satisfaction. I held her with curled fingers digging into the soft folds of her warm damp crotch.

The leggy blonde was hot, burning with the heat, squirming and twisting uncontrollably as I palmed her damp vulva, rubbing deeply while the passion-crazed girl gave out with urgent whimpers that soon became mumbled pleas. She gave out with a high-pitched keening sound as she strained back, elevating her hips as much as her bounds would allow, thrusting her sex against my palm while the tendons of her thighs stood out rigidly, the sleek powerful thigh-muscles tightening as she strained upwards.

Her cries increased in pitch and intensity till, with a sharp yelp, she suddenly tensed and a tiny spasm rippled through her stiffened body. Then a long shivering moan slid out from between her lips and that long, extended body went limp. Helga went slack in her bonds, closing her eyes to savor the delicious afterglow of the tiny climax that had rippled through her overtook her. I watched her laying there, face flushed, brow sheened with sweat, her slack limbs outstretched, breasts rising and falling in great trembling undulations, and I touched myself, because I couldn't help it.

* * *

Quick as a flash the ex-gym teacher launched herself, springing up to grapple with the taller girl. For a moment I sat enthralled by the wild cat fight. The wiry brunette jammed a booted leg between the blonde's stocking-clad thighs and held her in a death grip, while the taller girl struggled with all her might to free herself from the smothering embrace. Finally, the long blonde twisted free and lunged at her attacker. But the dark-haired girl was just a shade too quick for her, and she stepped aside to deflect the charging blonde while bringing up a gloved fist in vicious swing aimed straight at the solar plexus. The blow caught Allison squarely in the outstretched belly and she promptly folded over, falling to her knees, winded and gasping for air. Instantly, the other girl was on her, straddling the panting blonde and grabbing a fistful of her long blond hair. As Allison struggled to get up, her opponent wrapped her fist in the blond mane and yanked the girl back by the hair, hauling her to her feet. With a mighty heave, she dragged the limp girl forward till she could shove her slack body over a padded gymnast's horse that stood nearby.

Allison lay folded at the hips, still struggling to get her breath, as her attacker grabbed her wrist to slip on a leather cuff, then pulled it forward, stretching the girl up onto her toes. She quickly used a cord made of stiff elastic to hook the leather cuff to an iron staple conveniently placed in the floor well in front of the padded trestle. By now Allison had got some of her fight back and she was resisting more strenuously, but with one arm outstretched and tied down to the floor, there was very little she could do. In short order, her other wrist was banded and a second elastic cord secured, holding that long blond body in place bent over the thickly padded "saddle" of the gym horse.

The girl seemed properly subdued, but when Renata knelt behind her to complete the job, the blonde swung a vicious high-heeled foot up nearly missing the crouching brunette. This sudden kick infuriated Renata who leapt to her feet, grabbed the blonde by the hair, and yanked her head back as she leaned over to warn her victim against any further gestures of defiance. I saw the agonized look in those pale blonde features as Renata tightened her grip and twisted her fist to enforce her words.

This time when she relinquished her grip, the blonde head sagged in abject defeat. Renata than went about the business of securing the girl's ankles. Working methodically, in no particular hurry now, she circled each slim ankle with a leather strap, which, like the wrist bands, were equipped with D-rings. From these the cords were easily attached, and Allison's tall legs were pulled apart to be held in place with heels widespread. Now the eager brunette stepped back to admire her handiwork.

The long-legged blonde was on her belly, stretched out over

the padded top, her head dangling down between her outstretched arms so that her silken mane fanned out to almost touch the floor. At the other end, those lovely nyloned limbs were stretched taut drawing the girl up to balance on the very tips of her high heeled shoes. Renata allowed herself a smile of grim satisfaction.

At that point Allison turned her inverted head to look around and say something to the smugly self-satisfied brunette who stood behind her, regarding her with folded arms. It appeared that the fight had not gone completely out of the bound girl, for whatever she said only irritated the black-haired girl more, undoubtedly convincing her that Allison should be gagged, which she now proceeded to do. Not surprisingly, the girl refused the ball-gag, but Renata merely pinched her nose and held her nostrils shut till the girl was forced to gasp for air, and at that moment she found the hard rubber ball jammed between her gaping teeth, the straps quickly buckled, securing the gag in place. Now, with her victim bound and gagged, the dominating mistress of discipline began to toy with her victim.

Stepping up to the bent over female, she said a few words and lightly tapped the girl's nicely-presented rearend. For a moment she stood there, her hand resting comfortably on Allison's mini-skirted behind. then she moved the skirt around over those tightly drawn buttocks, easing the material up and down and around in slow circle. Finally, with a grin over her shoulder at the watching camera (and at me, I am sure), she took the hem of the little skirt between her fingers and lifted it to uncover Allison's tautly-stretched panties. The skirt was drawn up all the way and laid precisely over the bent back. The underpants now revealed to me were of metallic bronze. Smooth and glossy, the opaque satin was stretched to its limits, straining to contain the lovely swells of proud Allison's upturned bottom.

Renata patted that slick-pantied behind, than gave the girl a set of small but sharp slaps, spanking her all over her taut panties with that gloved hand. Allison of course, could do nothing but endure this humiliation though her hips twitched and her head shot up in reaction to a particularly vicious slap. But a light spanking on the panties was hardly the extent of what Renata had in mind for this miscreant. Did the bent over girl realize even then that her ordeal had only begun, or did that realization only come to her when she felt her panties being taken down. Slowly and deliberately, Renata drew those metallic underpants down, exposing the white swells of Allison's pampered young ass. The slim-hipped girl's narrow butt was drawn into elongated swells by the stretched posture she was made to endure. A thin dark slit separated those close-set, sleek-muscled mounds. Her underarch was held open and between the splayed legs, and one could make out the stretched, pouting blond vulva. Renata left the girl's underpants spanning her outspread thighs, just above the knees. It was an incredibly lewd, wanton pose. I felt my pulse racing; my solid erection surging with a wild thrill of lust.

* * *

The many sexual experiments upon which we had embarked during the past several months had paid off handsomely. We had diligently worked to find the secret of each of our girls, the one key which if turned, would turn her into a raging sexual animal. For Mona it was being tied up.

Now I should add that Mona, with that wry, seductive smile of hers, that lanky body and those low-slung hips, and that absolutely perfect ass, was one of the most sensual women I had ever met.

She might well have been that secret dream of every male— a genuine nymphomaniac, or at least as close to that dream girl as any female made of flesh and blood could possibly get. Always up for sex, and eager for men of all kinds, the girl had a voracious sexual appetite; I have never seen a woman so intense on draining every drop of pleasure from the men who found joy in that sensual, pneumatic body of hers.

The demanding position reduced Mona to a cunt, a sexual object to be well used, again and again by a parade of naked, feverish men, tripping over themselves in their eagerness to take their place of worship at the altar of Venus between those silky smooth columns of Mona's spectacular thighs. By placing that tall slender, and devastating beautiful brunette in bondage, we unleashed her raging passions, turning her into a wild woman. Tied down like this, she was insatiable—or very nearly so, as we were about to find out. For today she would be taken to the very limits by a half dozen lecherous, lusty males, who having satisfied that first itch in such a heated rush, were now prepared to more leisurely enjoy the pleasures of the flesh to their fullest satisfaction.

As we approached the hooded figure, we saw her stir as she sensed our encroaching movement. A single overhead bulb was shaded so that its light shown directly on her. A loose leather sack covered her head down to her lips, concealing her features, though there could be no doubt about the girl's identity as her body was unmistakable. That sleek, model's body had been completely oiled, so that her naked form gleamed under the light of the single bulb. Mona was a magnificent, a well-oiled, well-made fucking machine, the sinewy muscles of her thighs glistening and straining with tension, her high-seated Venus mound so enticingly displayed, open and vulnerable.

The aroused men silently crowded around the table, looking down on the hooded figure, all of them were sporting naked penises, obviously at the ready. At a nod from the Commander, I retrieved a small canvas sack holding four brightly colored marbles. Renata dipped her fingers in the bag and drew out all the first one. The sight of the Black marble eliciting a sharp cry of triumph from the associated man. The next three were drawn; the order of precedence thus established.

Mr. Black, grinning hugely, immediately stepped up between those splayed thighs, and with a single thrust plunged into the open pussy, getting a long low deep-throated groan from the restrained female, whose body quickened at the sudden stab of pleasure. Placing his hands on her slick thighs he slid them up to her hips, and holding her lightly, began to rock back and forth on his heels, pumping into the girl while she tossed her head from side to side.

Black didn't last long. He was pumping like a maniac, when he suddenly he threw back his head and strained upward, grunting and groaning as his shot his wad, and staggered backwards. His wet, depleted prick slid from Mona's superheated cunt and swayed obscenely as he made his way to a nearby couch. His place as taken by the randy Mr. Green, who enthusiastically fucked the girl with a lusty deep lunges which had her keening and moaning as paroxysms of pleasure rippled through her bound body. With a series of short, urgent grunts, Mr. Green came, powering into her to hold himself there, deep inside the girl as he flooded her innards with his surging cum.

Scarlet promptly stepped up to take his place, a goatish satyr with prick rearing up in lewd salute, he lunged at her, burying his sword deep within that velvet sheath with a single thrust. The impaled girl twisted as much as her bounds would allow, and the tiny, erotic moves she made fired the lust of the randy lecher who pumped into her, hips bucking furiously. Soon passionate moans and lusty grunts merged and both lovers came with a shuddering climax.

As Mr. Scarlet staggered back, his place was immediately taken by that sexual connoisseur, Mr. White whose prick was not quite upright, yet stuck out rigid enough to be slid into that thoroughly drenched and well-used vestibule. White's strokes were unhurried, methodical; he never changed the pace, and one wondered if he could go on all night at that mindless mechanical pace. Bringing Mona to orgasm now became a contest of stamina, and here it is possible that White's lack of youthful vigor gave him something of an advantage, for he was slow on the draw and seemed absolutely able to hold his fire. Mona made a low rumbling sound, long and breathy; it turned into a wavering moan that rose in pitch while the relentless drilling went on and on. The building orgasm seized her, and she flung her head about wildly, while from under the hood came the screeching, keening wail of a banshee. A massive, thundering orgasm shook her restrained body. The woman's shuddering climax energized her lover into a furious pace and he soon finished off, collapsing back and sagging weakly to find the same sofa occupied by his predecessors.

By now the nymphonic Mona had been driven to multiple orgasms, and her body seemed totally depleted. Sexual spendings were oozing from her gaping cunt, and a low throaty "oooh" of deep satisfaction came from under the hood. The endurance contest was judged a standoff; all were declared victors.

CURIOUS COUNTERPOINTS

VANESSA SLOWLY GATHERED herself together and drew herself up to resume her position kneeling before me. The effects of her recent orgasm lingered. Her face was flushed, her hair disheveled, perspiration sheened her brow and her small delicate breasts rose and fell in gradually evening undulations. I saw her take several deep breaths, swallowing rapidly; my eyes were drawn to the band of leather at her neck, as she knelt before me, with eyes closed, waiting to recover.

Cora, with booted heels set wide apart, hands on hips, stood watching Vanessa's heaving shoulders, patiently waiting until they quieted down. When she spoke it was in a voice that was soft, and once more matter-of-fact.

"Vanessa darling, you will observe that Mr. James seems to be interested in you." (This pointed reference to the obscene bulge that tented the front of my trousers, situated as it was only inches before the young woman's eyes, caused me to blush with mild embarrassment, even though I was already coming to realize that that particular emotional response had little currency at Ironwood.)

"Go to him; pleasure him, use those sweet lips of yours."

I felt the object of that wanton suggestion quicken with a hopeful twinge of anticipation. Over the girl's head, Cora's eyes sought mine, and her taut lips curled up in a deliciously evil grin.

Inching forward in the chair to bring my butt to the very edge of the seat, I opened my legs in mute invitation, as Vanessa shuffled forward, bringing herself up between my widespread knees. And now that wonderful submissive reached for my trousers, carefully lowered the zipper, and slithered a hand in, groping blindly for my rampant penis.

A tingling excitement raced through me at the electrifying touch of those cool delicate fingers that found, and then closed possessively on my straining manhood. She traced the phallic outline with a sure touch, expertly using only her fingertips before curling her talented fingers around the shaft and tightening them. Then she was squeezing gently, flexing her fingers and sending rippling thrills shooting through me, sending me to raptures of indescribable delight.

Now, those deft fingers had my prick out in the air. Freed from the tangle of underwear, it stood rigidly expectant, quivering only inches from Vanessa's pretty face. The exquisite pleasure of that light teasing feminine touch was simply maddening. She held me with both soft hands, using just her fingertips to lightly trace the outline of my fierce erection.

And then, as I sucked in a sharp breath, she wrapped those long cool fingers around my iron-hard prick and tilted the upstanding rod toward her pursed lips. She leaned slowly forward to plant a kiss squarely on the sensitive flesh just below the ridge of the crown; I moaned. With loving concern, my talented cocksucker let her lips linger there, softly nibbling, using lips and mouth and tongue, while waves of excruciating pleasure coursed through me.

My eyes fluttered closed; I let myself surrender to the delicious sensations generated by that incredibly soft, velvety tongue. With sure, skillful movements, this wonderful girl paid lavish tribute to my manhood, eagerly, methodically, nibbling with restless lips and working me over with that delightfully agile tongue. I heard myself groan as she used her flattened tongue to caress the entire length of my quivering prick, lapping in long broad strokes, only to spiral around the throbbing head and then to trail wetly down the other side. She nuzzled for a moment in the pubic hair at the base of my cock and then began the tantalizing journey all over again.

My hands clenched, my nails digging into my palms, as powerful thrills electrified me, surging though my body in rapid-fire succession. My hips bucked forward, my arched body straining up to seek even more of the heavenly pleasures of that wet teasing tongue. Blindly, I groped for the kneeling girl, clamped my hands on her shoulders, dug my fingers in as I tightened my butt and strained to hold on. For one long, agonizing moment of sheer delight, I arched back, tightening my grip on her naked shoulders, twisting and squirming uncontrollably, offering every inch of my rigid manhood for her slavish devotion.

Now, this highly-adept cocksucker showed her true form. She formed her sweet mouth into a small O, drew her lips back protectively over her teeth, and ducked right down onto my cock, taking the shaft deep into the enfolding warmth of her hot little mouth, engulfing me till I groaned with the sheer exquisite pleasure of it all. The ring of her taut wet lips slid up and down my length, and she was sucking me off with joyful enthusiasm, her cheeks hollowing, her head pumping in furious abandon.

This sudden escalation sent me careening to the edge of climax. My control was rapidly melting away, a warning upsurge of pleasure rushing through me. In desperation I grabbed at my throbbing cock, managing to extract it just as I came with a shattering climax. The first powerful burst of sperm hit the forehead of the kneeling female. Through half-lidded eyes I managed to aim my erupting cock right at her face, directing each pulsating burst so that my semen splattered Vanessa's face, decorating her pretty features with my cum till globules of thick cream dripped down her closed eyelids; ropy strands of cum painted her nose and mouth and chin.

The girl raised a tentative hand, to wipe her sticky face, but Cora stopped her in mid-air.

"No! Use your tongue! Lick it off!" she hissed.

I smiled weakly as, through heavy-lidded eyes, I saw that agile tongue emerge to rim her lips, straining to lick up the dribbles of cum coating her lips and chin. Only when she got every drop that she could by this method alone, did Cora allow her to use her hand to wipe up the remainder.

Dutifully, she was made to lick clean her sticky fingers, and after she had done a similar cleaning job on my poor depleted cock and tucked it safely away, we sent her off, still naked, to get us some drinks. Meanwhile, Cora and I blithely resumed our polite conversation, just as though that bizarre interlude had never occurred.

* * *

Now Monique beckoned Danielle forward and pointed to what I noticed as a rather incongruous addition to this starkly utilitarian room. It was a wooden carousel horse, gaudily painted with big wide eyes, flaring nostrils, and a perpetually frozen-opened mouth. The wooden horse undoubtedly had started life in some carnival where it had given children many years of pleasure, but now, in retirement, it had been ingeniously modified to provide another kind of fun, a very adult pleasure designed specifically for the young women of Ironwood. For sticking up obscenely from the center of the carved wooden saddle was a smooth plastic rod, a dildo that was hinged at the base to allow maximum penetration at any angle.

Little Danielle dutifully followed the pointing finger to approach her assigned mount and I watched as Monique helped the girl to place a bare foot in a dangling stirrup. She cupped a gloved hand under Danielle's sweet little rump, where it lingered for a moment before she gave the supple brunette a boost, urging her to throw a leg over the wooden steed and find the other stirrup so that Danielle stood high astride the saddle, her rigid legs keeping her taut body suspended over the wicked-looking dildo that waited less than inch from her poised crotch.

Monique now brought forth a tube of lubricant and proceeded to grease the shaft liberally, running her gloved hand up and down the shaft till it was well-coated. After a few minutes on the horse a healthy young girl would supply her own lubrication, but experience had shown the overseers of Ironwood that for the initial penetration, this simple precaution helped to get an anxious girl firmly installed.

Now Monique delivered a friendly smack to Danielle's naked butt and ordered her to lower herself onto the jutting shaft, reaching up with gloved fingers to separate the pussy-lips so as to assure a smooth insertion. I watched Danielle's face as she took a breath and closed her eyes, bent her knees, and then slowly impaled herself on the plastic rod. Her brow creased as though with straining effort as the rod disappeared up her gaping vagina, and she adjusted to the novel sensation. She shifted her hips and let herself relax a bit, more comfortable now with her splayed crotch pressed firmly against the wooden saddle, the phallus lodged well up her cunt.

She opened her eyes and looked down uneasily at Monique. The latter had turned away for a moment but now she returned and in her hands were a blindfold, and pair of manacles. The blindfold of black silk was placed over Danielles' eyes and buckled in back imprisoning a thick hank of dark hair. Then the girl was ordered to put her hands behind her, and the metal bracelets were snapped on her wrists, cuffing her so that her shoulders were pulled back as her hands were secured behind her back. This had the effect of forcing her to proudly throw out her little breasts and sit in an even more upright manner in the saddle. She threw back her head and swiveled her hips, undoubtedly trying to accommodate to the hard plastic shaft that was ensconced up her sex.

Now that Danielle was properly mounted, and she could do nothing but wait blindfolded and, no doubt, wondering anxiously what was to about to happen to her. Monique found a switch covered by a panel in the horse's belly and turned the ensconced dildo on, electrifying the girl with a sudden thrill that energized her rigid body and sent her bouncing as she began to ride the pleasuring staff, craning back, jogging in the saddle.

Cora turned to me to whisper that the device employed could be sent vibrating and with a further adjustment of the controls, the sturdy piston would begin to pump in and out of its sleeve, fucking the rider with slow steady deliberation. Monique fiddled with the switches and I noticed a pronounced bucking of the hips as the impaled girl's lust was fired, and her loins moved in instinctive reaction to the rhythmic thrusts of the fucking phallus.

Danielle was bounding up in the saddle now, riding erect, her shoulders arching backwards, her floppy little titties juddering as she was energized into a fucking frenzy. I saw her thighs spasm, and her brow creased in intensity as she rode with wild abandon, firmly taut breasts jouncing up and down in a most delightful way.

In this manner the little rider was driven to a string of multiple orgasms under the close scrutiny of Mistress Van Daam, who would turn off the devilish devices after each climax, only to re-activate it once she had judged that the spent and sagging girl had recovered sufficiently to be ready to driven along the road to yet another ecstatic climax.

Finally, after almost a half hour of this intense sexual stimulation, the wicked devices were switched off, and the room was abruptly silent save for the labored breathing of the girl who mumbled deliriously, pleading for an end to the unrelieved sexual stimulation of her healthy young body.

Danielle was slumped forward, neck and shoulders sheened in sweat, her lank hair falling down around her face. She was still installed on her pleasure toy, but so completely depleted, that when Monique playfully sent a short jolt through the joystick to test her, the only response she got from the poor girl was a low wavering groan.

* * *

The final event of the day was to be the most bizarre. This was a sort of harness race with teams of girls being chosen to take the part of "horses"; each pair being assigned a third girl who acted as their jockey. The "horses," on hands and knees, would be harnessed in tandem, and made to crawl along pulling a delicate light-weight buggy with one of the smaller girls perched atop.

Gretchen now set about affixing the harnesses to the "horses." I watched fascinated to see the way she fitted a set of leather trappings to the first girl, the tall blonde, Erika, who had once served as my dinner companion. With a single sweeping motion, the cool Nordic beauty nonchalantly doffed her tunic, and then calmly lowered herself to kneel in front of Gretchen who slipped a collar around her neck. Once collared, she submissively dropped down to hands and knees to allow herself to be properly strapped in harness.

She waited patiently, motionless, allowing the strange contraption to be fitted to her naked body. At the front a strip was laid across her back and shoulders, then passed under her arms and around to cross her chest just above her hanging breasts and there to be tightened down and buckled in place. From the center of that strap another thinner strip ran lengthwise under her body, up to be attached to the collar at the top, and down to pass between the dangling breasts to be bisected by a second crosspiece which encircled her slender waist just above the hips. The remainder of the lengthwise strip was left, for the moment, hanging down between her splayed thighs.

Gretchen, having arranged the strapped contraption loosely in place, now stepped behind the kneeling blonde and picked up the trailing strap, pulling on it so that the thin leather strip was drawn right up between the legs and along the narrow crack between the blonde's superbly shaped rearcheeks. The strap was threaded through the bisecting waiststrap and up the center of the girl's back to be threaded through the upper strap and finally attached to the collar in back, just beneath the soft mane of blond hair.

The harness was adjustable, and now that it was in place I watched Gretchen tighten it down, pulling on the straps till that splendid nude body was snugly bound with leather strapping. I saw her place a foot on Erika's butt and tug on the lengthwise strip, drawing it further into the rearcrack till it was lost to sight, embedded deep between those tight rubbery cheeks; only then was it buckled into place. Once satisfied, the overseer gave one final tug on the binding straps and, smiling to herself at the job well done, turned to see to the next "horse."

After all the "horses" had been harnessed, and backed up into the traces, there was still one item to complete their trappings. A set of reins had been attached to a hard rubber bit, and these were now inserted between each girl's teeth, the reins drawn back to be placed in the hands of the little drivers who had mounted up and were now ensconced in their seats, slender buggy whips in one hand, two sets of reins in the other.

The sporting fellows of our club immediately saw the possibilities. There was a flurry of lively betting action as wagers were eagerly laid on hastily considered favorites.

Now the contenders were at the starting line. Gretchen raised the starter's pistol. As the shot rang out the delicate buggies began to lurch forward, moving slowly and unevenly down the oval that had been laid out on the grass, and we spectators were treated to the sight of the naked girls crawling on hands and knees, straining in their traces, scrambling to get some momentum going on the slippery grass, all the while being urged on by their youthful jockeys who snapped the buggy whips, laying on light, whippy cuts across the twisting and churning behinds of their gamely struggling teams.

The stinging whips seemed to have a salutary effect as the more they were applied, the more the pace quickened. The little traps made their way uncertainly, teetering around the first corner, but the pace became smoother along the far stretch, where two drew away from the pack and now crawled neck and neck, while the crowd shouted its encouragement. Now the effort seemed to be taking a toll; some of the teams began to falter.

Down the home stretch the pack opened up and one team, arms and legs straining, churning buttocks striped from the crack of the whip, opened the distance to a full length. The little driver, caught up in the excitement of the race, was peppering the churning bottoms before her with maniacal fury. In a sudden burst, the rig lurched across the finish line; the "horses" stumbled and fell to the grass, and there they lay sprawled out on their bellies, panting and exhausted.

The crowd roared its approval, and we hurried off to congratulate the winners. The girls were exhausted, after their labors in hot sun; sweating profusely. Some stayed on hands and knees, still in the traces, their heads hung low, as the gasped for air. Others, released from their duties sprawled back, panting heavily, sweat running down faces and chests, hair drenched and disheveled. It was clearly time to call an end to the games, and send the naked athletes to the showers.

* * *

After the meal, the convivial company filtered through the double doors heading towards the ballroom at the far end of the hall. Here they came upon a scene, enchanted by Cora's dramatic flair for the inspired decor. For it was here that the headmistress had arranged to have four of our prettiest girls displayed in a most provocative tableau.

Stepping through the threshold and into the spacious rotunda beyond, the guests were astonished to find the four "living statues" that Cora had arrayed in a most lascivious display. The circumference of the room was inscribed with four pairs of pillars set with a three foot gap between them. These stood opposite of other, placed at each point of the compass. In the gap between each pair a female figure stood spreadeagled between the twin pillars and tethered by light chains attached to anklestraps and wristcuffs, chains which held them in place with just enough slack to allow some freedom of movement.

Except for a pair of stockings, long, sleek and shiny blue with thigh-high ridged topbands, each young woman was displayed delightfully naked, open and vulnerable under a single spotlight that illuminated her stark figure in the otherwise darkened room.

One further bold, dramatic touch had been added. (How like Cora, I thought.) The girls had been hooded! A loose leather sack worn on the head.

Cora's imaginative embellishment of the room's decor raised the simmering tension in that room, the almost palpable sexual excitement which sizzled through the crowd, igniting an obvious interest in the chained captives who, quite understandably, received increasing attention as the evening wore on.

I found myself mesmerized by a tall, elegant figure with proud breasts that sat high and firm; long streamlined flanks, and exquisite legs, dancer's legs with finely muscled thighs. The hooded woman must have been a blonde, for between her thighs the brazenly exposed vulva was furred with the finest pubic hair, pale silvery in color.

Like a moth unable to resist the allure of the flame, I was powerfully drawn to this striking beauty, my wandering gaze insatiably drawn back, again and again, to her sleek naked body, where my eyes would come to dwell on that lewdly displayed form. Gradually, I worked my way over to stand before this hooded creature. Her splendid nudity and the total vulnerability of her position, inflamed my passions. I could do with her what I would: reach out to her, to touch her, to caress her, provide her with the most exquisite pleasures, or the fires of sexual torment. Her beauty was irresistible! My hand came up, drawn to her naked flesh so near, and gently, almost reverently, my fingertips stretched out to sample a silken thigh.

The hooded girl flinched in surprise at the unexpected touch, handsome breasts rising as she abruptly drew in a breath. A quiver ran through her splayed form, and wiggled through her shoulders. She shivered like a spirited filly. Then she tossed back her head and straightened, and held herself perfectly erect, hardly daring to breathe, tense and expectant, waiting for the next touch.

I was burning with impatience to more fully satisfy my desires. I longed to trace those sleek flowing lines from bottom to top, using the pads of my fingers to explore each marvelous feminine contour. Squatting down before her, I reached down to lift and cradle one nylon-sheathed foot in my hand. Starting at the toes, I glided my fingertips up the arched instep, over the delicate ankle, over the band of leather and on up over the sculpted contours of her leg, relishing the sensual feel of the firm warm flesh encased in the smooth slick nylon.

Wrapping my fingers around the column, I slid my cupped hand upward, savoring the firm subtle curve of a sleek calve muscle; exploring the shallow indentation just behind the knee. I fitted my curved hand to the elegant feminine contour of her nyloned thigh, gliding over the silky smoothness of the stocking till I reached the wide elastic top band, and my fingertips went over the ridge of lacy elastic to touch the naked flesh beyond, seeking the very top of that long curvaceous limb. And there I paused, to linger for a while, luxuriating in the incredible satiny smoothness, feeling the moisture of her innerthighs.

Up to this point the tethered figure had remained motionless. Steeled with the inner resolve, that marvelous self-discipline of a well-trained Ironwood girl, the young woman showed not the slightest response to my silent tribute to her magnificent form. But now, as my fingertips slid between her thighs, skirting the very edge of her pale fleeced triangle, every fiber in her body tensed.

Her thighs twitched. It was a barely perceptible shift, a slight widening of the gap between her legs, a mere suggestion, a subtle invitation to allow her unknown lover even greater access to the sensitive innerflesh. But, for the moment, I chose to ignore the mute invitation, preferring instead to lightly trace up along one side of her triangle. Carefully avoiding her blond pubis, I crossed over to her pointed hip, then along the twitching flanks to caress the shapely outer curve of her extended leg, stroking up and down that sleek nyloned length. After a few passes, I reversed direction, back up her flanks and around to explore the slight shallow of her taut belly, tracing the bottom edge of her ribcage, before nosing upward toward her heaving shivering breasts.

Now, I brought my other hand into play, using both hands up to capture those enticing mounds, rising to my feet to cup her proud bosom, hefting the delicate weights in my palms, watching as the soft pink aureoles expanded with excitement, under the light rubbing of my thumbs.

Palming her satiny breasts, I slid my spread fingers straight up until I could enclose each neat globe in the curled fingers of a hand. Then I tightened my grip, squeezing and unclenching in a rhythmic pumping that soon had the girl tossing her head, squirming and writhing in fiery agitation. As she danced in her bonds, I could feel the little nubbins stiffening against my cupped palms, her nipples hardening with arousal in response to my firm fondling.

I heard a plaintive moan escape from under the hood, as the intensive breast stimulation electrified the tethered figure. She couldn't help twisting her shoulders, thrusting forward first one hip then the other, straining to thrust her breasts into my kneading hands. Her increasing agitation quickened my own mounting sense of urgency, and I toyed with the notion of trying to bring her off by this means alone.

I paused, letting my cupped hands rest lightly on those lovely curves, now slick with sweat. From under the hood came a long soulful sigh. Suddenly, decisively, I grabbed her vulnerable breasts, attacking them with renewed vigor, roughly handling those pliant mounds while my captive grunted in short urgent bursts, twisting sensuously and arching back in pure sensual delight. The hooded woman was losing all control now, her hips bucking in a furious parody of fucking while she gyrated wildly, thrashing about in her chains.

When I judged that she had been brought to the ragged edge of orgasm, I viciously grabbed those moist silken globes, clenching my fingers to squeeze tightly. The frenzied female moaned and shook, climaxing with a resounding shudder, rattling her chains in a passionate explosion which spasmed through her and caused her to yank frantically on her restraints to the point where I became alarmed that she might hurt herself.

By now a crowd had gathered around us, watching the performance in rapt silence. As the hooded woman climaxed, they broke into spontaneous applause. I turned with a smile, bowing to our appreciative audience, while my victim groaned and let her head fall forward to hang limply in her chains, panting raggedly, her shoulders heaving as she struggled to regain her equilibrium. She may have been thoroughly depleted, but I wasn't finished with her . . . not just yet.

Stepping around behind her, I contemplated her handsome bottom. Cupping one of the taut cheeks, I slipped my fingertips into the deep crack between them, causing her butt muscles to clamp instinctively. But I persisted, sliding two fingers down along the tallow valley, digging into the cleft till I could feel the lightly-furred centerseam of her crotch and the damp warmth of her soft vulva.

And there I spent some time, toying with her fleshy cuntlips, plucking and gently tugging on the dewy-slick labia, while the moaning female began to move helplessly, awakening to the first stirrings of rekindled lust. The abrupt insertion of a finger up her well-lubricated cunt drew a sharp gasp of breath, followed by a low throaty grunt from the impaled girl. Next, I stiffened my hand and pressed the edge back and forth in her splayed crotch, rubbing deep between clinging wet pussylips.

When I pulled my hand free I found that my fingers glistened with juices. Slipping the hand under the hood, I held the fingers to her nose, rubbed them all over her lips, giving her a good whiff of her own sexual spendings.

Now I leaned close to the hooded head, and whispered a lewd command, ordering her to lick my hand clean while I rubbed my sticky fingers over her lips and chin. A soft, lively tongue emerged to lap my palm like a submissive cat. Crooking two fingers I slid them over the tiny ridge of teeth and onto her palpitating tongue. On this offering she sucked greedily, drinking in her own nectar.

The perverse thrill of this oddly intimate act so aroused me, that I felt a sudden urge to see her face. In a rush of excitement, I yanked the hood off to unmask Erika, blinking in the sudden light, flushed and disoriented. Her long blond hair, which had been tied up under the hood, was soaked, her face sheened with sweat, her mouth and chin glistening with the residue of her own juices.

With her breath coming in great gulping heaves, she turned to confront her mysterious lover, and when her smoky blue eyes met mine, and she saw who it was, her lips curled in a wry, knowing grin. Her tongue came out to lick her lips like a great self-satisfied cat, and—and then that sluttish vixen . . . winked at me!

* * *

Without further ado, the crisply efficient schoolmistress got her equipment and proceeded to carry out her task. She held a small pot and a paint brush, as she squatted down before the first bent over figure in the bizarre lineup. I watched fascinated as she plucked the elastic waistband of the pair of thin white panties and bared the rounded cheeks of the first girlish behind. Leaving the twisted panties spanning the girl's thighs, she dipped the brush into the pot, and began to swab on a thick syrupy liquid, brushing up and down the small rearend with broad, lavish strokes. The tickling of the soft brush soon had the girl writhing and squirming her hips, but Monique ignored her victim's agitation, and couldn't resist adding to the poor girl's discomfort by running the soft bristles straight up the center valley in a thoroughly wicked stroke that electrified the girl causing her to jerk up and clench her hardened buttocks in instinctive reaction.

Monique smiled to herself as, apparently satisfied that she had thoroughly coated the clenching rearmounds, she drew the girl's underpants back up, pulling them up tightly before letting the elastic waistband snap back into its proper place. Methodically, she gave the pantied behind a final rub, using her fingers to rub the thin nylon all over that small bottom, plastering the panties to the girl's sticky butt before she moved on. Throughout this bizarre treatment, the well-trained girl didn't move a muscle. I knew it would take a few minutes for the hot sauce to do its work; then we would see how well she could stay put!

Now Monique squatted behind the next victim, a slim-hipped blonde with a narrow butt, and straight girlish legs, who wore underpants of soft apple green. The schoolmistress repeated the ritual in a workman-like manner, baring the girl's pert bottom, brushing her bare rump liberally with the sticky syrup, tugging up the panties and letting them snap back into place.

Finally, she moved on to attend to the third girl, who was already working her rearcheeks in fearful anticipation. Peeling the coral pink panties down a neat pair of high-set buttocks, the schoolmistress lavishly applied the glistening syrup to the two rubbery little cheeks, sweeping straight up the crack with a flourish, goosing her victim who bounded up in wild surprise. Monique was smiling to herself as she saw the girl clamp her butt tightly and wriggle her cute ass in a most delightful way. Without further ado, she grabbed a fistful of displaced panties and hauled them straight up, stretching the nylon to its limits, pulling the underpants till they snapped snugly into place. Then she was assured that they would remain well plastered to the assmounds once she had smoothened them over till it looked as though the girl's underwear had been glued to her small rearend.

Now we waited . . . but nothing happened! The girls stood stock still, bent over, holding on, as they had been told to do, waiting, with rigid legs pressed tight together. I was disappointed not to see the slightest reaction and I gave Monique an inquisitive look. But her lively black eyes met mine and she allowed herself a wicked smirk as she nodded knowingly. I watched her raise her hand and point a single finger to the first girl in line.

I followed the pointing finger to see that pantied bottom twitch once, twice, then there was a more definite move of the hips as the girl shook her tail from side to side. Now the second girl joined in, closely followed by the third, and soon all three bottoms were merrily dancing, as the girls wriggled, squirmed and shook, and the fires flared in their itching bottoms.

The girl in the white panties was shifting her weight from foot to foot, hopping about in fiery agitation. The second girl in line, the one with the apple green panties, crossed her legs, pressed one knee tightly behind the other and strained downward. Her sister in the pretty pink panties was arching up, raising her shoulders but managing to hold on, while she frantically waggled her bottom from side to side.

Now we heard a chorus of yelping and whimpering, as the girls, gyrating wildly, tried to shake of the burning sting the fiendish sauce had imparted to their cute little behinds. They were driven frantic by the prickly heat blazing in their rearends, and it was only a matter of a few seconds before the middle girl bolted upright and her hands flew behind her to grab her nylon-encased cheeks. She rubbed furiously, desperately trying to rub away the terrible itch. Immediately, the girl in the pink panties followed suit, yelping, jumping up, and clutching her stinging behind. The girl on the end just managed to outlast the other two, but she soon joined them, since for anyone to maintain the position under such dire straits would have been inconceivable. Now all three girls were hopping about, clutching their butts, and dancing frantically, much to the amusement of the rest of the class.

At last relief was forthcoming as Monique had some girls bring out three large pails of water. These were placed in a line and the agitated victims, caring not one whit about their dignity, squatted over the buckets to lower their fiery bottoms into the cool water, bringing instant, and much welcomed, sighs of relief.

* * *

Later, we snuggled together on the bed. With one arm slung around her shoulder, I toyed with her tit, fingering a nipple, while we shared a cigarette and laid plans for the evening. I told her about this place I knew of, a club actually, called the Bow and Arrow. It was a hangout for arty types, artists and their models, actors, actresses, musicians, with a sprinkling of the rich and beautiful people who went there when slumming on the town. The club was known for its wild parties to which non-members were invited, if they knew the right people. In my line of work, I of course, got to know the right people.

The bacchanal was a fancy dress affair, where guests came in outrageous costumes. My costume was that of an explorer, one of those brave stalwart souls who tramps through the jungles at the far flung corners of the Empire. This required a pair of jodhpurs, tight-fitted trousers that took a bit of wiggling to get on, and long riding boots of soft, highly polished black leather. Naked from the waist up, I strode around the room getting the feel of the stiff boots. Now I drew on the trim bush jacket, buttoning it up and then, on second thought, undoing a few so it was left half open down the front. The pith helmet would cause a minor problem I thought, causing a bit of a stir if worn through the more respectable streets of London. It would remain in its package, until we arrived at the party.

Nikki emerged from the shower, took one look at me in my outfit, and smiled her approval as she took in my booted figure. Still warm and moist and wrapped in a towel, she took her place at the vanity, sitting on the low bench in front of the glass, studying her reflection thoughtfully. I got her to drop the towel, as I could never get enough of seeing her naked, and from my place on the bed behind I could see both the back view and the front reflected in the mirror as she went about the feminine business of applying her make-up.

She toweled her damp hair, then applied brush and finally comb, shaking the silken strands into their natural fall, an even and slightly curved bowl of shiny black that fell to her shoulders. I watched fascinated as she fiddled with her bangs and then, obviously satisfied with the results, reached for her cosmetics case. I settled back on the bed, prepared to enjoy the age-old ritual as the naked girl carefully chose her cosmetics, brushing on the right blush to enhance the delicate ridges of those soft cheeks, drawing lines of rich dark sepia to define the arch of the brows and the almond shape of those large expressive eyes of hers, using the tiny brush to lengthened and darken those seductive lashes. The eyelids were dusted with flecks of turquoise, that gave them a slightly lurid, sexy gleam. Then it was time for the lipstick—dark maroon, a subtle gloss that would impart to her pouting lips a wet and gleaming look. I watched the careful double-arch tinting of the upper lip, the graceful seep of the lower, a pretty pout, the lips pressed together in a single tight line, then, the final blotting. Satisfied, she smiled at her image in the glass, well pleased with what she saw, a pretty woman, confident in her good looks. The scent was strategically applied from a little carved glass bottle, a fine spray behind each ear, down the neck, between the breasts.

Then she stood and padded over to her suitcase to begin a hunt through her lingerie. I stopped her. She would have no need of underwear tonight. I drew her attention to the bed, where I had laid out several packages for her. Now I handed them to her, each in turn.

First, there were the sexy pantyhose, black and gauzily translucent. I waited while she drew them on, pulling them snugly into place, smoothening the nylon over her hips. Slick and sheer, the skin-tight moulded her nether contours in a smoky film. Next, I had her step into a pair of open-strapped sandals, the kind with thin ankle straps and gleaming heels that were wickedly high. The largest package contained all that was necessary to complete her exotic outfit: a brief jacket of sleek black leather, hard and shiny, with a red satin lining. She held it up quizzically. At my nod of encouragement, she slipped it on and zipped it up to the collar. It fitted perfectly, tight, and just the right length, with the bottom band snugly constricting her narrow waist. The silken lining would feel deliciously exciting next to her naked skin, while the supple leather would mold her smooth curves.

Beckoning the girl closer to me, I reached up to lower the tab of the prominent front zipper, creating a delectable decolletage which exposed her upperchest, the rounded tops and a generous expanse of the sloping innercurves of those taut sexy tits. I couldn't resist reaching in to cup a cuddly breast and give the girl an affectionate squeeze. She bent her head to kiss my hand.

The last package was a small one. It contained a single short strap. Nikki recognized the leather strap. At Ironwood, such straps were used to band the neck, forming a 4-inch high collar. She knew what the strap was for. Without a word, she handed it to me, knowing I would want to place it on her, and then she lowered herself to her knees and bowed, bending down to offer her neck in a charming gesture of submissiveness. I placed the leather collar on her, slipping it up under the soft folds of her dark hair, buckling it in place and our preparations complete, we were ready to go.

Not wishing to be arrested on our way to the event, I took the precaution of wrapping my companion in a large raincoat, which hung loosely from her shoulders to her calves. Except for the half-hidden collar, she could easily pass for just another young woman out for walk with her date on a rainy London night.

Outside the hotel, we climbed into the first waiting cab. If the driver noticed the collar, he gave no sign of it. I gave him the address and settled in comfortably, my hand resting on Nikki's warm, silken thigh as the taxi crawled off into the night.

* * *

For dinner that evening, Nikki selected a simple black sheath. Daringly cut up one side, the slinky dress moulded her lithe smoothly-contoured figure and left a generous expanse of her pale shoulders to be admired. Although the loose bodice had only a shallow curving neckline, there was just enough of the topcurves of her small taut breasts left exposed to keep my interest as she leaned over to take a glass of wine. As the bodice fell away a bit in front, a nipple peeked out at me, Nikki often went bra-less. With those small tight breasts, the girl had no reason for support, but the realization abruptly sent a twinge of lust through me.

We sat close to one another in a corner booth of the hotel's elegant dining room, my arm rested on the back of the deeply curved both so that my hand could occasionally caress her bare shoulders, my fingers sample her fine black hair. Nikki looked devastating, and she had had the predictable effect when we entered the room and the heads of appreciative men and jealous women followed the seductive sway of the willowy young woman in the long black sheath. Now I studied her features in the soft candlelight, those pretty eyes with the long lashes, that she used so seductively and with such devastating effect.

As we sipped our drinks I reached down to lay a hand on her thigh, just letting it rest there, with a light, proprietary air. I felt a responsive surge of desire to the nearness of the dark-haired girl, and I shifted closer, moving my hand up her thigh, stroking her through the thin dress, rubbing the slippery silk over the nyloned leg. Nikki snuggled closer. I let my hand wander, slipping it under the dress, moving upward. I relished the warm slick feel of that firmly packed nylon. Warmly responsive, Nikki returned the favor, her small hand on my leg sending my temperature soaring.

I let my inquisitive fingertips glide up, over the elastic band of the thigh-high stocking, to touch the silken flesh above, blindly seeking and finding the overarching legband of her panties.

I tightened the arm that had been loosely slung around her shoulder and drew her to me. The intoxicating scent of the fragrance she wore rocketed through me; left me lightheaded. A wicked idea suddenly struck me! I leaned down to whisper in her ear.

"Nikki, give me your panties."

The girl turned her face up to scan mine, so near, her lips slightly parted, wet and gleaming in the candlelight.

"Give them to me," I muttered the words in her ear. Her gaze never faltered.

"Now?" she whispered, only mildly surprised.

"Yes, here, right now . . . do it Nikki! You can slip them off easily. No one will notice, if you're careful," I encouraged, hardly able to keep the excitement from my voice.

She returned my smile with her own, a amused smile that played across her lips and told of the sort of spunky readiness that I had come to expect from Nikki—a fun-loving girl who was always eager to play games. With an impish grin, she shifted down on her seat, raised her hips and, her movements hidden by the hanging tablecloth, reached up under her dress to quickly slip her underpants down to her knees. For a moment the attractive brunette sat there like that, the dress rucked up across her lap, accordioned panties spanning her thighs just above the knees.

"Take them off. I want them," I urged in a hushed voice.

Sitting tall and elegant, the young woman let her gaze pass serenely over the faces of our fellow diners; none of whom was paying the slightest bit of attention to us. Reassured, she leaned sideways, drawing her legs up so she might reach down and run her underwear down her folded legs. I watched as she struggled to tug the twisted underpants free from her high heels. Crumpling up the wadded lingerie in her closed hand, she slipped it across to me under the table, all the while sitting proper and erect. Her panties were still warm from her body as I took the silky scrap of flimsy nylon and stuffed it in my jacket pocket.

Now it came to me with the full force of a powerful turn on: this exquisite, fashionable dressed, young woman who sat beside me, her hands folded on the table, coolly surveying the elegant dining room—was sitting there without her panties!

I had her reach down and hike up the dress to pull it out of the way so that she sat bare-assed on the smooth padded bench. Soon she had arranged things so that her naked bottom was planted directly on the cool vinyl. There was no problem as the hanging tablecloth effectively shielded her from the roaming eyes of our fellow patrons. Only the waiter might be treated to a happy surprise, should he stand to one side, and then at just the right angle. Then he would see that the sophisticated lady's chic black dress was rucked up around her waist, her glamorous black-stockinged legs exposed for all of their entire lengths.

She sat with legs slightly parted and I found those splendid thighs absolutely irresistible. I dropped a hand under the table and curved my fingers around a thigh, intent on taking up where I had left off before the surreptitious removal of her knickers.

Nikki never flinched, but sat with folded hands calmly surveying the crowded scene; she knew all about the games randy couples played in public places. She knew I meant to put her to the test, call upon her for a demonstration of that magnificent self-control upon which the Ironwood girls prided themselves.

Our young women were taught to control their emotions (and their reactions) in even the most trying circumstances. The Ironwood girl served at the pleasure of her lover. Her body belonged to him; only he could determine when she would allow herself emotional release. I had seen such girls brought to the ragged edge and held there, forced to endure the exquisite torture of impending climax that they were allowed to yield to only at the nod of their lover.

And so Nikki sat there with that marvelous *sang-froid* of the well-trained Ironwood girl, perfectly upright, her lovely bare shoulders thrown back, a set, expression on her pretty face, perfectly composed, as though she were totally detached from what was going on under the table.

And in that way our dinner proceeded, me occasionally

reaching down to toy with her, nudging open her thighs, so that she sat with nyloned legs well-parted while I fingered her soft vaginal flesh. Of course, the healthy young woman could hardly keep still under this intense stimulation. Her hips were twitching, although she managed to maintain her poise prettty well, from the waist up.

This surreptitious playing around had the both of us hot and bothered by the time the coffee was served. I was sporting a massive erection; while the only observable effect on the pretty dark-haired woman was an occasional flutter of her long lashes, or possibly a sharp shivering breath drawn through clenched teeth. I studied her face, there was a slight blush that had arisen to her cheeks, and her wide dark eyes were shiny with excitement.

* * *

And so it was, that Allison and I found ourselves waiting in the wings beside the small stage in the main ballroom. To prepare her for her dramatic debut the attractive young woman had been stripped, her hard white body had been banded with highly polished black straps: the decorative leather collar, and wide slave bracelets banding slender wrists and ankles. As the house lights dimmed, I had her get down on her hands and knees. Then I attached a light chain to the D-ring at her collar. The house lights winked twice, and the stage lights came on. It was the cue for our entrance.

To increase the dramatic effect, I had dressed in tight black jeans, a white silk shirt, open down the front, and black boots—an outfit somewhat reminiscent of an animal trainer's. To complete the illusion, I carried a riding crop. Thus outfitted I strode onto the stage leading the nude woman who dutifully padded after me, like a big cat at the end of her leash. The audience roared its approval to see haughty Allison crawling on all fours, her little pointy titties dangling down, jiggling most delightfully, while her churning bottom swayed from side to side. Thoroughly embarrassed, she kept her eyes to the floorboards in front of her, trying to ignore the dozens of pairs of eyes eagerly devouring her naked body.

I stood at the center of the stage, hands on hips, and ordered my charge to sit facing the crowd. Obediently, Allison tucked her feet under her bare bottom, sitting back on her heels, hands hung loosely at her side. The once proud young lady assuming the requisite pose, head hung low, her eyes carefully avoiding her quieting audience, who were now treated to a superb view of her young breasts: two pear-shaped globes sagging slightly, with uptilted nipples, succulent and swaying slightly as she shifted back to sit on her heels.

Now I put her through her paces. First, I unhooked the leash and had her stand, ordering her to lift up her head and directly face her hushed audience. She took a deep breath, threw back her shoulders, and brazenly widened her stance, facing them with a look of haughty disdain. She knew she was to be humbled before this bawdy crowd of lusty men, yet she stood before them, unbroken, her face a mask of insolent defiance. Hands at her side, legs spread, she revealed her naked body openly to them, inviting them to stare, arrogant and proud, a single nude figure, daring her audience to look.

And look they did, for there was much to admire. Allison had sharp delicate features and boyishly short hair, giving her a crisp, clean-cut appearance. Her short golden brown hair was swept back along each side, curling over and around her ears. In the back it was cropped high, leaving bare her long graceful neck, banded now in the high Ironwood collar.

The subtle curves of her lean body flared to a neat pair of compact hips, sharp and angular, then down to the rounded contours of her thighs, the sculpted curves of her shapely legs, the dramatically banded ankles, and long narrow feet. Her exposed vulva, a narrow triangle of dusky fur, invited the fingers to dabble in the silky curlings. Tapping her heel with the riding crop, I had her widened her stance, boldly inviting her audience to examine her sex, the soft white flesh with the deep center crease shaded with soft brown pubic hair that thickened between her legs. I saw that her bush had been trimmed, neatly shaved to accommodate a low-riding bikini that must have once covered her furry little pussy. Such a detail was enough to convince me that this young lady was not above showing off her feminine charms. Undoubtedly, she was the type who liked to tease the boys, boys who would quickly find they could look . . . but not touch.

I whispered an aside to her:

"Turn around."

Without the slightest change in expression, Allison let her arms drop to her side, brought her legs together, and slowly turned in place offering her back to the audience. Now we were treated to a view of her slender shoulders, the long narrow plane of her smooth back, and those high-set hard little buttocks I knew so well.

"Bend over. Hands on your knees." My words were soft; a hushed order.

Slowly, the girl bent forward, widening her stance, bracing herself, presenting her audience with a superb view of her tightcheeked young bottom.

"Further than that, Allison. Stick out that ass of yours for us to see," I ordered, tapping the solid rearend with the tip of the crop.

Allison deepened the bowed curve of her back and thrust back her naked bottom.

"Now wiggle it for us. Shake that thing!" I hissed.

From my position beside her I could watch her face. The girl was blushing furiously now, but she swallowed and closed her eyes and wiggled her ass on command, shaking it from side to side like a well-practiced whore, eliciting warm applause from her most appreciative male audience who shouted and hooted their approval with crude encouragement.

"Enough," I cried. "Now bend down all the way. Grab your ankles."

Obediently, she did as she was told, folding her lean supple body at the hips, sliding her hands down the front of her legs and stretching down to clasp her ankles at the leather cuffs. She held the most humiliating position and waited, giving everyone a good look at what she had to offer. Bent nearly doubled, her neat ass was upraised in provocative display; the underslung pouch of her dusky pussy peeped out at us from between the taut rounded curves of her straining thighs.

I lightly tapped the jutting rump with the tip of the riding crop, tracing the lovely swells of Allison's upturned bottom. Then, on a sudden impulsive, I snapped my wrist, whapping her smartly across the proffered cheeks. The girl jerked up in surprised reflex and started to straighten up, but at my sharp warning, she settled back down, renewing the grip on her ankles, and looking over her shoulder at me with a sullen spiteful look. The audience roared its approval, clapped.

Now I teased her a little with the whippy rod, running it over her pale cringing cheeks, watching them clench in fearful anticipation. I worked the tip between the hard white hemispheres, tracing the tight crack, pressing between those firm pillows, probing between clenched cheeks. Allison jerked as if electrified at this impertinent intrusion, but she obediently held the mandated position.

* * *

I took her limp hand and placed it on the base of the vibrator.

"Go on. Do it!" I urged in a dry voice.

I waited, tense and keyed up. Then the hand that held the shaft moved, jiggling then evening out to pump up and down in a slow steady rhythm. Jane closed her eyes and slid back further onto her shoulders. I let her set the pace, watching the blonde girl fuck herself at my bidding. The lines of her face slackened in a dreamy reverie. Her lips parted in a long exhaled breath.

"Faster."

Obediently, the hand pistoned faster, and the increasingly aroused blonde began to squirm, twitching excitedly, rising up on her toes, calve muscles straining. Her twisting torso arched up off the floor as she began rolling her head from side to side, driven by the pleasurable sensations pulsing through her reedy body. Her eye lashes fluttered, eyes closed, tightened down, her jaw clenched. She moaned, a tiny moan through tight-pressed lips.

"Faster!" I hissed.

By now Jane was writhing uncontrollably, her pretty features screwed up, her eyes tightly shut against the rising tide of lust. She bit down on her lower lip with tiny even teeth, as the flood of sensations threatened to overwhelm her. I kept her at it till I saw the first beginnings of an unmistakable bucking of her pelvis. A shiver racked her straining body as the twitch grew to a decided thrust, and then her hips were bucking frantically.

"Now, turn it on!" I ordered hoarsely, my voice cracking with emotion.

She was so distraught, she had to use the other hand, to fumble for the activating switch. The angry buzzing sound, half muffled, told of the sudden thrill surging through the passion-driven female, whose eyes opened wide, her arched eyebrows shooting up at the abrupt cascade of electrifying sensations. I kept her at it, energizing herself with that delicious tingling that rippled from her core and radiated out to flood her trembling, pleasure soaked body. Wild-eyed, the girl whimpered and strained even further upward, tossing her head from side to side in a maddened frenzy. She shoved the buzzing sex toy all the way into her distended sex leaving it snugly ensconced, while her hands fell away to brace herself on the floor while her hips bucked in sexual fury. Now, the woman beyond all control, caught in the those of unrelenting ecstasy while her bounding ass bounced up and down on the carpet.

Of course, she was incapable of sustaining this incredible self-stimulation for more than the few seconds and with a plaintive whimper, she exploded in shattering climax which racked her straining form again and again. Then, with a long wavering moan, the young woman collapsed back on the mat in a depleted heap; the devilish vibrator still buried up her cunt hummed merrily away; she was beyond caring.

I stepped over to look down on the flushed and sweating female, as she lay there, panting like a steam engine. She was totally drained, her eyes closed, her face and upper chest sheened with sweat, her small breasts heaving in great, shivering swells. She lay with legs sprawled carelessly apart; one arm thrown up across her forehead, while the other lay across her belly, the hand protectively shielding her exhausted sex.

I raised a booted foot and set the toe squarely on her flattened left breast, lightly pressing down to squash the slight mounded rise, indenting the swollen nipple while I moved my foot in a small circle. But except for a gurgled half-groan, I got no response from the comatose female. For now she was done. I wondered perversely, if she could be made to repeat the performance.

* * *

The bevy of girls who now entered the room were all barefoot; identically clad, wearing a single garment: a simple white tunic, cut in the Greek style, which covered them from shoulders to hips. The sheer garment was a sleeveless, one-piece affair with a generous curving neckline that dipped low in front, and rose in narrowing shoulder straps to loop thin shoulders. The deeply-curved neckline left bare the upper region of the smooth girlish chest while the loose bodice fell in soft folds, the thin material gathered at the waist and there it was tightly belted to form a brief skirt which barely covered the tops of firm young thighs leaving bare legs pleasingly displayed. From behind, one could see that the little skirts were barely adequate to layer the female bottom, and then the thin covering stayed in place only if the girl held herself erect and perfectly still, for even the slightest movement would threaten to expose more than the undercurves of a pair of pert rearcheeks—a hint of which peeked out below with saucy impudence.

* * *

"You seem to find Miss Robin to be of some interest, eh, Mr James?" Victoria asked coyly.

I gave her a tight-lipped smile, not at all sure I could trust my voice to answer just then. But with a few quick swallow I managed to venture forth, in a voice that was strained and threatened to crack: "Why don't we have her play with herself a bit?"

Victoria beamed. "Of course. This one likes playing with herself," she assured me. And so poor Robin was ordered to engage in the rites of solo pleasures before our very eyes.

She was still staring at me, but her eyes seemed to have glazed over. Her lips parted; her breathing was becoming more ragged. I saw her take a deep breath and bring a hand down her belly, nosing her fingers through the profusion of dark curls over the mounded pubis and down into the exposed dusky pink furrow. When her fingers curled and her palm rubbed over the fleshy pad, I noticed her eyelashes fluttered, the lids sliding down till her eyes narrowed, and though she still kept them centered between my legs she regarded my cock now through slitted eyes.

The lurid sight of the lovely brunette burying her curled fingers into the soft folds of pussyflesh, cupping herself, palming her mound to stir the fires of passion, was enough to energize my thickening prick so that it rose and flared into full prominence with a sudden surge of lust.

If our little playmate noticed the erected tribute to her sexual prowess, she gave no sign of it; her eyes were barely opened and her head lolled back on the cushion, rolling slowly from side to side as she savored the warm waves of pleasure flooding generated in her loins and flooding through her healthy young body.

Victoria let this steamy scene go on for awhile, Robin slipping into her inner world of pleasure, oblivious to us, rubbing herself off with a slow circular massage and occasionally clamping her thighs on her deep rubbing hand. I watched the sinuous movements of her lithe torso and heard the soft moans of pleasure she uttered as her head rolled back and she sent it snapping from side to side flinging the pillow with silky black hair back.

I stole a glance at Victoria and found her sitting on the edge of her chair leaning forward, totally caught up in the rising heat of the girl's sexual performance.

"Use your fingers, girl! Go on, fuck yourself! Show us how you do it, you little whore!" she suddenly hissed at the passion soaked girl, startling me by the vehemence of her commands. Victoria, too, was becoming aroused by the solo performance.

I saw Robin curl her middle finger to slip it up between the slick folds; then a second and a third. And with three joined fingers inserted in her cunt, young Robin jiggled her wrist, diddling herself upon command and sending a wild thrill of excitement rocketing through me. I couldn't resist taking myself in hand at the explosive sight and I slowly fingered myself, carefully, just a little so as to not upset the delicate balance that Victoria had set up.

"Look at Mr James!" Victoria's command rang out, sharp and clear, startling me as well as the semi-oblivious girl. Robin's eyes snapped open, but they remained unfocused as she stared through me. Her hand was moving faster and faster till it became a pistoning blur, and her shoulders rolled back on the cushion. She arched up, her eyes widened and she flung her head back, whimpering in tight urgent whimpers.

Robin strained upwards raising her bottom up off the chair as she rubbed furiously, her whimpered cries turning into low moans of earthy passion. She was writhing in the heat of her onrushing orgasm. Suddenly, her thighs clamped down on the pleasuring hand and her eyes clenched shut against the incredible onrush of the flooding ecstasy. A shudder of pure pleasure jolted through her taut young body and, with a long satisfied groan she abruptly collapsed back into the chair, her thighs, fell loosely apart, and her shoulders heaved as her breathing slowly returned to normal.

* * *

Now I pulled a straight-backed chair around to straddle it, sitting in front of her, eager to complete her initiation into the world of Ironwood.

I had her sit back, tucking her legs under her, spreading her knees apart in blatantly obscene invitation. Admiring the top of her tilted head and the eloquent curves of huddled shoulders, I ordered her to reach back and clasp her ankles, thus drawing her shoulders back, and raising up her magnificent chest as if to thrust it out in offering. The collared woman dutifully followed my instructions: lifting her chin, and throwing back her head, so as to sit with naked bottom planted on her heels, unseeing eyes fixed straight ahead. It was the presentation position, one that Ironwood girls would learn to assume automatically, slipping to their knees to sit back on folded legs, offering to display their manifest charms, whenever they might be presented to male guests.

Now for the camera's benefit (and, I must admit, for my own edification), I took the time to indulge myself by placing Amanda in a series of provocative poses. I ordered the girl to rise up and straighten her back, kneeling erect once more, bringing her hands up to link her fingers behind her neck. Posing with uplifted arms elevated those enticing breasts, bringing them into ever greater prominence.

Up until now I had shown, what I believed to be remarkable restraint, considering that I was all alone with a pretty girl who was wearing nothing but her shoes, and who had proven herself wonderfully compliant with my every wish. Yet except for that brief encounter when I laid hands on her shoulders and forced her to her knees, I had not touched her at all. But now I was seized with an overwhelming desire to sample what she so eloquently offered to me. The aching longing I felt to get my hands on those lush, mouth-watering tits became so desperate that my hands seemed to have a will of their own. They reached out for those fully plump, softly rounded shapes—seductive curves that positively beckoned the attention of any red-blooded male.

My fingertips lightly grazed the side of her left tit, curving around to follow the alluring rounded contour. Amanda stiffened and gasped in a tiny shivering intake of breath as my fingers traced the shape of that perfect breast. The light teasing caress only whetted my appetite. I was instantly hungry for more. Bringing the other hand into play, I reached for both tits with curved palms to cup them from beneath, and heft their full heaviness. I palmed those gentle mounds as my fingers slid up the slopes and curved till my hands tightened on the soft warmth of that silken skin. I held her in my hands.

Some women's breasts have a liquid quality. Unlike those of their sisters, with breasts that are tighter, more taut skinned so that they move with only the slightest shimmy, theirs are looser, more like balloons half-filled with water. Such tits easily bounce and quiver, and are a positive delight to fondle. Amanda had such comely, and thoroughly enjoyable, tits.

I opened and closed my hands, digging in fingers to greedily grab full generous handfuls of softly pliant tittie-flesh, avidly fondling Amanda's lush, beautiful tits. I savored the feel of her, testing the bouncy resiliency of those choice mounds, pressing, petting, and stroking the kneeling woman's naked breasts, while she swayed in the rising heat. Thus I spent several minutes, thoroughly enjoying myself, lavishly feeling up poor Amanda who, still on her knees with arms upraised, found it increasingly difficult to maintain the pose I had put her in.

Of course, no healthy young woman could help responding to all this stimulating attention by such an ardent male admirer. I soon had Amanda breathing heavily, her shoulders squirming and heaving with the effort. I watched a quiver of excitement shot through her upper body; she worked her lips as though to swallow down the rising tide of passion. It took only a few minutes with my hands palming those jellied mounds before I had her excited nipples sticking out, thick and taut with arousal; the disks of her aureoles were expanded and tight, the tiny stems protruding stiffly, hard as little pebbles. I scissored those jutting nipples between my fingers; plucked at them, pinched them lightly while she whimpered; pressed the hardened nubbins into the surrounding disks of pliant flesh, while she groaned.

The sound that escaped her lips was more of a growl than a moan, deep throated and thrillingly sexy. The hot, flushed woman was damp with perspiration which sheened her brow, her upper chest and her quivering, shuddering breasts. She knelt with eyes closed, struggling with the repeated surges of arousal that shook her to the core, panting, long lashes fluttering under the ceaseless stimulation of my pleasuring massage.

"Nooo . . . please noooo.." she pleaded in a breathless voice that had thickened with sensual desire; she clenched her shut eyes and arched back against the creamy rise of pleasure. Then her hands feel from behind her neck and she shook her mane like a proud filly after a spirited workout. With a deep sigh, her head fell; shoulders sagged; her breath was coming in deep heaving gulps through open lips.

"Look at me!" I hissed, clutching two handfuls of silky soft flesh.

Her eyes flew open and she was staring into mine with excitement and obvious longing flooding those deep brown depths. "Hands behind your head," I reminded her hoarsely.

Amanda took a deep breath, and exhaled a long wavering moan. Then, breathing hard, with breasts rising and falling in ragged undulations, she slowly brought up her hands to once more take up and hold the mandated position.

My greedy hands filled with those warm, sweaty, marvelous tits. I began moving them in a languid circular massage, all the while admonishing Amanda for her shocking lack of control. For at Ironwood, self-discipline was the first step. A lady who learns to rein in her own raging lust becomes more adept at pleasuring others. And above all, Ironwood girls must dedicate themselves to the art of giving pleasure, wholly and unselfishly.

In this way I toyed with her, fondling those wonderfully floppy tits and pausing, every now and then, letting the girl have a bit of respite as I eyed up her heaving chest, that superb bosom with choice nipples that stood out, darkened and swollen with passion, as I spoke of control.

Even under such pleasuring manipulation of her bouncy breasts, she must learn to maintain her composure, suffering the sweet agony of intense foreplay, until she allowed her release by her lover. Much later, I was to learn from the women we had trained, that the resulting orgasm is unlike any they had ever experienced in its raw, earth-shaking power.

And as our first girl knelt there, her eyes on me, gritting her teeth at the sheer intensity of pleasure that welled up in her panting, sweat soaked body with my hands playing constantly with her delightful breasts, I couldn't help turning to look over my shoulder at the hidden camera; couldn't resist giving it a knowing smile.

* * *

Amanda's breathing was heavier now, naked breasts rising and falling in deep undulations. She still sat with eyes closed, but there were other subtle changes that attested to her growing arousal. The wide disks of her aureoles had expanded, and her voice slipped into the same dream-like quality I saw in her knowing smile. She liked to rub herself, she admitted, to palm her mons, to slip a finger or two up her cunt and in that way to bring herself off. I was wild with excitement.

"Show me! Do it!" I insisted in a hissed whisper.

Her heels were still hooked over the rung, as she shifted her butt forward to the edge of the stool, and let her knees fall wider apart so that I might have a better look. Spellbound, I watched her thighs slowly open, those long steepled legs spreading out before me, moving apart in obedience to my call, till she sat with her hairy womanhood on open display; bulging vulva stretched open to my eyes, the petals of her hidden flower fully revealed.

As I sat entranced, a hand came up to slide down her belly, extended fingers delving down into the thicket of dark pubic hair. The hand fitted itself to her vulva, long pointy fingers nosing towards her underarch as the hand curved and tightened on her sex, and Amanda gave herself an urgent squeeze. Then she used the heel of her palm to rub the softly mounded pubis, while two fingers pressed between the fleshy outer lips of her cunt.

"Look at me!" I demanded.

Her eyes flutered open and she looked down on me with half-lidded eyes; her lips parted and her head fell back as she arched up. She was breathing heavily through her mouth, shoulders twitching at the ripples of pleasure coursing through her body as she languidly rubbed herself off. It was a struggle to contain my wildly escalating excitement at the sight of this sensuous young woman playing with herself, palming her vulva, lewdly fingering her half-opened sex.

"Show me your cunt!"

Obediently, Amanda slipped her two fingers down along the protruding lips and pried back the petals, to hold herself open with fingers pressing back the dark pink lips of her cunt. The folds of her outerlips were pulled open to reveal the labia, ragged pink lips still closed protectively, the coral pink flesh of that feminine flower surrounded by tiny curlings of pubic hair that shaded her splayed crotch.

"Go on . . . play with yourself," I urged, burning with the heat of that singular erotic moment.

I watched, totally captivated, as her hand moved slid down to cover her cunt, and she started rubbing her palm down over her pubic mound, twisting her shoulders as she palmed her furry vulva in a deep, slow, sensual massage. Her fingers played along the centerline, teasing over the pouting pussy-lips, the fingertips rubbing, pressing, slipping into the slick inner flesh. I watched her press into the cowl of flesh at the very top of the lips, where the hidden pearl of her clitoris lay in wait. She fingered herself there, with light delicate teasing touches.

"Fuck yourself! DO IT!"

The writhing brunette curved her two middle fingers and slipped them up her splayed cunt. Her high brow winced, and her eyes snapped shut and tightened with the intensity of the sudden stab of pleasure she gave herself. But she immediately struggled to open them again, to regard me once more through dark slitted eyes as she began to jiggle her hand, slowly at first, then faster till her pistoning hand was a frenzied blur, and she gave out with a long quivering moan through opened lips.

"Fuck yourself!. . . . Fuck yourself!. . . . Fuck yourself!" I urged hotly, my control slipping away as I jammed my hand down my pants to clutch my aching prick, yanking, desperate to find some sort of relief. Her hips were rocking now, and the girl hunched forward, then threw back her thick hair, as she brought a second finger into play. Immediately, she slipped a third curled finger up to join the other two, and now she sat on the very edge of the round vinyl seat, three fingers jammed up her glistening wet cunt, her wrist jiggling in a flurry of motion as that handsome brunette writhed in surging passion, finger fucking herself for my edification.

A perverse thrill surged through my body as I sat paralyzed with my hand on my cock, utterly captivated by the hot sight of this lust-driven girl who hunched forward, jaw clenched, face contorted in passion, grunting through tightly-drawn lips as she diddled herself, jacking off, oblivious to all that was around her, even as over my shoulder, the all-seeing camera hummed merrily along.

Elegant Concertos

She came to me willingly, this lovely submissive girl; obediently let herself be drawn down to lay with her loins raised over my lap, one solid hip pressed firmly against my hardening prick. Her long lithe body lay perfectly still as I opened her riding pants and started tugging the snug material down her flaring hips. She moved only to shift obligingly, raising her hips up, so I could pull free the bunched material from between our bodies. It wasn't easy, but I managed to work the snug riding pants down to her knees, exposing a pantied behind that was encased in taut, cream colored panties.

Eagerly, I reached for her panties, slipping my curled fingers in the back of her underpants and grabbing a handful of fabric to peel the panties down over her lovely ass, revealing two tight-set cheeks, stretched into elongated swells, separated by a narrow slit. The tautly-drawn cheeks had taken on a rosy blush from repeatedly smacking against the saddle on the long ride. I placed a hand on them and found the skin pleasantly warm and velvety smooth to the touch. I ran my fingers over the upturned curves, and Marianne's hips gave a sexy wiggle. I bent down to plant a big wet kiss on her left cheek, and got a little low-throated sigh of satisfaction from my cuddly playmate.

Now I switched tactics, curled my fingers into a claw and attacked that vulnerable behind, digging my nails into that soft, malleable flesh; firm, yet yielding. I clenched my fingers; sunk them talon-like into the meaty mound, squeezing, wobbling the little mound, while Marianne grunted, her body stiffened and her head and shoulders shot up, heels fluttering up in back in reaction to my rough mauling of her naked ass.

Using a hand placed on the middle of her back to pin her down, I hauled off and smacked her ass, bringing my cupped hand down in an authoritative, stinging slap.

WHAP!. . . . WHAP!. . . . WHAP!. . . . WHAP!

At the first slap, Marianne kicked up her heels in fluttery agitation, but she soon settled in and managed to hold herself still, merely grunting and jerking reflexively with each juddering impact on my smacking hand. I was fascinated with the way the pliant mounds wobbled at each crisp slap. Flattening my hand, I gave her butt a glancing smack that sent the pert mounds shimmying most delightfully.

Now the red blush was deepening, as I kept at it, punishing that womanly behind, walloping her, not hard, but with measured steady slaps that soon had the big woman twisting in my lap. She squirmed, grinding her hips against my all-too-ready cock, wiggling her inflamed bottom in a vain effort to shake off the sting I repeatedly imparted there.

I gave the girl no respite, peppering Marianne's superb ass, spanking her squarely across both cheeks with my cupped hand till my palm was stinging from the repeated impact. I rested for moment, giving her a brief respite; then I began another round. Now she was squirming in hot lust, clearly turned on, making little mewing sounds through tightly-set lips.

When I stopped again my hand was stinging terribly, and Marianne lay quietly over my lap, her long body a dead weight, her well-punished behind throbbing and red. I laid a gentle hand across those tender mounds; her butt cheeks clenched at this teasing contact, but she never made a sound.

I urged her off of me, half shoving and rolling her so that her long body ended up over the log that I had vacated. Then I knelt down behind her, and brought my lips to her warm bottom, there to kiss and then to lick the recently-chastised flesh of Marianne's throbbing ass. A deeply satisfied sigh escaped her lips, as I continued to tenderly minister to those choice mounds, holding her by the hips as I lapped up and down those twin curves with broad, wet strokes that soon had the girl writhing with tickling excitement.

My prick was aching with intolerable readiness, and I could hardly control myself as I grabbed her by the shoulders and threw her, face down, on the grass. She lay still, her upturned buttocks smooth and warmly inviting, as I tore off my boots and ran down my riding breeches. With a lunge I was on her, flattening myself against her solid, inflamed ass, savoring the warm feel of her recently-spanked bottom against my groin. I wiggled my hips, pressing my cock deep into her crack to give her the full feel of my manhood between the cheeks, that clenched instinctively on its hardened length. The dark-haired girl groaned; I backed off, rolled her over. Her legs fell open and her knees instinctively rose up to welcome penetration. I fell between her opened thighs, lunging forward to drive my solid prick straight into her welcoming wet vagina. The leggy girl wrapped those sleek-muscled limbs around me and began urging me on with little strangled cries of passion; pounding my butt with her heels, beating a wild tattoo.

Now she was meeting my lusty thrusts with her own, her body hungry straining for me, as she craned back and arched up, then began bucking her hips furiously, all the while making deep throaty grunts, that punctuated each thrust. Fucking with mad abandon, I rode the wildly gyrating girl to a most spectacular climax, a roaring explosion that blotted out all thoughts of the other couple, or of anything else in the world.

As I came gently down to earth, I rolled off Marianne's hot sweaty body and sprawled back, my softened cock wet and depleted. Gasping for air with my chest heaving, I lay on my back, gazing up at the incredible blue of the summer sky above me.

* * *

Almost five years had passed since I first stood before the desk of Cora Blasingdale. Then, I was a just candidate for a choice position at Ironwood. Now our roles were reversed, and it was I that sat behind the massive desk, while the big blonde stood waiting before me.

Five years made this an anniversary of sorts, a time to reflect. They had been good years; Ironwood had prospered. Our business, supplying exquisite, perfectly-trained young ladies to various houses of pleasure by contract, or placing them in hands of private collectors for a reasonable finder's fee, was flourishing. Ironwood had acquired a certain reputation, albeit among a small select circle of connoisseurs, of offering the finest quality courtesans in the world. There was a mystique about the Ironwood girl that raised her to world class status.

I had to give due credit for our astonishing success to my one-time superior and now chief assistant, Cora Blasingdale. It was she who insisted on the strictest standards, and instilled the rigorous discipline that infused the regimen at Ironwood. It was she who fostered the Ironwood ideal: a young woman who was trained to freely subvert her own will, placing herself body and spirit totally in the hands of her lover in the unrivaled pursuit of sensual pleasure.

I thought about how much we owed to Cora now as she stood before me, dressed all in black as was her wont—the turtleneck sweater softly clinging to those firm high breasts, the tight jodhpurs that shaped her long elegant legs, and those knee-high riding boots, tight-fitted and made of soft polished leather. The image came back to me of the proud blonde on her knees, paying obsequious tribute to my penis; of majestic Cora Blasingdale, bare breasted and collared, humbled by me, before the entire Ironwood community.

She didn't seem to bear the slightest resentment over her public humiliation on that fateful day when the reins of Ironwood leadership had changed hands forever. To the contrary, the woman seemed more alive, warmer, softer, and decidedly more feminine. Her voice had lost its hard edge, and when she looked at me her pale blue eyes seemed to soften with sexual desire. Now she stood quietly before me, while I reviewed the accounts.

I could feel her eyes on me as I feigned unusual interest in the boring columns of figures. I could sense that she wanted to say something, but was holding back.

"Well?" I asked glancing up at her handsome face, meeting those inquisitive eyes.

"It's just that . . . it's . . . been a long time, James . . ." She began hesitantly, unsure of herself. I guessed at what she had in mind, but I wasn't going to help her.

"So?"

"Well . . . you see I thought, perhaps you'd . . . perhaps we could . . . make love."

"Fuck?" I offered.

She lowered her eyes; the blond head gave a tiny nod.

"That's all you think of, isn't it, woman? Sex. And I know the kind of sex you want. Your kind of sex . . . hard and dirty. That's it isn't it?" I waited, my eyes on her face.

A shiver went through the elegant blonde as she stood before me head hanging low. She held her body rigid and nodded dumbly.

"Well you'll have to ask nicely," I said teasing her. "Tell me what you want!"

There was a pause. She took a deep breath; her full bosom rose and fell in a deep undulation.

"Oh James, I want to fuck," she managed to get out in a voice that was low and breathy.

I smiled to myself.

"Sit down."

She turned to take a chair across the desk facing me, but I stopped her.

"No, first take off those boots . . . and the pants." I said it as though it were a casual, offhanded remark, like a request to pass the salt at the dinner table.

Cora would never think to question such a lewd request, such orders being commonplace at Ironwood, though it was rare for the Headmistress to be on the receiving end. But now she didn't hesitate, just perched obediently on the edge of the wooden chair and struggled to get her boots off. Then she stood, opened her riding pants, and without hesitation, shoved them down her legs, finally sitting again to draw down the clinging pants free. Now the tall blonde stood up, reduced to her sweater and pantyhose. I made a mental note to mention those pantyhose to her. In the future, I wanted her in stockings.

Still, I had to admit the black pantyhose *were* rather sexy. Especially since one could plainly see from the plastered hair of her blond-furred vulva, that she wore nothing under the taut press of elasticized nylon. The tightly-fitted garment clung to every curve and crevice, smoothening and shaping the elegant contours of her hips and thighs and butt. Just at the juncture of the thighs, the reinforced gusset was drawn into a tight crease that stretched along the folds of the fleshy cuntlips, molding the jutting pubic mound. The hazy triangle of pussyfur thickened into rich curlings that ridged the lips of her prominent labia.

I motioned her to a seat, and paused to appreciate the erotic picture she presented to me: The tall, well-built, 40-ish woman, with the short stubble of ash blond hair, stylishly cropped, sitting across from me, perfectly still, with her knees openly parted, her hands resting on the arms of the chair.

Quietly composed, she looked back at me with the even gaze of a seated monarch on her throne, the only trace of her excitement the peeking of her tongue as it made a quick pass to moisten her set lips.

I watched her slowly cross those long legs, letting a stockinged foot swing idly. When she saw my frown, she promptly moved to rectify her mistake, uncrossing her languid legs to sit once more in that shameless pose, knees well parted, offering me the unhindered view of her nyloned sex. For a moment or two we sat in silence, my eyes pointedly focused on her splayed crotch, as I let the anticipation grow. Then I spoke.

"Stand up now, and turn around," I spoke curtly, trying to keep my voice even although I felt the quiver of emotion and the dryness in my mouth at the closeness of this desirable woman so excitingly clad.

Cora slowly rose to her full impressive height and pivoted in place, presenting me with a choice view of her handsome bottom encased in the snug nylon, the narrow crack clearly visible between the prominent curves of that fully-curved buttocks. I remembered enjoying the bouncy, resilient, happily pneumatic ass of Cora's on more than one occasion, and I smiled now at the thought of those happy times.

"Bend over; hands on your thighs," I ordered, my hands tingling with anticipation.

Without a word the big blonde folded herself from the hips, placing her flattened palms on her thighs just above the knees and bracing herself like that, presenting me with a perfectly scrumptious view of her jutting behind, provocative curves tightly packed in straining black nylon.

"Now stick up that big ass of yours!" I commanded.

I watched the bending woman move to obey, raising her shoulders and deepening the curving slope of her back, moving sensuously like a big cat to eagerly adopt the lewdly suggestive pose I demanded of her.

"Now pull your pantyhose down in back. I want you bare-assed, woman!" I hissed.

Cora's hands came back and she hooked her thumbs in the elastic waistband. Slowly she peeled the clinging nylon down, exposing the meaty mounds of her mature womanly ass. She eased the nylon barrier down past her the smiling undercurves of her smooth bare bottom and down a bit further to leave the stretching twisted nylon spanning her sleek-muscled thighs just a few inches below her hairy crotch.

"Now . . . shake it. . . . Go on, shake it! . . . move that ass of yours . . . and tell me what you want, tell me how badly you want to be fucked!" I demanded, my uncertain voice cracking with emotion.

Where sex was concerned, Cora had seen it all. For the most part, she took it all in stride, and nothing phased her. I had seen enough of her in action to conclude that the woman was essentially embarrass-proof. Yet I knew the key to Cora Blasingdale. It was just this sort of sexual humiliation that always got to her, bringing on a heated rush of lusty desire. It was a powerful turn on for her, to be humiliated like this, to be made to perform, as I had discovered almost by accident one fine day. This sophisticated lady would turn into an animal when she made to grovel in sex, happily degrading herself in the most obscene manner, wallowing in sex like a lusty whore. And so I had her waggle her ass most provocatively for me now . . . and she loved it! The woman was insatiable.

I couldn't help smiling to see the elegant blonde obediently move, rotating her buttocks, wagging her naked bottom so wantonly in my direction.

"Tell me what you want, Cora!" I hissed.

"Fuck me . . . fuck me . . . fuck meeeee" The words came out in a heated rush.

By this time I was sporting a raging erection and I meant to comply with her desire, but there was one thing I wanted to do first. Quietly slipping open the top drawer of the desk, I extracted an 18-inch ruler. Of course, with her back still turned towards me, Cora didn't know that my hand held that lethal weapon as I stealthily got up and crept around the desk. She was still holding the pose I had put her in, her impudent bottom stuck up in air, when I stepped up and whacked her right across those vulnerable rearcheeks with a sharp crack of the pliant lath.

WHAP!

Cora yelped in shocked surprise; her shoulders shot upright at the stinging impact, but she managed to keep the position. I smiled to myself. How like a well-trained Ironwood girl, I thought, secretly pleased.

"That's just a reminder," I warned grimly. "Now get over there, and belly up to that desk. I want you over the desk . . . all the way over," I managed to get out in a voice that came out choked with passion.

The big blonde assumed the position, leaning over the desk, lowering herself till she rested on her elbows, legs slightly parted, still hobbled by the half-masted pantyhose. A pink welt had formed across the twin mounds where the ruler had met that solidly built rump.

My hands were shaking as I tore off my shoes and socks and trousers and hurriedly skimmed down my briefs, releasing my grateful prick, which sprang to instant attention. Then, dressed only in my white silk shirt, I stepped up behind the woman who was bent over so submissively before me.

My trembling hands reached out for her, clasping her by the solid hips. Curving my palms around, I fitted them to the sculpted contours of that smooth taut behind. The excited woman squirmed in the flush of arousal at the feel of my masculine hands on her bare ass. In her growing agitation, the big blonde shifted her weight from one foot to the other.

Now I allowed myself to fully savor that magnificent ass, toying with her, not playfully, not tenderly, but masterfully, letting her get the feel of my hard, urgent passion, my demanding lust as I dug my nails into those fleshy domes, till she arched up and back, whimpering in the grip of painful pleasure. Taking a firm grip, I mauled those pliant cheeks, pressing deep into the firm but yielding flesh, massaging roughly, occasionally giving Cora's superb ass a crisp decisive smack with a cupped hand, or a glancing slap that sent the wobbly mounds jiggling most delightfully. Cora released a deep-throated groan; after a few more minutes I had her moaning openly.

I leaned over her, draping the full length of my body over hers to stretch up and whisper in her ear.

"You love this don't you, you whore you?" I hissed, grinding my hips against her solid behind, tickling her along the moist crack with my swollen cock, following a lewd route that caused my prick to jump with the wild thrill of it all.

"You love it when I play with that big, gorgeous ass of yours, don't you?"

Cora craned backward, her eyes clenched shut. She could do no more than vigorously nod her blond head at the hiss of my lascivious words.

Her thighs were still hobbled. The pantyhose would have to go. Trembling with eagerness, I reached between her splayed legs and grabbed a fistful of nylon to yank the clinging pantyhose downward. Dropping to one knee behind the bending woman, I helped her to lift each foot in turn, while I pulled the clinging stockings off her feet. Now stark naked from the hips down, the long-legged blonde was an inspiring sight indeed! A tremendous surge of lust rocketed through me as she moved, opening her bare legs in mute invitation, inviting my hands and eyes, access to her womanhood.

Now I stood behind her, my straining prick was stoutly upright, pointing expectantly just inches from her rapidly moistening crotch. I sipped a hand between her thighs to cup the soft flesh of Cora Blasingdale's pendulous pussy. The woman uttered a softly plaintive moan as I lightly squeezed and fondled her needy sex in my cradling hand. I spent some time there, caressing the slick folds of her pussylips, fingering the wet, rubbery lips.

Bending my knees, I positioned the head of my cock just under her splayed crotch and spreading her labia I held her open as I lunged up, driving my erect penis straight up into her hot gaping cunt. Cora gasped at the swiftness of my penetration; a long wavering moan escaped her lips. I thrust upward till I was all the way in, buried to hilt. I savored the warmth and the slick tightness of that vaginal sheath that by now I knew so well. I wiggled my hips a bit, tickling her innards, letting her get the feel of me, while Cora threw back her head and gurgled in happy contentment.

Then I began pumping into her, holding the big woman firmly by the hips as I plunged in and out of her sopping wet cunt, slowly, methodically fucking the hot lusty blonde who squirmed under me, writhing in the heat of passion.

Now Cora was grunting with each thrust, making animal noises, tight-lipped guttural grunts that increased in pitch with each thrust. Soon she was moving with me, thrusting her loins back to meet my churning hips, fucking furiously, trembling, as I dug my clenched fingers into her hips and held on, white-knuckled, riding my magnificent mare to the ragged edge of ecstasy. The big blonde came with a violent tremor, a deep convulsion that shook her long body while she gave out with a low shivering moan. My own climax quickly followed, as I strained back to shove my cock all the way in and tightened my buttocks, holding myself rigidly while I skated along the ragged edge.

With blinding suddenness I exploded into her depths, my pulsating prick jetting thick wads of cum deep into the innards of the Mistress of Ironwood. I was racked with spasms of passion that seemed to go on and on. And then it was over for me, and I sagged weak-kneed, to collapse onto the still bent-over female, covering her body heaving with my own. We rested like that, gaping and gasping for air, panting heavily as the last waves of passion began to subside.

Wearily, I climbed off the bent-over woman, and fell back into the waiting chair. Cora let herself slide down off the desk to fall to the floor, and after a moment resting there, she crawled over to where I sat. Her long bare legs sprawled out as she sat up and leaned against my leg, resting her head on my thigh, content for now, to be in that place. She looked up at me with a genuine smile, her blue eyes soft and wonderful as though asking a silent question of mine.

"Welcome home, Mister James," she purred with the pleased smile of a contented feline.

* * *

We drove straight to the hotel, checked in, and went to our room to change for dinner. I took off my shoes and started to undress, while Nikki kicked off her sandals and stretched like a languid fawn. I watched her out of the corner of my eye as she undid her shorts and, with a girlish shimmy worked the snug shorts down over her hips, bending over and crossing one leg one in front of the other, so she could ride the shorts down to her ankles. The blouse was untied next, left to hang loosely on her slight shoulders.

I don't know if she noticed me watching her, but what she did next could well have been for my benefit. Quite casually, she reached up under her blouse and slipped her underpants down, stepping out of them in one quick movement. Then she opened the front of her blouse, but seemed to change her mind about taking it off, and instead padded across the room to retrieve her suitcase, with the loose flaps framing her willowy figure. Turning her back towards me, she tossed the suitcase on the bed and bent over to begin unpacking, opening her suitcase, and pawing through clothes.

I was taking off my slacks when I stopped in mid-gesture,

arrested by the wanton sight of my pretty roommate. Bent over as she was, the hem of the blouse had ridden up to expose the bottomcurves of two pert little rearcheeks which smiled out at me. The provocative invitation instantly fired my simmering lust. In a frenzied rush, I skimmed down my briefs, shaking in my eagerness to get my hands on the bending female.

Taking full advantage of the salacious opportunity she presented to me, I pressed up against those pertly jutting buttocks so that my rigid manhood rode up along the narrow slit between her cheeks. I wiggled my hips to ensconce it deeply between the snug mounds of her upturned bottom. Taken by surprise, Nikki started to straighten up when she felt my abrupt intrusion, but I immediately restrained her with a flattened hand placed firmly between the shoulderblades. Slowly, I pushed her forward, forcing her to throw out her hands to brace herself on the bed.

She stayed bent over while I ran my hands around to the front of her thighs, over her taut belly, brushing my fingertips through the wispy curlings of pubic fur I found there, before slithering up her front to clasp her loosely hanging breasts. Small and rounded, they dangled like two little pears, two tempting handfuls, just ripe for the picking. I cupped those luscious titties and gave her a friendly squeeze, all the while grinding my hips against her outthrust bottom, feeling her up happily, marveling in the texture of that tittie-flesh, the silken softness of those neat delightful handfuls. She shifted her weight, pressed her rump back against my loins, and caressed my snuggling prick which was now comfortably ensconced in the enfolding warmth of her rearvalley. Nikki tightened her butt muscles, clenching her cheeks on my rigid penis, and wiggling her sexy little behind in the most delicious way.

With some reluctance I pulled away and left her standing there, ordering her to hold the position, while I went to my traveling kit to retrieve a handy tube of lubricant. Without taking my eyes from my the rounded contours of Nikki's tempting tight-cheeked young bottom, I liberally greased my throbbing shaft and approached the proffered rearend once again, my rock-hard prick proudly, achingly erect. I reached out to grab the girl by the ass, slipping my thumbs into the crevice and prying open the twin mounds. Then, holding her open with one splayed hand, I used the other to dab a gob of gel right on her crinkled anus. At first the tiny muscle spasmed reflexively, contracting to resist my poking finger. But under my steady pressure it gradually yielded, giving way under my implacable assault. Now my finger was well inside the hot tight rectum. The impaled girl exhaled a long ragged hiss of breath as I twisted my finger, screwing it deeper into her rearend. She craned back, twisting her shoulders and gurgling from deep in her throat as I held it there, jiggling it, thrusting into the dry tightness of her inner heat.

Wildly excited now, I moved to replace my finger with my lust-engorged cock, placing the straining head directly on the tiny rosette and pressing hard till, with a sharp gasp from the bending girl, the tight ring of rubbery flesh yielded and the swollen crown of my lusty manhood was snugly inserted up her taut young bottom. Slowly, I pressed forward, easing my prick up the sleeve of her tight-fitting channel until I was halfway in and then, with a vicious thrust, I plunged into her ass till I was buried to the hilt. The savage thrust brought a tiny whimper from the girl's lips. She jerked upright at the swiftness of the sudden penetration.

With brutal impatience, I shoved her back down and fumbled for her dangling breasts, grabbing those hanging tit-bags like two handles to hold her as I withdrew almost my entire length only to drive back into her with another pounding thud. Nikki tossed her head back, reared up, and arched back, grunting through tight clenched teeth.

Then I was fucking her in the ass, and that randy young woman was moving with me, meeting my deep thrusts with her own, as her tight little asshole clenching my prick, spasming on me, sending delicious sensations rippling through my body. I clutched the silken flesh, holding on to two neat handfuls, while I wildly rode her to a thundering climax, my ragging prick pumping furiously into her churning behind.

The power of the massive explosion came welling up inside me, and then my prick was erupting, sending throbbing jets of cum deep into her core while Nikki shook in a single violent tremor, whimpering, crying out in ecstatic delight. I fell forward onto her bent body, my eyes closing in blissful surrender. Below me, I could feel a series of rippling contractions racking her thin, reedy body, tiny aftershocks from her own orgasm.

I stayed in her for a few minutes longer, and then withdrew my depleted cock, to stagger backwards and collapse into a welcoming chair. Nikki started to stir, but I told her to stay there, and ordered her not to move as I reached for a cigarette. I wanted to admire that lithe girlish figure, bent over in lewd display: the taut, nicely-rounded bottom, the straight slim legs, the bulging purse of her vulva, shaded with wet dark curls, a tell-tale smear of juices drying on her eager young thighs. When I finished my cigarette, I smacked her on the haunch and told her to get dressed. Suddenly, I was ravenously hungry!

* * *

To make sure the awakening woman wouldn't kick out once she became fully aware of her predicament, I quickly cuffed her ankles with two leather bands which I then attached by small chains to a pair of conveniently-placed staples set in the floor behind the trestle. This widened her stance further stretching the tangle of lingerie that still hobbled her legs. The girl mumbled and stirred once again before quieting down.

Working quickly now, I reached for a jar of hand cream, knowing that some lubrication would be necessary to ease my way up that virgin territory. I slipped off my pants, and skimmed down my briefs, stepping out of the tangle, swollen penis swaying heavily.

Stepping up to the proffered ass, I generously greased my hard prick. A wild shock of excitement shot through me at the thought of fucking that tight little asshole. If the haughty and proud young woman awoke to find her anus being happily violated, the rude awakening was sure to leave a truly lasting impression.

I leaned in against her butt, snuggling my stiff prick deep into her crack and rubbing it up and down that warm moist valley, all the while grinding my hips against the hard jutting mounds.

I was powerfully aroused now, palms tingling, hard cock throbbing with lust. Stepping back I opened her up once more, this time to insert a glob of lubricant on her crinkled anus, pressing hard till the tiny muscles yielded and my finger suddenly slipped up the girl's ass. At the sharp stab the girl jerked her hips and let out a shocked "oh," a yelp of surprised violation, that told me the probing finger had goosed her awake. Working quickly before she could react, I extracted my finger. Holding the rubbery cheeks apart with the splayed fingers of one hand, I grabbed my stiffened penis in the other and aimed the crown at her little asshole. With slow, relentless pressure I bore down on the anxious resistance of the little gate. The girl wriggled and tried to clench her cheeks, but I held her open, pressing inexorably forward, until her resistance began to yield and inch by inch, I penetrated her hot tight channel. At last I was all the way in, my rigid shaft lodged up her clinging rectum.

Now the skewered girl was wide awake and she could have no doubt that she was about to be taken up the ass. She let out a bloodcurdling scream at the impending violation, followed by urgent demands that I stop immediately, her invective punctuated by angry curses. She tried to straighten up and it was then that the full reality of her precarious position sunk in. In frantic desperation she tried to shake me off by wriggling her butt, tightening up and clamping her rearcheeks in a futile effort to expel my well ensconced prick. But the spasmodic grip of her hot channel only served to excite me more, and I thrust into her with a tight grunt.

Ignoring her threats, I pulled my hips back and then drove my prick in up to the hilt, burying it deep up her ass, getting a braying protest from the inverted head of the captive woman. I began pumping, slowly in and out, pressing the little ring of rubbery flesh inwards until it yielded to my inexorable pressure, and drawing back as the clinging circle tightly sucked the length of my withdrawing penis.

At one thrust I stayed motionless buried in the girl, her ass against my pubic hair, while I ground my hips against her tight mounds and she hollered and cursed like a raunchy whore. At last, realizing that her protests were having no effect, she switched tactics. Now between grunts she was offering to bribe me, pleading with me to name a price.

I continued the slow fuck, swallowing down the rising excitement, struggling to keep control and hold off from shooting my cum up Allison's bouncy ass. I concentrated on prolonging my pleasure.

After a while, the girl seemed to resign herself to the inevitable. Trying threats and bribes, and then begging for mercy, and seeing that none of that altered her fate, she seemed to calm down. The rigid stiffness drained from her body as she accommodated to the rhythmic pumping of my prick right her snug little ass. But then a surprising development occurred. Allison began to squirm in a ripple of sensual excitement, at first just a little twitch. A more massive quiver ran through her; her hips started bucking in instinctive reaction. Suddenly, she was pushing back against me, lustily matching her thrusts to mine. The randy bitch was hot, and clearly enjoying herself.

Her sudden burst of enthusiasm sent me over the edge, and

I felt her tight asshole rhythmically milking my cock as she got into the spirit of the thing. I could hold out no longer. As I neared my climax I pulled out just in time to spurt wads of milky sperm all over her lovely ass, decorating those elegantly curved domes with thick gobs of ropy cum. My knees sagged; I fell forward onto her stretched-out torso, gasping for air, resting on her bent undulating back.

After a few moments resting there, I staggered backwards to collapse on a convenient bench, and sit contemplating the arcuate legs; panties and nylons tangled at half-mast, were a reminder that she had been humiliated, her body shamelessly used. Now I saw with some surprise, that the inner surfaces of her thighs were sheened with juices, attesting to strength of the healthy young girl's arousal and the power of her climax. I smiled to see those taut jutting rearcheeks, liberally smeared with dribbles of drying cum, still lewdly presented by the helpless young woman who was stretched out, half-inverted, in the humiliating, but excitingly wanton, pose.

It occurred to me that probably for the first time in her young life, the willful lass had found herself forced to yield to a will stronger than hers. I lit a cigarette and smiled. It would not be the last time.

* * *

Warm and responsive, Helga slipped an arm around my shoulders and bent down to bestow a kiss, and this time it was a long dreamy kiss, her lips gradually falling open, yielding to the press of mine, while her tongue ventured out to play. As I kissed her, I let my hand ride up her smooth nyloned thigh brushing back the loose skirt to uncover her stockingtops, the wide bands of embroidered elastic that snugly encircled her splendid thighs. When we broke our kiss, Helga's head fell back and she melted in my arms, arching her back to offer up her breasts to my adoring lips.

I kissed and nibbled my way down along her craning neck while my fingers explored the fancy embroidery, then the lacy edge of the snug topband and beyond to find the silken band of flesh at the top of her leg, the incredible smoothness of the topmost part of those choice mouth-watering thighs—thighs which now parted for me to ease my access.

Now I fell on her greedily, kissing her everywhere, delivering hot feverish kisses, as I plunged in to revel in the touch, smell and taste of her fine young body as I made my way with mouth and lips and tongue down her neck and shoulders over her smooth chest and onto the sweetness of those small taut globes. And I spent a lot of time there, licking her breasts, lapping up over the delightful slopes, till Helga was squirming excitedly in my lap, and I could feel her inner heat through the layers of our clothes.

Driven frantic by our passionate lovemaking, Helga cupped the back of my head with one hand, digging her fingers in my hair, while the other fell to my crotch and she desperately clutched the tented outline of my cock. The thrill of her sudden touch electrified me, and I came very near to losing it right there and then. Reacting quickly, I clamped her wrist, and tore her well-meaning hand away. Then I pushed her back. It was time to come up for air. Helga's face was flushed; she sat regarding me through half-lidded eyes, her ripe moist lips parted, her slender chest heaving in rapid undulations. My eyes fell on her heaving breasts, wet with my saliva, the excited nipples stiff and taut with excitement.

"Let's get you out of these," I managed to croak, fingering the thin nylon panties.

The tall blonde obediently stood up, swaying slightly, slightly drunk with passion. I watched her take a deep breath, delicate breasts rising and falling as her ragged breathing evened out. She smiled down at me, while her hands went to the catch at the side of her skirt, undid the clasp. Her breasts dangled down from her bent torso as she lowered the little zipper, and then worked the loosened skirt down over her hips, raising each knee in turn to step free of the collapsed skirt.

Helga's slick hip-huggers were made of bronze, metallic-like nylon, shiny, and high cut at the sides. As she straightened up, I drank in the sight of that long, lean body resplendent in nothing but the low slung panties banding her hips, and the thigh-high stockings that still sheathed her long, elegant legs.

Those stockings were next. Helga slipped off her heels and raised her right foot, setting her toes on the front of my chair, as she reached for the topband. But I stopped her. The dusky stockings would not be in the way, and I rather liked the way she looked in them. I wanted her to leave her stockings on, but drop her drawers. With a sly grin, she brought her hands up to the elastic waistband of her underpants, hooked her thumbs inside her panties, and eased them down her hips, bending over and riding them down her legs all in one efficient movement. Straightening up, she raised each foot in turn to free herself from the collapsed underwear. An ache of desire shot through me as I watched her step out of the silken puddle with calm, delicate grace.

Now she stood before me, only inches from my chair, her tempting blond pussy shamelessly exposed, a lightly-furred vulva with its neatly embedded centertuck. I couldn't resist touching her there, running two joined fingers down the soft wispy curlings of pubic hair, to lightly trace over the half-hidden ridge of her pussylips. Already, she was moist between the legs.

I brought the other hand up behind her and, holding her by the back of her thigh, drew her loins to me, as I leaned over to plant a kiss on that dewy cunt, breathing in the heady fragrance of her arousal, deeply smelling her damp, slightly tangy, womanhood. The kiss I bestowed on the exact center of Helga's plump little triangle was short and perfunctory, a mere brushing of the lips through the blond puff of hair, but it elicited a sharp gasp through clenched teeth. Helga closed her eyes and swayed, while my tightening fingers held her close to me, digging into the back of that firm nylon-encased leg.

I rose up, and for a moment we stood eye to eye. The tall blonde was only an inch or two shorter than me. I wrapped my arms around her naked body, and drew her in. Helga threw back her head, offering her lips as she melted in my arms, pressing her sex to mine. We kissed and I ran my hungry hands up and down her bare back, finally cupping her firm rearcheeks, pulling her loins towards me so that I felt the soft press of her naked belly rubbing against my still clothed prick, exciting me beyond belief through the layers of clothing.

I had to get my clothes off! Releasing her, I turned her by the shoulders, and with a crisp smack on the bottom, sent her off towards the bed, while I started tearing open my shirt. The naked girl bent over to pull down the bed covers, and then climbed up into bed to wait for me. I told her to lay down and roll over onto her belly. And while I stripped she lay there with legs loosely parted, head resting on her folded arms, her face turned so she could watch me with keenly interested eyes.

In a heated rush, I tore off my shirt and undershirt, my hands trembling with eagerness. I fumbled to get my pants open, and skimmed them down quickly. My socks followed, and then my briefs, and at last my prick was free, bobbing in front of me, its head raised in proud salute to the naked woman who waited sprawled out on the oversized bed, with the seductive little smile of pleasure.

* * *

Now, I had the docile nude assume what at Ironwood we called the "presentation position." Without hesitation, she slid to her knees, in one smooth motion kneeling before me, then sitting back on her heels, legs tucked up under her, hands loosely at her sides. I was fascinated by those appealing little tits she displayed, with their uptilted points—soft pink and inviting, barely rising and falling with her shallow breathing. With calm deliberation, I got to my feet, stretched languidly, and slowly began to unbutton my shirt, aware that Beth's eyes were following my movements as I stripped before her, skimming down my pants and slipping off my briefs, to free my long-suffering prick.

Once undressed, I stepped up to where she sat on the floor, watching her gaze, fascinated by my bobbing manhood, which stood tall and ready just a few inches from her downcast eyes. I could have taken her right then and there, pressing my swollen erection to her lips, rudely inviting her to take me in her mouth and suck me off, which, being an Ironwood girl she would have done without hesitation, but that was not what I had in mind.

First, I would have this marvelously compliant girl perform for me. I beckoned her to her feet and as she stood there, her naked body so close to mine, I couldn't resist grabbing and kissing her. The suddenness of the hard kiss took her by surprise, for though the stiffness quickly drained from her body as I pulled her to me, her lips though rich and full, remained pressed together as I bore down on them. That angered me, and I gave her a stinging slap on the bare bottom which brought a delightful squeal.

"You know better than that," I warned sternly, digging my hands into her hair and drawing her head back by a fistful of silken strands.

Beth's eyebrows arched up, her eyes widening in alarm, but she let her mouth fall open to receive my second kiss and this time she greeted me with more enthusiasm, her tongue darting into my mouth as she pressed herself to me. The feel of the girl's naked body against mine, the warm softness of her breasts, the press of her groin against my upstanding prick sent a wild thrill rocketing through me, bringing on the exciting threat of imminent eruption, so near that I had to abruptly push her away and back off to collapse in my chair, knees parted, feet flat on the floor, prick throbbing with lust after that near miss.

I said not a word, just sat there studying the little tuft of silken burnished hairs that furred the plump triangle cozily tucked between the rounded columns of her enticing, young thighs.

"Spread your legs now. Show me your pussy," I ordered quietly.

Beth gave me a fleeting smile, then tossed back her head to look at some distant place, far over my head as she brought her hands up to place them with joined fingers pointing down along the sides of her triangle. I watched the elegant pointed fingers, tipped with red, as they nosed through the thicket of auburn fleece. Quite deliberately, she widened her stance and bent her knees slightly as she pressed along the bulging purse of her vulva, opening the petals of her delicate pink rose for me.

For a moment she stood perfectly still, thighs spread, knees bent obligingly holding the pose I had put her in, while I eyed her splayed-open womanhood. I was curious to see the girl's reaction in thus exposing herself to me, but when I glanced up, I found that she had closed her eyes. For some reason, that annoyed me.

"No! Look at me! And keep your eyes on me while you're showing me your pussy!"

I studied the slick folds of pinkish brown so openly revealed to me. It was obvious that this sort of exhibitionism was not one of her turn-ons. Still, I thoroughly enjoyed seeing her in such an erotic pose, and she, again thanks to Ironwood's rigid conditioning, had developed an overwhelming desire to please.

"Okay. You can straighten up now . . . and turn around."

Calmly, her hands abandoned her sex, and she brought her legs together, and turned in place offering me a superb back view of her nude body: the angles of shoulderblades under the smooth skin of her back, the traces of the gently bowed spine; the long waist and smooth taper to the shallow dip of the lower back; the delectable mounds of those pert, compact buttocks.

"Now I want you to bend over; place your hands on your knees, and hold that pose!" I managed to get out in a hoarse whisper; my throat gone suddenly dry.

Beth did as she was told, bracing herself with hands on top of her knees while her appealing young bottom jutted straight back at me, as though begging to be taken in lewd invitation. I couldn't help but admire the tautly-rounded curves, the smiling undercurves, the trim and agile thighs, between which the dark fur of her bulging vulva peeped out with seductive impudence.

"Spread your cheeks for me."

Once more, the Ironwood training showed, as again, without hesitation, those obedient hands came back to curve around the jutting rearcheeks. Pointed fingers dug into the crack, and she pried back the pliant cheeks, exposing the hidden valley and letting me see the dusky pink rosette embedded there. I decided that the girl might not have been Ironwood's most enthusiastic playmate, but like all the others, she would dutifully follow orders, no matter how bizarre or perverse. I wondered what went through her head as I kept her like that, holding the straining mounds apart so as to expose her most intimate secrets to me.

When I released her it was only to place the young woman in still another lewd pose for me, this time having her spread her legs in a widened stance, and then bending over, all the way, so she could clasp her ankles. The girl folded her supple body at the hips, lowering her head as she reached down to clasp her ankles, and I watched her long mane fall forward, fanning down between her opened legs. The jutting cheeks rose up to even greater prominence, the curving skin pulled taut by the stretching pose that strained the rigid muscles of thighs and calves. With her legs spread she provided a more generous view of her pussy, and I couldn't resist bringing up a hand to clamp her crotch and there to fondle her soft, thickly-furred vulva till she twitched in growing agitation.

Having the submissive beauty pose for me had the predictable effect of making my lust-swollen cock painful with the throb of expectation. Barely able to contain my excitement, I had her quit the pose, turn around and get down on her knees before me. This time I had her kneeling upright. I opened my knees and beckoned her to shuffle forward between my wide-spread thighs, till she knelt only inches from my straining cock.

* * *

Anne was a delightful picture in nothing but that sleeveless white blouse that hung loosely on her narrow frame, the pale fleece of her vulva peeking out below the hem that fell halfway down her bare hips. I grabbed her by the upper arms, drew her to me and kissed her, letting her get the full feel of my hardened penis pressing into her soft underbelly. She returned my kiss with surging passion, and her hand slithered down between our tightly-pressed bodies to seek my rock-hard cock. The electric feel of that first touch thrilled me to the core as her slim fingers found me and deliciously wrapped themselves around my lust-swollen shaft. The dear girl let me feel her mounting need in the urgent squeeze she gave me, tightening her fist till I heard myself whimper; my knees weakened and threatened to collapse.

I fought the wild surge of excitement that welled up in me, as I hurriedly pushed her away, tearing loose my primed and ready cock from the lusty girl's determined grip. I propelled her back against the desk, forcing her backwards till she lay sprawled half way over the desktop. Clamping my hands on her hips, I lifted her up further onto the desk so that only her bare legs were left dangling down over the side.

She lay back, looking up at me through half-lidded eyes, her gaze fixed on my upright cock. As I closed in to stand before those loosely parted legs, her knees rose up instinctively, seductive thighs opening slowly to welcome me in.

I contemplated my estate agent's gaping womanhood, a pale coral slit with ragged cuntlips nestled in a light sprinkling of dusky pubic hair. Grabbing her by the ankles, I folded her steepled knees even further back, rolling her back on her shoulders so as to serve up her exposed pussy. Driven half crazy with lust I dove into that inviting cunt, burying my face in the soft slick folds of Anne Ludlowe's vagina, while she gurgled happily from deep in her throat. I caught the unmistakable smell of a woman in heat, and drank in her scent, fully savoring the raw muskiness. With nostrils flaring with that heady odor, I extended my tongue and fully licked her cunt, lapping along the insides of her silken thighs, edging the thick outer lips, then using board strokes of my flattened tongue to run up her slit, pressing insistently between those juicy, wet petals, to probe her very core.

"Ohhhhhgaaddd yes," the passion-driven woman moaned, tossing her back her silky mane, and urging me on in a heated whisper.

I had to have that juicy cunt! Straightening up, I picked up her slack legs and holding her open, I aimed my painfully ready penis right between the gaping folds of her vulva, and fell on her, plunging into her; a single brutal lunge that drove my prick smoothly right up that slick, wet, pussy.

Anne gave out with a long satisfied groan and arched back and upwards, twisting her shoulders at the swiftness of the penetration. I slid in to the hilt, grinding my hips against her splayed crotch, while Anne's soft little moans turned into whimpers of delight each time I wiggled my hips, letting her get the full feel of me; my prick tickling her innards.

I luxuriated in the delicious sensation of my prick sliding easily up the silken walls of that enfolding womanhood, felt her cunt muscles milking me, as they spasmed with jolts of pleasure. As I held myself still, deep inside her, her legs instinctively rose up to wrap around my waist. The muscles of her surprisingly strong thighs tightened; she was embracing me with her lithe legs clamped around my hips, pulling me even deeper, more desperately, into her hot, needy sex, urging me on with whispered pleas in my ear.

For a long moment I held myself perfectly still, my cock buried deep in Anne's hot tight cunt, savoring the exquisite pleasures she generated in my loins whenever those velvety walls tightened on my well ensconced prick.

Then I moved, rocking back on my heels, pumping into her with a slow, steady pace that I had to fight to maintain, as I thoroughly fucked Anne Ludlowe on the schooldesk at Ironwood. She was thumping my bare butt with her heels; meeting each lunge of mine with instinctive pelvic thrusts. Our ride quickened. My hips were bucking in crisp staccato, the girl bouncing and gyrating beneath me, moaning with increased urgency in her voice, as she tossed her head from side to side like a wild woman. I reached out for her. Curving my fingers around her svelte hips, I clasped her firmly, and held her while I pounding into her, fucking now with furious abandon, while she twisted and turned, arching back and straining upward.

Suddenly Anne let out with a tiny yelp; her body straightened and she held herself with muscles were taut as bowstrings, hips arching high up off the desk. She quivered with pleasure, and then came with a long wavering moan and a deeper, more profound shudder that ran through her rigidly held body.

Seeing the passion-driven woman climax sent me careening over the edge with a wild escalation of pleasure. I powered into her . . . all the way, twisting my hips, screwing delighted Anne with a deep rutting lunge. I held myself buried to the hilt, and ground my crotch against her churning mound, grimly determined to squeeze out that last once of pure pleasure, as my thundering orgasm overtook me. At that supreme moment, I threw back my head and came, just a pure ecstatic thrill tore though me, obliterating everything but my throbbing, pulsating prick.

* * *

By now I was practically on top of the blonde, climbing up on the couch on my knees to straddle that outstretched nubile body, bringing my manhood up to her face so that my swaying balls brushed over her chin. Whitney's eyes fluttered open and she looked up to see my rigid penis quivering just inches from her wide blue eyes. I brought my swinging balls up to her mouth. She might have been the younger of the two, but she was just as experienced as her older playmate; she knew just what to do. Opening her mouth she extended a small pointed tongue and licked all over my hairy scrotum, and then that sweet girl gently took my balls into her mouth and softly suckled them. It was heavenly! I sighed with profound satisfaction to feel that warm wet mouth cuddling my balls. A warning surge of passion caused me to abruptly draw back, extracting my wet and gleaming manhood. It was a perverse delight to move up against her, rubbing my hardened cock and my wet balls all over that slim girlish chest. I slithered up her slender body, this time slipping my hands under her small blond head to raise her up off the pillow, tilting her cradled head so that she lay at the proper angle to receive my rude offering.

I eased myself slowly over the tiny ridge of teeth and into the warm sanctuary of Whitney's inviting mouth where a velvety tongue welcomed me, slithering along the underside of my shaft, sending excited shivers of pleasure through my body. Moist lips tightened and the charming little blonde obediently began to suck. She looked up at me with those big blue eyes as she drew me in deeply, hallowing her cheeks, moving her head in a gentle bobbing rhythm. I grabbed her by the pony-tail to slow her down, controlling her bobbing movements as I started moving my hips, pumping in and out slowly, methodically, thoroughly enjoying the tight ring of wet lips as they slid up and down my hard swollen prick, delighting in the quick fluttery movements of that adept tongue as it teased the sensitive underside of my shaft just below the crown. In an abrupt surge, the tingling pleasure rose up in me and threatened to spill over. I tightened my butt against the creamy rise of pleasure, and stiffened every sinew of my body, determined to hold on, for I was resolved to prolong things till I had drained every last once of pleasure from this juicy little piece. And although my eager and willing playmate would have gladly have continued her slavish devotion till she brought me to the point of climax with that adorable mouth and tongue, I was in the mood for a fuck, and a fuck I was going to have!

A jolt of unexpected pleasure rippled through me, sending me bouncing backward, to abruptly extract my throbbing cock from that sweet haven. For a moment my pulsating prick stood upright before her; a ripple of pre-cum erupted weakly to dribble down on her chin.

Immediately I slithered down that hot moist body and came up again right between those slack legs, driving into the gaping wet pussy in a single lunging thrust. The swiftness of the penetration caused the girl to gasp a shivering intake of air. She groaned; her head fell back and craned into the mounded pillow; she clenched her eyes against the sudden stab of pleasure. Whitney's pussy was small and tight and held me like a velvet glove. I luxuriated in the slick wet feel of those silken walls pressing on my buried cock. Rising up on my straddling elbows I slowly extracted myself till just the bulbous head remained between the sucking labia, and then I drove in again, powering into the writhing girl, who whimpered like a hurt kitten. I looked down to see that pale innocent face contorted in passion.

Glancing over my shoulder, I saw that Renata was

clenching two handfuls of blond hair at either side of Margo's head, grinding her sopping wet pussy all over the blond face of her subservient lover who knelt before her. I knew, that for Renata, this was the height of her pleasure: she was only most fully alive when she was able to dominate another woman, and if that woman was herself strong and independent, as Margo most assuredly was, and she was still able to force her will on her, well that and that alone could account for the smile of supreme ecstasy that curled her lips as she threw back her mop of dark hair, to fully savor that exquisite moment of triumph.

Meanwhile the limp girl who lay beneath me was becoming more animated. With each stroke of my slow measured fucking, her smoldering passions were being re-ignited. She was making tiny little keening noises, and her hips began to buck, instinctively matching her pelvic thrusts to mine. Supple arms wrapped around my shoulders; small hands feverishly feeling their way along the muscles of my back, before clasping me as those arms tightened in a welcoming embrace. With a sudden surge of arousal, her movements became clearly more excited, her legs came up to wrap around my waist and she squeezed me, letting me feel the full intensity of her burning need, drawing me into her hot, needy core with fiery urgency. The sensuous blonde was well on her way to her second orgasm, one that was even now gaining in terrible power.

The sensual movement of her healthy young body, and those soft tiny moans, urged me on, and the sudden upwelling of pleasure that powered up from my loins told me that I couldn't hold out much longer. Struggling to prolong those heavenly feelings that wracked my rigid body I strained back, fucking the writhing blonde with furious abandon. It was enough to send her over the edge. Abruptly her slender blond body straightened and jerked convulsively; she yelped and twisted up beneath me. At that moment, a second, more profound shockwave slammed through her; I felt the girl tremble beneath me just as I felt the wild thrill that rocketed through me to mark my own onrushing climax. With a final plunge into the hot churning depths of Whitney's sweet little pussy I came, shaken by a blinding jolt of pure pleasure that obliterated everything else.

NOW AVAILABLE

Confessions d'Amour
Anne-Marie Villefranche

Confessions d'Amour is the culmination of Villefranche's comically indecent stories about her friends in 1920s' Paris.

Anne-Marie Villefranche invites you to enter an intoxicating world where men and women arrange their love affairs with skill and style. This is a world where illicit encounters are as smooth as a silk stocking, and where sexual secrets are kept in confidence only until a betrayal can be turned to advantage. Here we follow the adventures of Gabrielle de Michoux, the beautiful young widow who contrives to be maintained in luxury by a succession of well-to-do men, Marcel Chalon, ready for any adventure so long as he can go home to Mama afterwards, Armand Budin, who plunges into a passionate love affair with his cousin's estranged wife, Madelein Beauvais, and Yvonne Hiver who is married with two children while still embracing other, younger lovers.

"An erotic tribute to the Paris of yesteryear that will delight modern readers."—*The Observer*

Ironwood
by Don Winslow

The harsh reality of disinheritance and poverty vanish from the world of our young narrator, James, when he discovers he's in line for a choice position at an exclusive and very strict school for girls. Ironwood becomes for him a fantastic dream world where discipline knows few boundaries, and where his role as master affords him free reign with the willing, well-trained and submissive young beauties in his charge. As overseer of Ironwood, Cora Blasingdale is well-equipped to keep her charges in line. Under her guidance the saucy girls are put through their paces and tamed. And for James, it seems, life has just begun.

NOW AVAILABLE

Addicted
Ray Gordon

Housewife, Helen Hunter, has it all. An attractive, successful husband. Money. Looks. However, things go wrong when her husband leaves on business. She becomes tired, nervy and anxious...panicky even. But on his return—after a hearty 'welcome'—the symptoms disappear. Something bizarre is happening—she has become addicted to sperm.

The supply from her husband soon becomes insufficient. She embarks on an incredible sexual journey to satisfy her desires. Unfortunately it soon becomes apparent that too much is never enough...

Slave Girls of Rome
Don Winslow

Master eroticist Don Winslow takes an erotic look back on the Roman Empire during its ascendancy in the world. This is a tale of power and pleasure. Never has a city been as depraved as Rome—and never have women been so relentlessly used as were Rome's voluptuous slaves! With no choice but to serve their lustful masters, these captive beauties had to perform their duties with the passion and purpose of Venus herself.

Lusts of the Borgias
Marcus Van Heller

Italy, during the Renaissance, was a time of culture but also of uninhibited corruption. And no powerful family of the age was more depraved than the infamous House of Borgia. Here is the story of their cruel, passionate, erotic adventures.

"One of the few historical erotic novels worthy of being called a classic. [It is also] a novel of outrageous sexual indulgence."— *Evergreen Review*

∽ NOW AVAILABLE ∽

The Intimate Memoirs of an Edwardian Dandy
Anonymous

Raised in the English countryside, fifteen-year old Rupert is ready to savour the traditional sporting delights of privileged English gentleman—and to master the equipment needed for them. Who better to introduce him than lusty, libidinous country girls? A fine upstanding young man and a quick learner, Rupert is soon au fait with the hidden talents of parlor maids and damsels in delicious distress. He attends revealing hypnosis sessions, and indulges in team games they don't teach at school...

Jennifer and Nikki
D. M. Perkins

From Manhattan's Fifth Avenue, to the lush island of Tobago, to a mysterious ashram in upstate New York, Jennifer travels with reclusive fashion model Nikki and her seductive half-brother Alain in search of the sexual secrets held by the famous Russian mystic Pere Mitya. To achieve intimacy with this extraordinary family, and get the story she has promised to Jack August, dynamic publisher of New Man Magazine, Jennifer must ignore universal taboos and strip away inhibitions she never knew she had.

Burn
Michael Hemmingson

Nicholas Wilde is a 50-year old painter shunned by the art elite for his unflinchingly representational depictions of the female form. Rose Selavy is the 24-year old muse who refuses to let him own her. When they meet, their passions burn red hot, then bloody and inspire one another, but when Rose leaves, Nicholas is left impotent, unable to seduce the slew of women he encounters because none can stimulate him with the heat that Rose had provided.

Wet Dreams
Anonymous

A collection of vivid tales to spur the imaginations of uninhibited men and women. These stories offer a cornucopia of sexual delights. In Wayward Venus, a young man is seduced by his governess. Another is initiated by a countess and her maid. In the merry ménage a mother and daughter invite the attentions of a gentleman of dubious reputation, and a girl is taught the pleasures of spanking.

"An intoxicating sexual romp." –Evergreen Review

∽ NOW AVAILABLE ∾

"Frank" and I
Anonymous

The narrator of the story, a wealthy young man, meets a youth one day—the "Frank" of the title—and, taken by his beauty and good manners, invites him to come home with him. He quickly discovers that his charge displays an unacceptable lack of obedience and consequently he commences to flog him in the traditional and humiliating English manner. One can only imagine his surprise when the young man turns out to be a young woman with beguiling charms.

Eveline II
by Anonymous

Eveline II continues the delightfully erotic tale of a defiant aristocratic young English woman who throws off the mantle of respectability in order to revel in life's sexual pleasures. After returning to her paternal home in London in order to escape the boredom of marriage, she plunges with total abandon into self-indulgence and begins to "convert" other young ladies to her wanton ways.

Best of Shadow Lane
Eve Howard

Here at last are the very best stories from Eve Howard's ongoing chronicle of romantic discipline, Shadow Lane. Set in the Cape Cod village of Random Point, these stories detail submissive women's quests for masterful men who will turn them over their knees. At the center lies the mischievous Susan Ross, an Ivy League brat who needs a handsome dominant to give her the spanking she deserves.

Slaves of the Hypnotist
by Anonymous

Harry, son of a well-to-do English country family, has set out to "conquer" all the females within his immediate reach. But no sooner does he begin his exploits than he encounters the imperious beauty, Davina, who enslaves him through her remarkable power of hypnotism. Thus entranced, Harry indulges in every aspect of eroticism known to man or woman.

NOW AVAILABLE

The Memoirs of Josephine
Anonymous

19th Century Vienna was a wellspring of culture, society and decadence and home to Josephine Mutzenbacher. One of the most beautiful and sought after libertines of the age, she rose from the streets to become a celebrated courtesan. As a young girl, she learned the secrets of her profession. As mistress to wealthy, powerful men, she used her talents to transform from a slattern to the most wanted woman of the age. This candid, long suppressed memoir is her story.

Jennifer
D.M. Perkins

His touch released a dark flood of sensation in Jennifer. It coursed through her body and changed her from a rational, intelligent, career woman into someone else: a woman who would do anything—move to any primitive sexual level—when she was aroused. She'd always had an active fantasy life. One of her earliest sexual scenarios was a daydream of being kidnapped by a strong ruthless man.

Mistress of Instruction
Christine Kerr

Mistress of Instruction is a delightfully erotic romp through merry old Victorian England. Gillian, precocious and promiscuous, travels to London where she discovers Crawford House, an exclusive gentlemen's club where young ladies are trained to excel in service. A true prodigy of sensual talents, she is retained to supervise the other girls' initiation into "the life." Her title: Mistress of Instruction.

House of Lust
Ray Gordon

Lady Hadleigh likes to think she can abuse anyone on her estate at will. But when she seduces Tom, her ambitious stable boy, she discovers an adversary determined to rise by mercilessly exploiting his tremendous sexual prowess at every opportunity. 'Breaking in' Lady Hadleigh's two teenage daughters is just a step in Tom's rapacious progress. There's a lot more to come as he thrusts his rampant way to the top.

Order These Selected Blue Moon Titles

Souvenirs From a Boarding School . . $7.95	Red Hot $7.95
The Captive $7.95	Images of Ironwood $7.95
Ironwood Revisited $7.95	Tokyo Story $7.95
The She-Slaves of Cinta Vincente . . . $7.95	The Comfort of Women $7.95
The Architecture of Desire $7.95	Disciplining Jane $7.95
The Captive II $7.95	The Passionate Prisoners $7.95
Shadow Lane $7.95	Doctor Sex $7.95
Services Rendered $7.95	Shadow Lane VI $7.95
Shadow Lane III $7.95	Girl's Reformatory $7.95
My Secret Life $9.95	The City of One-Night Stands $7.95
The Eye of the Intruder $7.95	A Hunger in Her Flesh $7.95
Net of Sex $7.95	Flesh On Fire $7.95
Captive V $7.95	Hard Drive $7.95
Cocktails $7.95	Secret Talents $7.95
Girl School $7.95	The Captive's Journey $7.95
The New Story of O $7.95	Elena Raw $7.95
Shadow Lane IV $7.95	La Vie Parisienne $7.95
Beauty in the Birch $7.95	Fetish Girl $7.95
The Blue Train $7.95	Road Babe $7.95
Wild Tattoo $7.95	Violetta $7.95
Ironwood Continued $7.95	Story of O $5.95
Transfer Point Nice $7.95	Dark Matter $7.95
Souvenirs From a Boarding School . . $7.95	Ironwood $7.95
Secret Talents $7.95	Body Job $7.95
Shadow Lane V $7.95	Arousal $7.95
Bizarre Voyage $7.95	The Blue Moon Erotic Reader II . . . $15.95

Visit our website at www.bluemoonbooks.com

ORDER FORM
Attach a separate sheet for additional titles.

Title   Quantity   Price

_____   _____   _____

_____   _____   _____

_____   _____   _____

_____   _____   _____

                        Shipping and Handling (see charges below)   _____
                                   Sales tax (in CA and NY)   _____
                                                  Total   _____

Name _____

Address _____

City _____ State _____ Zip _____

Daytime telephone number _____

❏ Check   ❏ Money Order   (US dollars only. No COD orders accepted.)

Credit Card # _____ Exp. Date _____

❏ MC   ❏ VISA   ❏ AMEX

Signature _____
(if paying with a credit card you must sign this form.)

Shipping and Handling charges:*

Domestic: $4 for 1st book, $.75 each additional book. International: $5 for 1st book, $1 each additional book
*rates in effect at time of publication. Subject to Change.

Mail order to Publishers Group West, Attention: Order Dept., 1700 Fourth St., Berkeley, CA 94710, or fax to (510) 528-3444.

PLEASE ALLOW 4-6 WEEKS FOR DELIVERY. ALL ORDERS SHIP VIA 4TH CLASS MAIL.

Look for Blue Moon Books at your favorite local bookseller or from your favorite online bookseller.